ALSO BY OONYA KEMPADOO

Tide Running

Buxton Spice

ALL

DECENT

ANIMALS

ALL
DECENT
ANIMALS

OONYA KEMPADOO

FARRAR, STRAUS AND GIROUX   NEW YORK

Farrar, Straus and Giroux
18 West 18th Street, New York 10011

Copyright © 2013 by Oonya Kempadoo
All rights reserved
Printed in the United States of America
First edition, 2013

Library of Congress Cataloging-in-Publication Data
Kempadoo, Oonya.
    All decent animals / Oonya Kempadoo. — 1st ed.
      p.   cm.
    ISBN 978-0-374-29971-2 (hardcover : alk. paper)
    1. Trinidadian and Tobagonian fiction (English)   I. Title.

PR9320.9.K46 A79 2013
813'.54—dc23

                                          2012034573

Designed by Abby Kagan

www.fsgbooks.com
www.twitter.com/fsgbooks • www.facebook.com/fsgbooks

10   9   8   7   6   5   4   3   2   1

FOR ROGER AND ROSEMARY

To express is to drive.
And when you want to give something presence,
you have to consult nature.
And there is where Design comes in.

And if you think of Brick, for instance,
and you say to Brick,
"What do you want, Brick?"
And Brick says to you,
"I like an Arch."
And if you say to Brick,
"Look, arches are expensive,
and I can use a concrete lintel over you.
What do you think of that,
Brick?"
Brick says:
". . . I like an Arch."

  —LOUIS I. KAHN (1901–1974), ARCHITECT

ALL

DECENT

ANIMALS

FROM THE TIME ATA CAME TO VISIT this place as a shy child she told herself—this is a place for adults. From the time them lovely Maracas waves first chewed her up, when she saw teenagers dressed like big people, rich homes flashing TV style—everybody rushing, buying food, driving and eating and drinking, picong talk flying—she promised herself she would come back to this prancy, peacock island. But she never trusted the perfumed strutting. And Trinidad never promised her anything. Never once invited her. No matter how many times Ata came from her island home. Because Trinidad is a metropolis, she thought. A complicated process and a place busy keeping up with itself, carrying on at a rate. Horrendous rates. Every time, in the taxi from Piarco Airport to Port of Spain, she could see the mess of it right there. All along the road, without shame or design. Ignoring her arrival.

Today the customs man doesn't bother with her bags, he glances at Ata's mixed-race complexion. "Yuh come back home?" he asks, just after Immigration finished giving her hell for visiting the *Home of the Greatest Show on Earth*, yet again.

"Yes," she says. She does live here now.

Outside the shiny cheap-tiled airport, the Indian taxi driver has her bag. "Where you going—is up a hill? Because my car does cutout on steep hill."

No need to answer. Business as usual. Down the highway. Ata looks out at familiar gaudy shopping malls and incomplete housing schemes, factories, fast-food chains, mosques, the Hindu girls' school. On this island of oil, with its asphalt sun and pothole roads, the highways are packed with cars crawling like shiny lice.

They inch through the junction by Nestlé's compound. It's midday and diesel-dark-skinned vendors comb through heat waves of glittering cars, dripping plastic bags of red pommeracs. Air-conditioned windows roll down. Cool bills for hot fruit. None for the limping polio beggar with his black cracked palm. The taxi man turns up the radio slightly to catch the latest news. A neutral voice offers, "Four victims were murdered in the country's latest fatality . . . A seven-year-old, who survived by hiding under a bed, reports that his father and brother were tied up while his mother and sister were brutally raped in front of them by three men and chopped with cutlasses. All were then shot several times . . . Police say . . ."

The taxi man switches off and sucks his teeth loud. "Every day is some nonsense, yuh know. What de hell really going on in this place?"

As if she, the newcomer/returnee, should know the answer. He doesn't need an answer. Like any Trini living in Trinidad, he has had to find a way to live with the unanswered questions. The same ones that bring Ata back, again and again.

They pass big Indo-Greco homes with icing-cake concrete balustrades, lots of sliding doors, curly wrought iron, and de-signer "features," all locked up; patches of farmlands, with

4

Gramoxone-dead grass borders. And plenty of billboards. White-teeth-smiling Miss World dressed in her airline uniform waves from hers. Bright multirace, happy people gulp down Orchard juice, cheersing each other. Trendy cricket heroes toast, with Pepsi and cell phones. Restbest Mattress is De Best.

They bypass town and the ex–railway terminal, the Sea Lots shantytown stretching up to Laventille, and the La Basse dump that leaks human scavengers and corbeau vultures, heading over the hills. "Some people don' like passing this way, yuh know," the driver tells Ata, "'cause of what them fellas used to do up so."

"I know," she says, and shifts herself to admire the Northern Range. There, behind Barataria, Tunapuna, and Arima, in the distance. These hills are the ones to watch. Blue-gray soft in the rainy season, hard and fire-scarred in the dry season, they talk. Incessant, annoying, fanning and waving and calling. They laugh, they mock the radio, echoing whatever they hear. They are part of it, she knows. Plumage of the peacock island. How to live with the ugliness of the beauty we love? Or die with it? "If you think living is difficult, try dying," Fraser had said.

She had walked straight into Camp Swampy, on her return to Port of Spain as a young adult, eight years ago. This was the worst of Slinger's Carnival-costume centers. But it was work that Ata had negotiated wages for. She felt she had a right to enter any Caribbean territory, or anywhere in the world for that matter, and work and participate and carry on as normal, and not feel like an illegal island immigrant. Growing up hearing about Caricom ideals and global citizenship, Ata felt "Caribbean," not Dominican, not Guyanese, not Trinidadian—a true no-nation.

This in-between feeling, neither one nor the other, moved her from island to island, from Europe to the Caribbean, without obligation to either. A nonbelonger. Unrooted in place and race and in herself. Each island, each time, as she saw the secrets of the land and the lying creases of the culture, she found out something about herself. Unsettling things, not to be proud of, detaching until she sometimes felt outside her own body. But at the same time unretractably entwined in it all. A disappointed accomplice locked in but able to share remarkable, particular treasures.

She walked away from her village cocoon of books and dreaming, from alien European attempts to draw out the talent in her hands, talent that she felt was there like green juice in a leaf, pulsing. Practice and apprenticeship, she thought. Her father had warned her, "Independence is only real when you are outside of the rat race! Work for what you want, Atalanta, but don't worry with this nonsense of working your way 'up the ladder.' Hierarchy is oppression!" But Ata knew that money is what bought independence. So she took what she could of her father's words, gathered the strength and patience her mother used to cope with her father—and stepped into Camp Swampy. Straight into the cussing, roughing, gnarly hell of Carnival production boiling day and night to the explosion.

Ata stops, tentative, just inside the gate. The ugly old house with its burglarproofed veranda is crammed full of cloth and poles. The small, scrappy yard exhales a mouthful of bad breath. A stench of glue, fabric paint, stale sweat, cigarette butts, alcohol, piss, and stress. Prepared in cap and overalls, she climbs the littered steps and enters. The floorboards give under her slight frame. She moves forward cautiously and stops at the scream of a cutting machine controlled by a shirtless man. On a huge table, thick layers of bloodred fabric are spread with cardboard shapes, laid like a puzzle. The cutter man guides the blade, pressing and pushing the heavy beast. It whines and chews, spitting out red dust. The man shoves a sliced wad out of his way and braces himself again, cigarette dangling out of his mouth, ignoring her presence. She waits for a while, hearing more commotion in other rooms above the noise. Eventually she calls out to the cutter man. He is the same mix as she is but darker, straight dougla, black and Indian, wiry and tough. After a while he turns off the machine, brushes cigarette ash and red fluff from his chest, and finally grunts at her. He shouts to the back of the house, that a young boy is here to see Francisco.

She steps deeper into the den, overflowing with paint tubs, buckets, brushes, sponges, rags, and dirty Styrofoam cups. Another room full of decorated poles and standards, bracing the walls. A moon and a man's face top the poles, strips of lamé, chiffon, and crêpe, hang from them. Spray-painted calabashes of all sizes lie on the floor or dangle by leather thongs from nails in the walls. Year of Gold Callaloo. The end of Slinger's brilliant trilogy of masquerade bands transforming myths and legends. Four thousand people had joined that year—fifty-seven sections each in different costume. Meaning four thousand accessorized costumes paid for, to be finished by hook or crook.

"Just two weeks to go and I don't know how the fuck we go finish!" Francisco bursts through the back door laughing his nasty laugh and strikes a Hindu-dancer pose for Ata. "You like it?"

His T-shirt, cut into shreds, and short dhoti stick onto his short chubbiness, completely covered in wet green paint. His head, shaved and painted gold, is well disguised as a calabash, but the hairy legs and whitish patches of skin shining through show him up as Po'tagee.

"Fellas" —he turns to them huddled in the back room over a

joint—"this girl is my good-good friend. Yes, is a girl, you see?" He whisks off her cap. "And, I will pussonally kill any one of you who touch her or trouble her. You hear?"

The fellas laugh and take in Ata's short, curly hair, boyish features, and shy eyes. Laughing at Francisco's empty threat.

"Yes, laugh! Allyou know I fucking crazy, when I ready. Come, girl." He leads her out into the yard full of tables of fabric waiting to be painted. Miles of spinach-green wet cotton hung drying on fence, lines, bits of lumber, and propped-up zinc sheets. The smell of the fabric paint was the bad breath. But it's not toxic, Francisco reassures her, that's why he could put it on his skin.

Ata dips her hands into the green paint and squeezes the sponge a couple times. The cold sliminess feels good. Splattering it freely over the fresh white fabric feels even better. Liberation and new-found creativity fill her young heart. Dreams and visions miles long. Cotton realms of rainbow gauze, like Francisco's "floaty dhotis." She imagines more than beauty. Clothing long brown fashion-model limbs, draping homes. A business built on the patterns of tropical flowers, shadows of leaves, textures and tones of earth, skin, and the rippling Caribbean Sea. She daubs and streaks, brushes and splatters, the black, the gold, the green, working her way under the skin and into the churn of Camp Swampy.

Catching a few hours' sleep under a table, she tries to figure out the rules, the hierarchy and upper echelons of this king-dom. Or fiefdom. The kings and queens of the band are not leaders, only puppets. There is a God of Design and he is King of Mas. An impetuous genius out of the wrong color and class, in this world of black independence. Slinger, the "real artist," came home with all his London classical-actor training, all his appreciation of the cultural fabric that he grew up with in Trinidad, bringing overstretched intellect and endless vision to transform the masquerade. This God of Design set about changing up everything in the arts—doing away with the commercialization of mas, not worrying about profit or loss—determined to re-create a costumed identity and the way ordinary people celebrate their body, their freedom and ancestral genes. The struggle nearly killed off God of Design. But "as he going off—is so he getting better." According to Francisco.

Flood, the first year of the trilogy with the thirty-foot puppet, Tantie the Washerwoman, and her charming Sugar Boy. Streets of white fabric rippled a river over revelers, shuddering to the stampede of socalypso and thousands of feet. Full flounced skirts, headties, loose shirts, and wide pants—more pure white cotton than was worn in petticoat days, or dreamt of as costumes in this age. Blinding in the sun. Then Fire Crab scattered sci-fi smoke on the Savannah stage and drew pyrotechnic blood as the awed nation watched. Buckets and floods of paint burst onto white. Rainbow colors washed the river like one big coolie Phagwa festival. The crowds went mad, the island shook, and mas changed forever. The next year he floored them again with a band called Cascadoo, named for the armored fish that will bring you back to the island if you eat it. "But they didn't give him Band of the Year then," Francisco said. "Because he white. But you just in time now, for the cooking up of Gold Callaloo. And with all these calabashes . . . this might be the golden egg!"

Despite the prejudice, this prolific creativity fashioned devotees, Slingerites—loyal followers who would never play with another band. These made up the masses. Visiting royal guests came from far and wide and blessed elite performers had direct contact with the King of Mas. Ata wonders if it is His profile stamped into the plastic discs crowning the poles, to be carried as staffs. Francisco watches her eyeing the work suspiciously. "I call them bobolees, these pole things," he declares.

"Bobolees?"

"Yes, a bobolee—a stupidy, a joker. And every band member has to have one. Pure boboleeism. We still have two thousand to finish. So . . . I am the Bobolee King." Francisco looks at Ata, gauging. "And you are a gofer. Yes, you now start—so is go for this, go for that—a gofer."

Not the cute little animal that came to her mind. She stares at Francisco's googly eyes behind thick glasses and his crooked, stumpy-teeth grin, and has to laugh. He is as mad as this crazy Carnival kingdom. And what does that make her?

The Port of Spain traffic behind the wall continues its stinking rumbling and she shouts over it, "What flicking hellhole is this?"

"Whaaat?" Francisco stops stacking the painted bobolees in the yard. "You cussing now?"

"What the fuck you think I have to do?" she shouts back. "Think I can survive if I don't? Nastiness flying around here like paint."

"Yes, Lord. Hallelujah, yuh baptize!"

Ata stumbles through the squalor after a week deep in Camp Swampy. Slimy, painty nights without sleep. Living on curry roti, channa doubles, and soft drinks. The dank house steams and sweats, continuously. Fueled with fire rum, crack, weed, whatever it needs to feed on. Vomiting green rejects to the putrid yard and batches of bobolees, calabashes, and wads of fabric to the master mas camp, two doors away. Women would visit the front yard, bringing money, food, whatever the men needed. Sometimes demanding money for child support. Once a fight broke out between two women arriving for the same man—

clothes ripping, thumping and tumbling on broken beer bottles and cigarette stubs, while the men cheered. Francisco broke up the fight and was left standing there trembling as the women cussed his "faggot hands" for touching their bare flesh. They disappeared then, covering their shame with a shield of foul language.

Now early evening feels like eternal damnation to Ata. She can barely focus on balancing down the front stairs, to the gate. She steps carefully, trying to hold something in her heart from bursting. A violent grunting, a man and woman jerking together, stop her dead. Right there, against the concrete steps. The woman's head, bowed, bumps on the cutter man's shoulder as he pounds himself into her. His snarl and red eyes roll to meet Ata's shock. "Walk, girl, don't fucking watch!" He continues pumping.

She bolts out of the yard straight onto the nightstreet. Her thumping heart pushes her feet fast round the corner pub, past the cars and limers outside. She stops at the door of the mas camp showroom suddenly, gazing blindly at the Gold Callaloo emblem on the plain glass door. Staring right through it for a moment. Floating, like the delicate Carnival-costume drawings framed and titled in there, all along the air-conditioned white walls. A middle-class couple step past her into the showroom, chattering with anticipation. Cool, neutered air wafts out onto Ata's face and she wraps her frail arms around herself. The pounding is still there.

She walks past Ma Pau casino, crosses Ariapita Avenue, to the quieter side streets. Near the police station, she stops at a neglected square. Woodbrook's vagrants live there. She passes the sleeping forms huddled against the public toilet and sits on a swing. No tears spill because she doesn't know what she would be weeping for. Anger and then a surge of extreme exhaustion and futility fold her into a hungry, homeless, vagrant figure. Suspended there.

Where do the vagrants go for Carnival? The places they rest in are taken over. This square becomes the assembly point for Slinger's revelers to adjust their costumes; help each other fit and pin, comparing how much pounds they had to lose; and stamp new gold boots to break them in. Where are the vagrants then? They blend into the dirty "ole mas" dawn of Carnival but are pushed aside, ridiculed, and pitied for the rest of it. While rich folks prance in their home square, the few brave homeless who dare to dance in their everyday costume are given a wide berth, out of fear or scorn—"respect"—in the once-a-year show of equality. *What is it all for, now? And why do people put themselves through slavery to make mas, or slave for the money to buy the costume—to "free up" for a few days? Two days of bought identity? Why the last-minute scramble and the stampede over dignity and dying skills?*

And what is she doing here? She knows the answers are back in the chaos of Camp Swampy. In the experience, the music and rhythms of Trinidad. "Is we t'ing," people tell her. *But who is "we" when so many Trinis pick up their families and run from it? When the Indian population hardly embrace it? When Carnival bands are associated with class?* Vagrant questions move her again. Vaguely. In the direction of the Slingerite artists' house, a tiny white fretwork asylum, tucked into a small yard packed with banana trees.

Three beautiful dancers, male dancers and local actors no less, one red, one black, one white, welcome her warmly with their usual tone of alarm. "Oh Gawd! What happen to you? You need RESS. Laus! Take a break, child. You can't keep up with dat madness right through, yuh know. Or else it go kill you. Is true. Come." And they share. Generously.

She showers and eats and sleeps on a bed in the tiny bedroom, in their clothes, their protection, their little house full of throaty banter, incense, gentle music, and rumbling laughter. Grateful, she breathes deeply in her sleep. And outside, the wide banana leaves cluster, pressing close, filtering the Port of Spain night air before it enters the jalousie windows, before it enters her.

The hills breathe and settle round the ex–swamp nest of a town. Spore-thick moist warm nights. Silk cotton trees with "shining eyes" line a street called Mucurapo. One of these old trees rots in the botanical gardens and a young straight one stands guard on the hill above. Breeze tugs off their white cotton-hair tufts and spreads their magic far. Soucouyant and Lagahoo. Old spirits and superstitions lived in them. But not now, the hills sigh. Look how things change and rearrange.

BRIGHT, SPARKY, DUSTY AIR and the sound of steel-pan tinkles through fretwork into Ata's home on Marli Street, four years later. Francisco spins around: "Look at this woman now—you born with a golden spoon in yuh ass! A real job, in a real office with nice people. No shithound stink work no more. A good girlfriend. And look at this place . . ." He looks about for the last time, at the little cocoon he helped her weave.

Magic. A wooden antique dream of a house. From the time she saw it, to agreement and key—it came true. Right around the corner from her work, Francisco, and the Savannah. Tall narrow doors graced the dusty front steps, ginger lilies colored the yard. As fragile as it looked from the outside, it was elegance inside, to her. A delicate palace. High ceilings lengthened her spine, white everywhere dressed her regal. Fretwork lace partitions, layers of gloss paint, the care taken to cut each detail so long ago. It didn't need much more than the few things Francisco had helped her furnish it with. They had boarded up the rotten bathroom window and put a new bolt on the front door.

He draped gauzy white muslin around the sunroom and she spread old cotton curtains on the floor there, to cover the holes. They cozied it up into a heavenly nest, weighted with smooth river stones and scented with vetiver. Her haven. His shelter, sometimes.

Ata looks at his lopsided face, his bottom lip, busted and trembling slightly. "You have to go?"

He can't stop the tears gathering in his puffy, hurt eyes. "Stay here and wait for what? To . . . to get stabbed next time?" Spreads his arms wide in mock sacrifice. "I look like I ready to die for being gay?" He tries to grin but his smile cracks as she hugs him.

She squeezes him tight tight and lets herself cry quietly with him. His neck smells slightly of paint and a sweet oil—and fear. She hugs tighter.

A bunch of fellas had stoned him as he walked home from his sister's place the other night. He was dressed in normal clothes but his tight gait must have given him away. They chased him down. He stumbled and fell but escaped. This time. Now he's migrating to an aunt in England.

"But it will be better there for you," Ata says gently as Francisco stops shaking and wipes his face with his T-shirt. "You could pursue your acting and you'll fit in just fine with all that's going on there—you know, the streaking parades and all."

He tries to chuckle and snorts hard. "I know, I know, I know." The trembling is gone but his lip is more swollen, the bruise on his chin red.

"I'll miss you bad though."

"And I will miss flicking you, girl." He squeezes her hard again and stamps his feet, notices a soft corner of the floor. It crackles when he prods it with his toe. "Wood ants feasting like—eh!" His eyes run up, to the attic. "You could imagine what going on up there? The other day, right in that office over so, thieves came in through the roof and t'ief out all the computers. T'ank God dese windows have burglarproofing." He goes on, urging her to take care of herself. She should socialize more, get to know people, the ones always inviting her out—go out. But be careful, especially as a woman living on her own, especially when coming home at night. Watch out for the strangers roaming around here like rats.

She watches him crossing the street, shouting back to her with his mashed-up smile, "Remember Camp Swampy days? Remember your survival skills, girl!"

She waves and sends kisses from the steps. Standing on the thin skin of the peacock, tucked close under the feathery shifting beauty, she feels fine bones moving beneath her bare feet.

The next day at work, Ata sits at her tall drawing table and pushes the slide rule up to the top, slowly, then brings it back down over the draft paper taped down in the center. Her friend SC, at the next table in the art room, looks at her taking her time to select the right-sized Staedtler pen. It's only the three of them in the art room at the back of the small advertising agency. Ata, SC, and a tiny mouse of a girl, Claris. Claris has to climb and hop up onto her stool, she's so tiny. But she is good. Cheerful, with straight short brown hair and pale skin that never sees the sun, quiet, efficient, and just good. SC is the moody one, always stomping hard and making the tables shake, slamming things on her desk and roughing up the felt-tipped markers. She's the sultry darkie of the bunch of women that make up the office staff. But she is good, too. Quick with pre-press, she churns out and delivers. SC had warmed to Ata, not sure what to make of her quietness at first but liking the fact that she was not from this place. When she realized that Ata also worked with *real* artists *and* that she gets crude humor—they hit it off.

SC cackles and crows at her own jokes on a good day, louder than anyone else, shaking up her tits with a particular gobbly laugh.

"I know. Is sad, eh?" she says gently to Ata now. SC had met Francisco and was getting to know all that went on in Ata's life.

"I miss him already."

"Is not sadder than this rahtid Happy Cooking Oil shitting artwork we have to redo again, though."

Ata glanced at the Happy logo at the top of her desk and realized that she should have taped it under the draft paper on her drawing board. The client wanted the *y* slanted and the whole thing set at an angle.

The day passes like a proper office day. Clean, neat lines glide from her nib along the slide rule. Stencil font from the big gray catalog. Happy Cooking Oil. Ideal Flour, *for all your baking needs*. And the never-ending annual report for CariCo Insurance. Helen is in charge of that, so she has priority at the square old Macintosh computer they share. Transparencies are the thing. And color separations done by hand, crude flash-card ads for TV that you can't spend much time on 'cause they're cheap. Tedious, monotonous, and unimaginative. Every now and then, they get to design something from scratch. Not today.

Drinking instant Nescafé with Carnation creamer after lunch at her desk, Ata refocuses, to get through the day. She has gotten used to the musty air-conditioned carpet and cow-gum smell; it even comforts her, now mixed with the coffee steam. Claris sneaks up to the tape deck and slips in one of her endless U2 and Queen cassettes. On certain days this kind of music makes Ata crave any other kind of sound. But now it's Friday. Next week will be end-of-month and she will collect a check for a small amount, barely enough to pay her bills and eat. Nothing more.

"What you need is a man," SC says finally at four-thirty as they're packing up. She goes out with Ata sometimes to her jazzy arty events and feels that, with Francisco gone, Ata might become an even better best friend. "I mean, a *real* man. Sex. Is good for the hormones."

"Right, and the first five men I take a liking to in Trinidad all turn out to be gay."

That made the mouse giggle as she scuttled out the door.

"I know. And the next good-looking ones married or they just damn stupid or *ordinary*. You telling me, girlfren. Anyways, cool yuhself and I'll see you tomorrow afternoon, right? Six p.m."

Ata halts abruptly, just outside the open kitchen door of the apartment SC had directed her to.

"*The Perfumed Garden. Concerning Praiseworthy Men.* The virile member must have at most a length and breadth of twelve fingers, or three handbreadths, or at least six fingers, or a hand and a half breadths."

A recognizable, high-pitched turkey-gobble laugh shrieks above other laughter, cutting across the deep voice of the man proudly announcing this.

"Lawd, Fraser, you too much!" SC splutters. "Oh my God . . ."

"And that's Arab men," the carefully cultured voice goes on to boast. "So you could imagine the dimensions . . ."

". . . of black men!" SC cuts in, her cackle rising again.

"And as Sir Richard Burton went on to explain—the how-many-fingers breadth represent nine inches, 'which is rare in the Englishman, the Frenchman, and other Europeans.' Do you know they went and did thousands of measurements, and this was in the thirties and forties, concluding that the average American and European is between five and seven inches?"

"Well I would'a like to be there with the tape measure!"

Ata steps into the doorway to see her ridiculous friend bent over, miming the measuring action.

"Soldiers," the owner of the deep voice says.

"Of course—is easy to get them up!" She happily jerks off another imaginary one, quickly, shrieking again and flapping an arm at Ata as she notices her.

"Come in, my dear," Fraser welcomes her.

A few people are seated at a blue table full of drinks watching SC in the middle of the kitchen floor, near Fraser, trying to control herself. She hugs and kisses Ata, then turns to introduce her to Fraser.

"My best friend I been telling you about, Ata."

"Delighted." Fraser's eyes twinkle frankly.

"Shocked." Ata smiles broadly, shaking hands.

"Don't worry with her, nuh. She only playing decent, if you know what she calls me . . ." SC mock whispers to Fraser, "I can't tell you in front of people."

He only raises his eyebrows but she can't contain it. "SC! You know what that stands for? Small Clit!" Before he could begin to guess. "Clit as in 'clitoris.'"

"Yes, yes, I think I get the idea."

SC's clucking, ready to burst again, delighted at the opportunity for rude talk. In fact, this is the only kind of conversation that brings her to full-form life. "My word!" She sniffs, straightening her tight clothes. "Well . . . this is a party, isn't it? When the people coming? I should have a drink right about now, I think."

Ata and Fraser watch her prance her shapely self over to the drinks table and the amused set of people there.

The flat is small but feels spacious with the open kitchen

almost the same size as the living room. Bare sliding glass doors open onto the veranda with a view of the steep valley. A white tiled floor throughout cools it. Fraser points out what he has done—removed a wall here, replaced the windows there, created this odd-shaped table, built in the chunky concrete shelving.

"Is nice, eh?" SC swans into the living room. "I told you he have style."

Ata takes in the books and well-positioned art pieces. A deep-red painting rests casually against a wall and a bizarre purple candelabrum hangs, dangerously low, over the couch and Persian rug. The party now begins arriving, in new cars, from their well-off homes in better parts of Port of Spain. The "ho-to-toes," according to SC. And Fraser gracefully greets and introduces them around. Ata watches him stretch his neck out from his broad shoulders and tapered bulk, trying to look some-one square in the eye, intelligently. A turtle. And returnee. Fraser Goodman. A big creative lump of an architect, from good Trinidadian middle-class stock, properly educated in England. "Great virtue in intelligence," he'd later quote. Looks like he feels he's in the presence of it now, blessed to be able to entertain such people. Sucking in his large stomach and trying to calm himself, to become an eloquent, British-accented gentleman. For a while.

"Marriette, my dear! You made it. How wonderful of you to grace us with your presence this afternoon."

Marriette slinks into the room and offers Fraser her cheek, exchanging a sly and secretive smile with him, like a cat that loves the game. Her voice is husky as she casually hello's all round. She perches herself on the kitchen counter against the window light, superciliously watching and swirling her drink, as Fraser welcomes and introduces more guests. Eyebrows permanently arched high over skin-colored eyes, silky hair in a sharp jaw-length bob, framing her almost Egyptian, perfect face.

Marriette crosses a bare bronze leg and slickly hooks some hair, swiping paw behind ear. Her presence had silenced SC.

"Marriette works with the French attaché but is destined to become one of our ambassadors. The woman speaks five languages. Don't you, dear?"

Marriette just grimaces at their little charade and shakes the hand of a very tall man who had just arrived—Terence, the professor. Bespectacled, dark, and low-spoken, he seems almost embarrassed to be present. Marriette picks this up immediately. "So this is the Terence you were telling me about, Fraser," she drawls, eyeing his wedding band and watching him turn away hurriedly. Arching her long neck and smirking, she eyes the next arrivals.

Fraser motions in a Trini-White, French-Creole doctor, pointing out people she already knows. A Chinese-lawyer couple step in. A striking blue-black dreadlocked relative of Fraser with his friend. An American old-school architect colleague, with his bejeweled upper-class wife. And Helen, "Helen the Greek Goddess of my life." Fraser's childhood love and best friend. Less hoity-toity others straggle in and it seems to Ata that Fraser had selected a cross section to deliberately bring the most diverse couples into contact with the most conventional. But they all know Fraser well, from the extremely long-haired Indian woman with her poor-white, hippy-rock husband—tattoos, leather, greasy ponytail, and all; office workers Dhiraj and Sunil with their matching, quiet girlfriends; a sci-fi-punk Syrian designer with her *Star Wars* makeup, head shaved, bodybuilder muscles popping from hot-pink shorts, trailing her chubby Afro-Trini husband; to Marriette's louder-than-all half brother, who heads straight for the beers. They all know Fraser well enough to quickly dismantle his pretense at formality and start up a good Trini opinion-dominated chatter and commotion of food and drinks.

The Greek Goddess smiles, floating through it all, coming attentively to the rescue of the delicate wine discussers while Fraser spins around on command, looking for more ice for the rum drinkers. Sangria lashers finishing the big bowl quick and slackers hauling Carib beers from coolers under the table.

"Wha' happening with de music? How you could have a party without music?" Marriette's brother shouts over the clamor.

"I will do it, I'm the DJ! Your muuusic-machine self, yaow!" The designer's hyper husband jostles his way into the living room.

"Play something nice and background," Fraser yells, then asks Marriette, "Why everyone came in through the kitchen door? I have a perfectly decent front entrance that's hardly ever used."

"When you will stop yuh assishness, Fraser? That's just it—which one of your friends ever came in here through your blasted front door? This man loves nonsense." She turns to Ata chuckling, exhaling a plume of cigarette smoke.

Ata stares at her easy confidence and suddenly feels completely self-conscious in her makeshift outfit, a piece of saffron sari fabric, wrapped and tied into a halter getup. She had cinched it with her sister's broad belt and tortoiseshell buckle, but the fabric was plain cotton with a nonshiny, simple border. She had even pulled up her curls and hooked on a leaf-shaped bronze earring that curved around her ear and along her jaw. Most people commented on her earring or unusual style of dress, but this near to Marriette it just feels cheap and overdone. Ata tries not to look at her and moves away toward Fraser's staff and the comfort of office conversation.

Dhiraj the draftsman and Sunil the all-rounder were both young and modest about their roles but quick to let you know that they know—they are in with something terribly unique.

"People don't understand," they whisper. "You see the new buildings going up, that look like they come straight out of Miami? Off-the-shelf designs? Well, not like that!" Apart from Fraser's style being ultramodern, "is just *different*" and they are proud and privileged to be part of it.

Ata lets on that she has a sense of it, from what he'd done with this flat.

"Exactly!" they both agree emphatically, nodding yes to SC's offer of more intoxication.

Ata suddenly feels worldly and sophisticated because of a familiarity with what seems so celebrated on this island. She half listens to someone's gorgeous rasta friend, who SC had pointed out as prime eye-food.

SC nods at him now. "Boring boring and overly *ordinary,* on the inside. Don't mind all this world-music kind'a mix, nuh."

"Aaaah let's do it, let's dance! Shake your booty right to the ground . . ." blasts out suddenly from the music set.

"What de hell!" SC cranes to see the DJ bobbing and grooving away in the living room. "Turn it down!" she shouts.

The DJ obeys, slightly. And the last remnants of cocktailpartyness disappear as some people begin shaking it. Alcohol confidence moves Ata toward the lawyer couple, who had been looking curiously but welcomingly at her. The look when people want to start a get-to-know-you conversation. SC is already gyrating her hips and wriggles off toward the living room.

The couple are interesting enough but conversation is an effort over the music and noise. The arrival of a latecomer gives them something to look at. He stamps and stamps on the doormat, wiping his feet energetically the way a dog does on grass after his ablutions, sniffing and jerking his sharp chin up in the air. Gripping a bottle of wine as if it were a walking stick, he hitches up his trousers and steps into the kitchen looking absolutely delighted to be invited. A foreigner. Most people could spot one a mile off. Exactly how they are spotted, before they even open their mouths, cannot be pinned down. This is a real skill, mastered by island-vibe detectives who zoom in on the clues between a stranger and foreigner, between visiting overseas family member and returnee, expat and tourist. The experts claim *we know everybody, is a small place*. Impossible with a population of a million. Or *we can smell fresh meat*. Ata wonders, does this make her a local, since she has the sense? But she's detected as a foreigner too, sometimes.

She watches as the latecomer glances around, eyes lighting on hers, raking her body. A stealthy wolf. Tall, skinny, and hunched but good-looking in a Gypsy way. His accent is slightly French as Marriette introduces herself and offers to find the host. He stamps his shoes some more, adjusts his spectacles, and swipes his longish hair back as Fraser comes beaming up to him. "Pierre, you're here, you old dog! You didn't even call me."

"I only just got in to the hotel. Had a bit of trouble with the taxi finding this place . . ."

Fraser embraces his rib cage warmly and he bends, wrapping arms and bottle around Fraser's shoulders. They thump and box each other, grinning away in genuine boyish affection. Marriette lounges off again, close by, smiling her drop-dead perfect smile. And the lawyer couple have faded off to chat with others.

"So you met the lovely Marriette already?" Fraser turns away from her, adding under his breath, "She's the stunner I said I wanted you to meet."

"But who's this?" Pierre's eyes are drinking in Ata. He pads over to where she stands alone now, trapped.

Fraser introduces them and returns to his duties.

"So what do you do?" Pierre asks, seeming less interested in the answer than in the detail of her collarbone and sharp bare shoulders.

Heart like a bird in a cage, she stutters and mumbles about graphics, design . . . Marriette's eyes glitter cruelly as she trails off.

"Umn." He nudges in closer to her. "Very graphic indeed."

After the dancing dies and the drunk and polite leave, the party becomes a sit-down affair. Marriette sits on a tall stool, comfortable as the ornament on the bookshelf behind her. Suave comments and her low, throaty laugh drift out and, glass in hand, sipping, she glows amber at them. At Pierre. Fraser, merry himself, checks her gleam. Spreads himself in his chair so he can see better—from her, to Pierre, to Ata. Then Marriette's well-lubricated brother is accidentally set off when someone asks about his surveillance work on other islands.

"Well, boy, soon small-island people can't afford to live in they own home. Is either you working in service—servitude for imported millionaires, building luxury villas for them—can't pay yuh bills 'cause yuh pay is shit, *or* you sell yuh piece'a heritance for U.S. dollars and get de hell out'a there. Is colonialism all over again, yuh understand? But dis time the owner not responsible for de slave. Whereas, long ago, the owner had to feed, clothe, give house and land, make sure they don't get too sick—or else is his loss and fire in he skin. Now the government self, the blasted politicians, only selling out every last piece'a crown land, and is every man for theyself."

Three others try getting a word in but he outshouts them. "But wait, nuh—ah now start! So, while all this craziness going on—inflation—people just putting up price 'cause they feel they must get a piece'a de dollar. Man who don't want to serve can't get work. In fact, is less jobs for he anyway 'cause they prefer to hire women—less pay, less trouble—man must do physical labor like construction and farming and t'ing. But man can't get a start-up loan 'cause banks only lending for secure business and tourist development anyway. So, is more violence. Man can't feed he family so he beat them, take a drink, and stab-up a next man. And woman sexing more than ever for money and whatever they need, 'cause is easier. But is service still, yuh check wha' I mean? Heh. Meanwhile, is damage. Damage all round de islands. Down to de damn 'eco-habitats.' Less food production, more importation. Food more cheap in England and de U.S. than in dese islands! So people must migrate to survive. They even joining army and navy, to migrate again."

Everybody breathes as he takes a sip, thinking the speech is done.

"Well, more Caribbean people will be coming in to Trinidad," the lawyer-lady finally inserts. "Especially with the CSME."*

"CS who? Caricom Simple Minded Economics?" Marriette's brother bellows. "Even though Trinidad have oil and t'ings looking good here—the TT dollar is shit! When they convert they minimum wage—and ours is lower, and they ain' even getting that—when they convert it, they can't send home shit. You see that CSME farce? Trinidad making up they own rules 'cause we don't really want nobody here, specially small-island people. If is foreign companies like BP and Shell and t'ing—well, that's a different matter. 'Singapore of the Caribbean' my ass."

"I guess the crime puts people off too," lawyer-lady mumbles.

"Exactly right! When they see Trinis hustling to move to other islands, buying homes, and sending they children to school there, 'cause'a the kidnapping and murder—who in they right mind go want to come here?"

*Caricom Single Market Economy.

"All the hundreds of convicts the U.S. deported back to the Caribbean, perhaps?" Fraser raises his wineglass.

"You damned right!" Marriette's brother clinks it with his beer bottle, hard.

The Trini exclamatory way of talking, overdramatizing everything with unpolished wit and raucous emotion, sometimes overwhelms Ata. Yet she feels prudish when she recoils. Somehow, the chaotic Spanish clamoring, the Indian clannishness and cutlass temper, the African skiving danceability, and English peasant/French farmer crudeness all blend together into a confused, brash way of life and language. But mostly, because it's an excuse for another party, everything is celebrated. Brian Lara, cricket, and steelpan—so much talent here. Unique art. Derek Walcott—we claim him. We reach World Cup football—we lose. But celebration is "we t'ing." God is a Trini. And creolization becomes the obvious answer for everything, more t'ing to celebrate. Piss-taking Chinee-parang, chutney-soca, rapso, fast-food curry and roti . . . "Douglarize the nation!" said one politician, responding to racial politicking. The "redskin" Trinis, though—the ones like the hot-stinging Jack Spaniard wasp, named after the bold, murderous pirate in search of El Dorado, the ones who think they're local white, like Marriette's brother—they always were the loudest and most boastful members of society.

"But it's not just here," Marriette says. Her cool voice comes floating out of the corner. "Things are getting worse everywhere. And Trinidad is no exception."

Ata thinks this is a good time to escape to the bathroom. She stoops under the hanging candelabrum but bounces it, spilling hot wax onto the carpet and her back, setting off "ouches" and everyone feeling it for her. SC clucks and Fraser fusses about how he should really hang it elsewhere.

"But only you would hang it so low."

Ata claims it's not that bad, glad for the ridiculous object taking center stage as she gets away. As soon as she returns, though, the foreign wolf makes room for her at his end of the settee, insisting she sit there. She sits, cautiously.

The wolf smiles, crinkling crow's-feet. He nudges the pack. "So what's . . . what's the forecast for this place, then? If it's so grim in the other islands?"

A loud groaning starts—to shut up the know-it-all brother.

"You *really* want to know?" the orator booms.

But SC jumps up and claps a hand over his mouth, holding it there.

"It's a mess," the lawyer-lady laughs.

Muffled agreement comes from under SC's hand and she renews her hold, bracing her body against him. He raises his beer bottle and the five Trinis raise theirs. Pierre and Ata raise glasses too.

"To a lost cause!" Fraser toasts.

"To all lost causes!"

Marriette's brother nestles back against SC's breasts. "Well, I don' mind getting lost here at all."

She boxes him and prances back to the settee laughing, just as Pierre's hand touches Ata's skin above her knee, where her wrap had slid back. Just resting his paw there briefly, but long enough to register the current between them. Her leg burns.

Others are standing up but Marriette is still as a sphinx in the corner.

SC straightens her skirt. "Oh boy, time for me to get this one home. Come, Ata, let's go before dis white man take a bite out'a you. I seeing, yuh know!"

Pierre laughs and slyly taps Ata's ass as she gets up, uncurling himself and stretching, before saying goodbye to the others.

Ata doesn't realize until she stands that she's had too much and maybe too many different drinks. Overdosed on the assorted company. She's glad for SC.

Fraser sees them to the door, inviting Ata to come see his office, anytime.

"Of course, thanks. And thanks for inviting me tonight," she manages.

"Is me who invited you, girl!" SC hugs her with one arm. "This fool thinks she could drink, but she have no flesh to absorb it. Bye, Fraser. See ya. And keep that one in check, he houngry, man."

In the Roses Advertising art room, *where ideas blossom*, SC keeps catching Ata's eye and winking hard at her. "De girl ketch white t'ing, yuh know, Claris."

Mouse squeaks, "Un-huh?" grinning mischievously but not missing a beat at her desk.

"Don't worry with this dramatist. Somebody was flirting with me, that's all."

"And you wasn't flirting? I could find out where he staying and his number from Fraser, if you want," SC offers generously.

"You see, Claris?" Ata smiles as SC winks at her again. "No, thanks."

"Jeez, man, I just trying a little nurturing. Like our dear boss-lady likes to say, *'We nurture you to full bloom!'*" She hooted the ending as they all cracked up.

The whole office shared the private joke about the corniness of their boss-lady's plug-line, and her taste. All eight employees were women, her bunch of roses, as she liked to call them. And when they had PMS they were allowed to show their thorns in this female-friendly environment. "You must feel comfortable to be productive. Think of it like yuh home. We are a family and must always stick together—to show them what we women can do!" Fiercely competitive, Angelica Diaz held her own against chauvinist businessmen. She had a natural combination of business head and body sense, and used her female charm all the time. Even with her bunch of roses.

When Ata first came to her office Angelica declared she only hired women. "So you may be lucky one time already. Who needs men?" She laughed, crashing bracelets and ring-heavy hands onto her desk. Her gold tooth glinted. "You know what I mean? Have a seat. And you, Mira," she shouted to her secretary, "stop passing up and down outside my door!"

Her desk was like Ata imagined the inside of her car—a box of tissues, fresh-scent potpourri, a little dog with his head on a spring sitting on a doily. Her office, like the inside of her home—gilt-framed cheap prints of stylized flowers, a pink curly vase with artificial roses, and two proud photos of perfectly handsome children, in graduation caps and gowns, of course.

"Your portfolio is unusual," she said to Ata. "I mean, is good." Closed it, jangled her hands, and puffed her cleavage up and down above the desk. "But what you have here has nothing to do with what we need. I mean, you talented, I could see that. You's a artist!" She puckered her orange lipstick, raised plucked eyebrows, and blinked mascara-heavy lashes at Ata.

This was one of these women who must sleep fully made-up, with foundation, blush, and all. She would wear a frilly negligee over her full-body Spanish shape, be born with long lacquered nails, and take her first steps in stilettos. Ata knew these kinds of women were born to rule. Right away, they run things.

Angelica looked at Ata trying to find some confidence and sit up straight and decided that she might be able to do the graphics Roses Advertising Agency needed. "I know you never done this but what we need most is flip cards. Is easy, you could pick it up quick. What I like is how you trying something different with yuh own kind'a style. And I does give anybody trying a chance. Yes, Mira! Yuh still up and down out there. I said I would give she a chance!" she shouted to the open door.

"You called for me, Angelica?" the tall, smiley secretary said as she appeared.

"No, I didn't call for you, Miss Fastness. This is Ata. She'll be joining us soon, part-time. There we go—official."

The girl smiled welcome at Ata. "Another female for the department."

"Yes, I wasn't looking for a man, I have a husband now, yuh forget?" She laughed rich and throaty and patted her piled-up hair vigorously.

Ata liked how this lady so plum vulgar and full of herself.

She looked at Ata square and hard. "Well, I giving you a chance. But is only part-time. You might get some other freelance work from stupid clients sometimes, I don' mind. But you brave, girl—to come and live here on your own. Trinidad rough, it only looking so fancy and nice."

Mid-morning Ata uses the gribbly lump of cow-gum waste to erase pencil lines. It is a satisfying thing, rubbing away blemishes to leave pen marks only. Clean, precise ink on translucent paper. Adding the final touch—a little circle, right over the alignment cross lines—like the target marks of a sniper. The same symbol when you look through the lens in the movies. Dead-on. When all three layers of artwork line up perfect over each other and the target marks come into alignment, she feels just as complete as the marksman might feel. Perfect shot. She bends over the template, relishing the rifle feel of the 0.25 steel tip, with its tiny ball gliding round the inside of the plastic rim. So smooth and quick. Neat.

The door opens abruptly and Janice bangs in as only she does, with her ugly poker face. "A special delivery for you, Ata," shoving a big bunch of roses wrapped in cellophane at her. She takes in Ata's shock, raises her eyebrows, and twirks thin lips in what could be a smile or a grimace of pity, then slams the door on her way out before SC can utter a sound.

SC flies across to Ata's desk, exclaiming and inspecting the gift before Ata can even touch it. "My word! Who they from? What a t'ing! Atalaantaah . . ."

Even Claris creeps up close.

Ata had never received flowers from an admirer before, but guesses who this is from just as quickly as SC does, even as she opens the little card.

"Is him!" SC confirms as Ata reads to herself *Can I see you tonight? Dinner? Yours, Pierre.* "Who else would buy roses? And where he find so many roses here, anyways?"

Claris ventures, "Er, a florist?"

"I mean, who would look to go and buy so big a bunch of roses in the first place? A foreigner. A Frenchie at that—ooh!" She hugs Ata hard, crowding her up with her breasts and trying to get a look at the card.

"But how he knows where to find me? I didn't . . ."

"You stupid or what? The man knows Fraser. That is what I call a hunter. Count them, I sure is a dozen. A local guy would'a send a bouquet. Or a single rose—a fake one at that."

Ata knows what SC means by *bouquet*—one of those mixed-flower arrangements, with five different colors, leaves and sprigs stuck stiffly in a green oasis sponge, in a white plastic dish. She's glad it isn't that.

Mouse sniffs to see if the flowers are real and SC demands to see the card as the rest of the office tramp in, led by boss-lady.

"Romance!" Angelica announces. "How nice! He must have got the idea from the name Roses, ha! I like the man already. Who is it?"

Some of the girls think Ata should have some privacy while they join in the gossip-maco pressure. With SC leaning up on her, Ata has no choice.

"Is a white man she meet the otha night. He is a Frenchie-English, works with the U.N." SC accepts the nods and raised eyebrows on Ata's behalf and turns to face her when Mother Rose asks outright what it says on the card.

This time Ata blushes as the bunch of women squeal more ridiculously. They enjoy their *Sex and the City* moment of fun while she's dying of embarrassment, thinking about the answer. Tonight?

"Is easy, of course," SC explains after Mother Rose shoos everyone back to work. "You shouldn't refuse. For what?"

Ata knows there is no real reason to say no. She wants to see the man. She stares at the imported flowers, peels back some of the cellophane, and touches the dark-red soft petals. They fall off in her hand. A bloom ready to expire. She agrees in her head, with SC's ever-ready advice about accepting but not doing anything too rash, keep him courting, check him out. But she needs to know a little more before tonight. She asks her friend if she would call and take her around to see Fraser.

"But what stupid stupidness is this?" Fraser shouts at his secretary as Ata pushes on the curved steel door handle. "What he has to talk to me about? What's wrong?"

"I don't know! Father McBarnette just said that he spoke to Father Gonzales, he's been looking at the drawings and wants to talk to you. That's all." Unruffled by Fraser's temper. "I mean, I can't read the man's mind over the phone." Muttering softly, she packs up her desk for the day.

Fraser felt the waft of warm air and glances at Ata slipping in cautiously. "That's what I'm talking about. I don't know if he thinks he is God 'cause he building a church, or what, but *he* is always the problem. AFTER Father Gonzales and I AGREE on something, *he* has to come, 'Why can't this be like that? Do we have to have this?' Come in, girl." He snatches open the door to his office and leads the way. The secretary waves goodbye silently, grimacing, as she creeps out the front door.

Fraser flings a hand at the beginnings of a white cardboard model on his desk. He knew what Ata had come for. "Sorry. This man is a real pain in the ass, though. Father Gonzales is higher in the church than he, Gonzales could be the difficult one. But no. This is the third time now he, McBarnette, is calling to carry on about some major or minor thing. And then we have to talk. And then we have to meet. And I have to try to convince them all over a-bloody-gain. Wasting my time! My time is precious, you know. And expensive! I already told them I'm doing up a model for a presentation to the committee . . ."

"How you know he's calling to change something?" Ata ventures, checking out the gray walls and angles of his modern gingerbread office space.

Fraser sucks his teeth and turns away. *How will she ask?* he wonders briefly. He watches her holding in the little excitement of her afternoon, clutching her roses, trying to take in his bigger problem. I will let her ask, he decides.

The cardboard building site of a church sits between them and the plywood base covers most of his desk. A curved wall stands erect on layers of terraced white land. One square column is the only other thing standing. Bits of construction card and paper are strewn about. A Corbusier book rests atop a stack at the edge of the desk. Photocopies of a curvy church are stuck to the wall close by, details of a dark interior with rectangle shafts of sunlight streaming in through holes in the wall. Fraser's own deft sketches—a cluster of shapes, the single strong line of a roof among a tangle of black marker strokes—are pinned up too.

"What's that?" Ata points at some contoured bits on the model.

He explains the steps, shallow and wide along the whole front of the building. And that the thing is—how many chances would he get to build a church? A Roman Catholic one at that. It's not just a house or an office, it's something for the people. And that he had had to ask himself, *What does church mean to me? What are the contemporary and eternal resonances of it?*

"Where will it be built?" she asks.

He told her—Maloney. And now it was her turn to look at the dreams lying bare on his face.

"In the housing-scheme area. By the highway," he adds, apologetically.

The miles of hot little concrete boxes, crammed into a grid off the highway, are an outstanding government eyesore. Faded, inner-city-style council blocks tower sadly above the dry field of packed boxes, not a space for a tree between them.

"I know, I know." He hurries on. "But this is it! The government gave them a plot of land to do something—for the community."

"Government gave the Roman Catholics?"

"Yes, but it's not a very big piece."

"And they build a church?"

Fraser is surprised by the sharp side of this deer, talking as if she knows him from some long-gone forest days. It makes him feel like he knows her better somehow too, like she senses his base position. Her wide gaze boldens him to remind himself—as he had convinced the priests with this architectural opportunity of a lifetime—that the church *will* be more than a place of worship. It will become a real community center, as any church should actually be . . .

"Planning and religion can't force 'community'—people have to want it. Government built a rat-racetrack of a ghetto suburb, relocating people from all over. Can children even play in the streets there?" Ata asks

"That's why it's needed!" He sees from her ferny smile that she really does understand, and can see the task before him. What does church mean to Maloney? Among broken bottles, telegraph poles, and wires? One can be true in this situation.

"Look, look at this." He grabs the Corbusier book and flashes pages at her. "This man, in his own way, created something *genuine*. Something as true as the Ethiopian Lalibela rock churches. And then there's the question of faith. Faith there was in a God. Faith lost. The architect's own faith . . ."

He sees on her face that he's going too far, beginning to preach his own lush pastures. She glances at her flowers resting on the settee. "Forget about him for a minute," he mutters.

"Who?" She jumps, startled. Flight or fight.

"The Frenchman who's after you . . . He's okay," he adds, flopping himself onto the small settee wearily and offering her the other half. She sits awkwardly. Her eyes still hesitant. "Have fun, go on. I've known Pierre awhile now and he's a decent soul really, as far as Frogs go."

She wants to say that she should call him, to give her answer, but suddenly feels juvenile, even while so comfortable with this strange, charming turtle. Pierre can wait, she shouldn't rush.

Fraser sees her slight relief and picks up again, needing practice for the priests. Yes, the Catholic Church is the most hypocritical, self-interested, powerful organization. But a church can offer an earthly ecstasy. A moment when worldly life is suspended and *something else* enters. Lots of people have written about it, he says. "And there will be a piazza."

She listens to the Cambridge tone creeping into his voice.

"Look at the roof, I wanted to make it mobile but they were against that. This lets in the afternoon sun and makes the space seem almost open-air, bigger than it actually is. On this side, the walls don't touch.

"(Come in under the shadow of this red rock),
And I will show you something different from either
Your shadow at morning striding behind you
Or your shadow at evening rising to meet you."

He insists that Eliot's "red rock" is the Ethiopian rock-hewn church. And that Africa is in Maloney, needing to be sung and praised even though the sky is strung with wires and the shape of hope is the heat-shimmering peaks of the Northern Range in the distance. *An African Elegy* from his latest obsession, Ben Okri—the turtle was on a roll, surfing.

"That is why our music is so sweet,
It makes the air remember.
There are secret miracles at work
That only time will bring forth.
I too have heard the dead singing.

"Once people can gather the elders will find their voices again. It will have served a civic purpose. Not like one of them dingy concrete sheds they call community centers. No doors, and the floor slopes down toward the altar. White tiles. Everything will be white and the roof—curved, bare, galvanized sheeting."

He sees her watching his vision unfold, glorious words melting, landing on architectural scrolls, the fish-scale wind chime twisting slowly in the draft of the air conditioner; on a rainbow of felt-tipped markers, pink anthuriums in a blue vase. Proud and pleasured by his own world of beauty, he notices her hands and wonders if she plays an instrument, with those long long fingers. He imagines his friend bringing those fingers to his mouth, them touching his friend's strange white chest, brushing the thin skin above his hip bone. He sighs and throws a leg over the arm of the settee, grunts, and closes his eyes.

The leatherback nestles down, right in front of her. "Think of," Ata whispers, "all them old ladies with they Sunday hats and skatie shoes, sliding on the slanted tiled floor, skating right down and bunching up by the altar!"

He cracks a peek at her mischievous face.

"You sure a playground, a patch of grass and some trees, a sports center, wouldn't be more useful?"

He chuckles and she laughs, just as Fraser's phone rings and he digs at his tight jeans pockets to pull out one huge old cell phone.

"It is he speaking," he says into it, drawing up his best British accent, beaming at Pierre's voice on the line. "She's right by my side . . ." Holding her eyes as she clues in. "Of course, she said she would love to . . . and can't wait!" Shielding himself as Ata launches at him. "She's saying . . . yes. Eight o'clock, her place." Laughing his head off as he leaps from the settee to escape her assault. "Yes, yes, I'll send a taxi for you. Cheers!"

Breathing hard, she's laughing, objecting, happy all at once, and Fraser envies her. She babbles, about not having anything to cook . . . and he shares, for a moment, the pre-first-date excitement. He offers his taxi guy and suggests she order something in.

"But I don't even have a dining table yet!"

Fraser smiles outwardly at what she thinks she doesn't have and what he can see she possesses—something he will never have. He calls Sammy the taxi guy for her, but her mind had already left his office. He will order terrible Chinese from round the corner again and work a bit more on his church. Maybe he might find some company tonight himself.

Sam was deep in Independence Square when he get the call. Liming with full-time taxi drivers for a few, passing time, before heading for a sweat on the Savannah with the boys. Vigorous dominoes stirring up elbow grease and dribbles'a cow-heel soup on the metal table, good and proper. Sam just looking on. He like to see everything and hear everything. Is his "learning" he tells people. He would laugh and listen and join in with the talk sometimes, 'cause talk is cheap, even free in his taxi. But he is one man that love he Trinidad, and so when shit happening and he seeing wrong things going down, he does get real real aggravated. It does get him rile, just rile. Then he have to find a way to cool heself and mind he own business. Sometimes he goes and check he lovely girlfriend—look upon she lovely, cool, sweet, and smooth face. Or sometimes he take a extra sweat with the fellas. But this afternoon, nothing riling Sam. He was just listening, and going for a regular football practice, soon.

"Tiny Winey" was playing on the big old scratchy speakers by the door. And that was another reason Sam like to come by this corner bar—they like to play a lot of ole-time soca and calypso. He can rely on that. And is mostly ole fellas always there. Even though Sam is a young fella, he likes to be around older people 'cause they have more learning and they see plenty more things, and they talk less shit about woman, woman, woman. Sam have all them old kaiso tunes on he lil' cassettes and now on CDs too, but is a different thing altogether when you hear them songs between old folks who appreciate them. Together with the rum jokes sparring double entendre and domino competition and suchlike.

Sam watch them men laughing, stamping they foot together with the slamming, scattering hidden flies from the sticky floor. And he look at Rosie round face shining down in the back, behind the dark dark bar. And he think, *Trinidad sweet, boy. Ah love it*.

"Yes, this is he," he say, quick-draw style, when his phone ring. He had pick up that line from Fraser. Fraser handy for a good few lines. But Sam feel when he say it fast fast so—it sound like business. He smile as Fraser say something, teasing him as usual. Then he tell the domino players he heading out to make a turn.

He had park quite over so, by his friend's lil' car park. But he don't mind the walk. He walks quick anyway, just like how he talks. He like pedestrianizing this part of town. That's right, pedestrianizing—footing it—in the "heart a Po't a Spain," as he sees it. It always have action and t'ing going on, making it feel like a real city, to him. He like to see them decent office girls at this hour, going in and out'a KFC on the corner, buying they lil' dinner-pack-to-go. This is the working-people hour and time to start making tracks home. Time to buy the few groceries you missing from the Chinee shop or pick up repaired shoes from the leather vendors in the middle of the square. He pass them now packing up, crinkling big plastic huckster-bags, stuffing them with they sandals and calabash ornaments, coconut pendants, and all sorts of Trinidad souvenirs. By this evening, the smell of leather and incense go be gone from around these tight stalls. But for now, as he stepping into the open boulevard, under the high, sparse old poui and flamboyant trees, the sun ain't too hot and the traffic flowing and the corn-soup lady setting up, and he just get two extra turns to make for the day. *"Wine Miss Tiny, roll back Miss Tiny . . ."*

Sam pull up screnching the gravel in the courtyard, park he faithful Nissan Sunny, and hop out, heading to Fraser' glass door. She already coming out though, Fraser kissing she cheeks just like how he kiss every damn woman. But like he give her flowers? Sam never see this one before at all. But she buss Sam a big smile and say thanks, before she even get in the car. In the front seat. Sam smile too. He like smiley people and better yet ladies but he pride himself on never getting too fresh. Always know how to hangle t'ings—right through.

"Eh heh, where we heading? Your wish is my command and Fraser say you want me to pick up and drop somebody else later?"

The woman watch him like she seeing a small brown rabbit instead of a man. She listen to Sam nasal voice and watch he squingey self and long cheerful face. Sam hands must be lil' paws mastering the steering wheel, the dashboard, the phone and tape deck. Two feet must be hind legs stabbing quick at the clutch and accelerator. She watch the Pizza Boys soft-drink cup and half-empty bag of granola between the seats homey-like, and she maybe notice his number plate is private, not hire car.

She start explaining her address and right away Sam know it, nodding, ginching heself forward onto the steering. "So you is from where? You not from here? I never see you round here before and I see alot'a people . . . You feeling nice you get flowers? That's nice . . ." Sam thinks he might as well make chats. This one look open to that. And she looking excitable. "Right, right, right, you now meet Fraser—I say dat! 'Cause I know he a long time, I do alot'a runnings for he, errands nuh. You could say I is he office gofer. Not chauffeur, mind you. And I would'a notice if I had see a nice lady like you here before. I don't forget people. Dat is just how I is. Since I small, I never forget a face."

The woman, Ata, introduce herself, surprising Sam for a second with a handshake move. But then he quickly accept and extend a paw, the one with the long lil' fingernail.

"So." Sam cut through the quiet back streets of Woodbrook. He know the one-way system, all the potholes and crossroad dips in the road, like he know all four white walls of the Laperouse Cemetery close by. "So, so what time you want me pick up this person? From where? Oh, right, I know the hotel. Yes. So he is a visitor, right. And where I bringing he to? Okay, okay, same place. That's easy. Good. And dat's a nice time 'cause I will finish me lil' football practice by then. Is perfec' timing. Fine." Sam see why the woman looking excitable now. He smile when she smile at him again. Something nice going to happen tonight, he know so. And that's why she fidgeting so before she ask—if he works late. Sam couldn't resist. "Is a kind'a date, nuh? The flowers. But I didn't want to be so forward as to say something, yuh know? Not everybody does appreciate a friendly comment. That nice—he give you flowers—men don' do these t'ings enough again, these days. Me, I is a ole-fashion kind'a . . ."

Her mind in fast-forward. Trying to plan for a type of date she had never had—bringing a man she didn't know at all into her home. Ata is thinking she could still suggest they go out to eat. She doesn't even bother to ask Sam about his football or keep up the chats.

End-of-the-week bare kitchen stared Ata straight in the face. She looked around the "dining" room and six o'clock weariness washed it sad, workbench with scraps and brushes sagging in the corner. She'd start with the dishes, make up the bed, bathe, and dare to look forward to the night—to when the light patterns of her pinpricked eggshell turned inside out.

She used to balance a shiny knife on the windowsill to put on eyeliner but had upgraded to a little piece of mirror. Holding it at arm's length, she angled it up and down her frame, checking how much her embroidered top covered, the length of her Javanese brown wrap. But should she dress to go out? Her big flat feet stuck out stupid down there. A bra? No bra? She should seem comfortable in her own house. Casual even. Cool, calm, and . . . jumping jitterbug at the sound of the gate opening, she peeped through the fretwork and braced herself to open the front door. There he was, stamping again, almost hopping and wiping his shoes on the step, in a frisky shaking-off-snow kind of way.

"Allo!" He jerked a big grinning chin up at her. "Allo again. Ah ha, look at you!"

She leaned forward for a kiss on the cheek and Pierre hopped inside onto the mat, wiping shoes again. Ata wondered if invisible rain was falling or did he step in something?

That night, that Frenchie-English walked in with a bottle of wine and romance gripped tight in a paper bag. Ata watched Pierre struggle with the kitchen knife and a fork handle—she had no corkscrew. She ordered Chinese delivery and he stumbled out to the gate to collect it. But it seemed he had never eaten a meal without a table, never eaten this close to the floor. He looked at the cushions and chose the single decorative stool, clutching his plate uncomfortably on his knees. She tucked her feet under her, closed her wrap to stop her leg glaring out.

The jalousie glowed with streetlight like pleated rice paper and talk didn't crack the tension or stop the night hours from seeping out. Didn't stop her from saying "Oh no, it's not so late" when he mumbled he should be going because of the time. Politeness was why he said it. His eyes weren't decent. The wolf's greediness licked them over her slowly. He slunk over and stretched out on the cushions next to her. Pink shins! She had never seen such a thing on a wolf, nor human being. Hairless, too. She stared at them in amazement, half-horrified and half-curious at how delicate they were, the skin tight and shiny. His feet—high arches, fine-boned and feminine. What a thing. A Gypsy wolf, braced up against the wall, breathing in and out of a big deep chest.

Which animal lets a wolf into their home? This close? Greedy and charming, disarming with a laugh and ease, Pierre lay on his back, vulnerable. Waiting for her. Ata trapped her skittering deer-heart and smothered it fiercely. She reached out touching soft, silvery, khaki fur and a hard flank flinched. Pale ribs. A lean smooth stomach. Rippling throat and the gentlest nuzzling. A tongue at her lips.

It was she who crawled tiger-tense over him, tested her

weight and pinned him, tasting more of this strange creature. Her back arched, she bit. And didn't know what she was tasting. Couldn't care. Just for that night. Every drop of his saliva, every piece of his strangeness—she wanted. Wanted to maul and stroke and rest her head on his big rib cage, under his heavy warm paw.

PORT OF SPAIN spreads below Ata, sitting on the little stone wall at the edge of the lawn. The hills wrap her back, curving into the distance on either side. They cradle the suburbs and town gently down to the waterfront. The Gulf of Paria is resting, against the belly of the island stretching south. The sea is still this morning, "flat as a millpond," according to Pierre. For four years she'd heard him say it and Ata always remembers that now whenever she looks at the bay. It bothers her slightly because it is such a European description, for such a tropical scene. She tried again to compare the scene to an imagined English millpond. No reeds, no millhouse in sight, with the big wheel or windmill always in the paintings. No. The only similarity is still water. And maybe the color sometimes. But the expanse, the long smooth lick of it, far away and shining out to the solid horizon. The promising sky clear against it, clean and innocent, there. Baby blue, tinged with the white of heat to come, vaulting higher, trailing scanty clouds way over the hills. Innocence, at this hour of the day, making the tankers and cargo ships look like children's toys, parked on watercolor paper. The fluffy fronds of the gru-gru bef palms and bamboo foothills close by give the scene a Cazabon touch, she thinks. An illusion of colonial pastoral bliss. The beguiling tropics. Is maturity compromised beauty?

Ata focuses on the traffic circling the big green savannah. The line of glittering toy cars along the west side. She feels the hills watching her, as they watch everything. Scrutinizing. The line of traffic down Maraval Road past the Tatil Insurance tower disappears in the downtown cluster, emptying bodies into their work holes; the Guardian news building, the Red House of Parliament, Excellent Stores, Central Bank twin towers, more office towers built by millionaire Syrians. Construction sites waited on the waterfront with cranes to be operated, the docks—containers and goods boats to unload. T&TEC generator silver chimneys puffing, National Flour Mills silos to be filled and emptied. And the National Stadium—nothing going on there but the highway around it crawling with cars, shuffling more people in from the richer suburbs of the West. No cars on the hills of the East. Trees, small houses, and tiny streets make them picturesque now too, hiding the torment of poverty and anger curling away to the South.

The hustle and knivery, the fumes and ugliness of the town— all of it is hidden from this wonderful open house and garden. A blessing. Luck. That she and Pierre had found it when they decided to live together. She scans again. And once more the watercolor virtue drifts . . . detailed landscape paintings and faded prints, by settlers and their descendants, the old photographs that preserve a false innocence, glimmer in this morning-soft view. The gentleness still exists, for archival moments. While the terror and violence of unstoppable undergrowth continues forging new-world progress and exotically dangerous new breeds.

A breeze must have fanned the millpond. A flicker of ripples runs lightly across the bay. "Cats' paws," Pierre calls them, and Ata likes that name. Wet prints tripping over the surface, disappearing on a warm wooden floor. Fleeting, is what makes it more beautiful—something you immediately want to see again. It will never happen in exactly the same way, though, and you will never know when it may. So you keep looking for that thing or moment, a shooting-star streak of emotion, wishing you could just keep it, for a second longer.

A heaviness moves with Ata from the warm stone wall toward the house. The grass feels slightly tough against her soles. It hasn't rained in a while. The sun bounces off the pool, blinding, as she steps onto the pebble-textured concrete around it. The clean little bumps feel good, before the rough-cut stone along the guest room. The room's drapes are still drawn, shutting the morning out. She stops briefly outside the French doors and listens for a moment, then continues on inside to the cool, smooth terrazzo floor. She can see that Thomas has already cleaned the living room. The floor shines beyond the beaming patches of sunlight. The settees are smooth, colorful cushions perfect in the low morris chairs on the veranda. Red anthuriums in their clay pots, and the glimpse of yellow lantana finish off the frame for the magnificent sky and view. Yes. Fixing it up with Pierre had given her more pleasure than she expected. Gardening, teaching him about tropical plants, packing beds with ferns and yuccas, spathiphyllum, night jasmine. The tall skinny palm tucked into the corner of the house, flat-leaved philodendrons crawling up the pillars—it all helped them fit together, better. She inhales deeply and turns back to the guest room, pausing briefly outside before knocking.

———

"Good morning," Ata whispers, entering the guest room.

Fraser's foot waves from the bed. The mosquito net is half off, sheets kicked into a heap.

"You okay?" She goes up to his bedside, trying to bring the morning in on her face.

He reaches a hand out for hers as he croaks, "I made it to the bathroom by myself—shhh." He presses as she moves to object. "It's just the damn net, though; I had to fight it off. It was like a nightmare trying to hold me back."

She squeezes his hand and can't help telling him off for taking the risk, with no one close by to hear or help. She untucks the rest of the mosquito net, pulls it back, and ties it up. "We could get rid of this but then you'll have to use the fan or AC for the mozzies." Straightening the bed, she nods to his twisted boxers. "The latest style?"

He chuckles as she helps him straighten them. "Only safe with silk ones, girl. Castration otherwise."

"How's your new navel string this morning?" She checks the dressing just below his belly button that covers the tube inserted for peritoneal dialysis. The dressing is intact. "You up to coming outside for breakfast? Or you'd like it in here? It's a bit late but it's not too-too hot. Bright . . . let me open the doors for you."

Fraser's hand stops her, trembling slightly like his voice. "Not just yet, Ata. Thanks, though." He asks if he could have one of her tofu smoothies for breakfast and agrees to have his face wiped.

She wipes his features with the warm washcloth and he sighs softly. Tired eyes close. Royal turtle nose, jowls, and finely shaped lips breathe. His big brow and silk-fuzzed bald head smooth, long ears flatten. The still, warm room sighs, then stays silent.

That Friday, Ata had rushed about with predeparture excitement. It thrilled her every time, even when she planned her travel. She had worked late nights to hand in her jobs to Roses Advertising and finish Slinger's costume prototype. That morning she double-checked that Thomas had what he needed, before they left.

"Breakfast is getting cold!" Pierre shouted from out on the lawn.

"The money for the topsoil delivery is on my desk," she told Thomas and paused in the kitchen with him. She could see he was trying to remember something else.

"Everything is cold now!"

"Coming!" She tapped Thomas's broad shoulder, grinning with him as he chucked his head in Pierre's direction. They would laugh behind Pierre's back at how prompt and particular he got around mealtimes, especially when he had prepared it. As if food cooled off in a second in this heat, or as if everyone felt the need to eat it piping hot in a strict sequence. At first Thomas was alarmed, but Ata reassured him that Pierre was not really angry, it was just him trying to hold on to a piece of his culture.

The breakfast was Pierre's. The same toast, butter, jam, and café *noir*. He had long given up trying to find quality pastries and French foods, didn't have time for that, and had kept his distance from regular French expats by deliberately not fussing about food or wine. Just get the best when you see it, and drink it. It was the one thing he refused to go without—wine.

There was a gesture of fruit on the outdoor table for Ata— one solitary mango on its own plate. More crockery than nourishment, she sometimes thought. She sat and pushed her cup forward for the steaming, bitter liquid.

Fraser had arrived as they were finishing, dragging himself out of his beat-up Land Cruiser.

"You're too late," Pierre welcomed him, "breakfast's finished. Sorry, old dog."

"Jesus. I sure is the same dry ole toast and jam. I'm not too late for breakfast, am I, Ata?"

She offered to heat up the coffee and Pierre headed for the shower.

"I know the English part of you is stingy, that's okay," Fraser shouted after him. He cut open the Julie mango, curling the cheeks inside out. It was perfect. He bit, almost dribbling over the heavenly fruit. "Unh, delicious. PIERRE, you up there on yuh throne? Mangoes and other fibrous fruit help, you know. You should try them sometimes." Laughing with Ata and groaning.

"If you'd like eggs or anything else, help yourself—we have to leave for the airport in half an hour," she told him.

Toast and the mango was fine. He was just teasing. But even Ata didn't know sometimes when Fraser was serious. He was exhausted as usual and by the time she came back out with the hot coffee and toast, he was stretched out on the bench in the shade, sleeping.

He scrambled up when she placed the tray down, rubbing his face hard and gesturing quickly at the bamboo, the metal copper with water lilies close by. "Youall moved it. The table is nice in this corner, eh? Very relaxing."

A breeze rustled the sharp leaves overhead. Ata said nothing but looked at Fraser closely. He looked like he'd been overdoing it again. Burnt-out and not ready for the day ahead. But that was nothing new for him.

By the time she and Pierre had showered and come back downstairs with their one wheelie case, Fraser was fast asleep on the bench again. The coffee hadn't worked. Thomas was clearing the dishes noisily but that didn't stir him either. They managed to rouse and maneuver him to the nearest settee and he kicked off his shoes, mumbling, "Bye, have a great time."

Don't worry about Fraser, Ata had told Thomas as they left, just let him sleep. Fraser had stayed at their house before, not only when they traveled, but regular time-out from his clients and lovers. He enjoyed hiding and luxuriating in what he called their bohemia, their great combination of tropical and cosmopolitan living, even if they did have some vestiges of colonialism—with a butler, as he called Thomas, silver cutlery and all. He always teased Thomas mercilessly. "Red T'ing," inspecting Thomas's friendly features and square build, "you putting on some size, yuh looking thick, man. That bottom looking round and chunksin. And yuh like wearing them sexy little short pants to tempt people, eh?"

Thomas died every time, grinning embarrassedly, dipping to pull his tennis shorts out from where they bunched up between his thighs.

"Yuh sweating? One day I must ketch you, when Pierre and Ata not around . . ."

Sleep had Fraser in its grip, curling its poisons through weary veins. He couldn't move—half-aware of the sound of a car leaving, washing-up noises in the kitchen. The office could wait. The world could wait. He had to sleep. Just to get rid of this terrible tiredness, for now. Sweet sweet sleep, he welcomed . . . and swam deep, into a borrowed heaven. While the Chancellor Hill rolled Pierre and Ata down its curves to the green belly of the Savannah.

———

Ata didn't bother with the Lady Young Hills judgment that Friday morning, as they wound their way out of town. She was still mentally checking what she had packed or maybe forgotten.

The guardian hills of Port of Spain arched their neck high over the swamp-basin town connecting to the ridged backbone, the Northern Range. The treacherously beautiful route cut through the lookout on the edge of ruffian Morvant territory. It sped you through the Never Dirty bottleneck housing scheme, giving way to Neal & Massy Autos and factories, down to the throbbing Eastern Main Road artery. They crossed the Priority Bus Route, looped onto the highway, and turned east to the airport.

Ata began to relax then, looking forward to a purely pleasurable little trip. Pierre had suggested it. She watched him driving. Sure, strong forearms guiding them easily. She loved the soft curly hair over surprisingly hard, bronzed muscle, thick, tight wrists—so different from his pale, softer upper arms. His one indulgence, an antique gold Rolex with its tan ostrich skin band, so suited its position that his wrist appeared almost ugly without it. The idea of a real gold Rolex on a white man's wrist bothered Ata. But she hadn't known it was a Rolex until she looked closely. This one was old. Understated. The type of wealth that Pierre liked and worked hard to acquire. Something he associated with aristocracy and value and style, the substance of history. Something she was not sure about but was now exploring, with him. She could see the same beauty, though. In a particular piece of antique furniture, selecting the one he would choose—purely by her eye for proportions, and attraction to nonelaborate authentic.

He caught her looking at his arm in the sunlight and winked at her. She reached out and stroked his fur lightly, up to his rolled-up white oxford cotton sleeve, stretched over to kiss his sharp jaw. "Love you."

He sniffed, stretching his chin out. "I know. I love you too."

They relaxed a bit more, rushing forward in the cool, silenced comfort of their new car. Happy for these insulated moments. A whole weekend of lovemaking and oblivion ahead.

Ata ignored the hill's brooding and the little guilt she felt for taking a long weekend off from what was not heavy in the first place—working from home. Pierre had insisted on supporting her to work freelance and explore whatever art form she chose. She had bought a computer and camera with her pay, playing around with photography while apprenticing with the best graphic artist in town. She felt lucky and pretty. Blessed once again with good fortune and subconsciously deeply guilty of it even though she'd had her hard times. Leaving and reentering Trinidad, so many times. Wanting to stay. Leaving for better. Coming back for worse. The island like a good lover/bad spouse to her. Love. Hate. Tabanca history.

That sleep, the sleep, the drugging, sluggish power of it. Fraser could feel it coursing through him, tugging at his muscles, his organs, forcing them to relax. *Shhhh. Let go. Release.* He could hear Thomas asking him something about dinner. *Shhhh. I'm fine. Shhhh. Just need ress . . . 'll help myself. Yess.*

Through closed eyelids, day became night, became day again. And sleep still held him in its deadly sweet grip. Stroking him. Soothing. Shutting, shuttering . . . He heard the phone ring, far away, shhhh. Heard Thomas saying something . . . sweet, dreaming, ocean-deep sleep . . .

Thomas passed again by Fraser on the couch, and heard a voice coming from the telephone receiver, "Hello? Hello?"

He picked it up and told the Dr. Lady that he couldn't believe Fraser dropped asleep again. "No," he answered her questions quickly, "it don' look like he eat anything since yesterday.

I thought he was helping heself but I don' know if he even drink anything neither . . . No." His panic rose with the urgency in her voice. "I trying, he answering but he not getting up, like he can't even open he eyes! No! . . . Okay. Okay."

She instructed Thomas to forget the ambulance, call Fraser's taxi guy and get him down to the private hospital. She'd meet them there—Fraser must be dehydrated and slipping into unconsciousness.

Sammy was there in no time and the two of them half lifted Fraser into the back of the car. All the way, Thomas kept repeating that he thought the man was at least drinking something. He never suspect anything—the man could'a died on him there and he wouldn'a know, 'cause he always see Fraser come there and just sleep.

"You wouldn'a know," Sammy confirmed. "No way. But I see he was looking real real tired, these last few days. Check, check he breathing, Lawd . . . We go reach soon."

Ata was glad that they did take the break to Saint Lucia—the fake honeymoon. Their love, compatibility in bed, in taste, humor, and intellect—needed celebrating every so often. Especially now that their differences were beginning to leak. In the ex-luxurious Grande Beach suite the terra-cotta tiles were shedding some of the clear sealant. The furniture in the living room and veranda was covered in the tropical floral print that is made specially for mediocre hotels—the ones that try so hard to supply paradise but have been having a little difficulty in recent times. Ata noted the dated light fittings and Pierre supplied the period—rusting seventies. The fake antique four-poster bed with its turned-wood pineapple motif looked fake because it was varnished instead of polished, the headboard too thin. But it didn't matter.

Damp all over from the heat outside, Ata stripped off as soon as they entered the room. Pierre dropped the clunky coconut tree keyring onto the side table and flopped onto the bed, shoes and all. He likes the luxury of breaking the no-shoes-in-the-house rule in a grand way—shoes not just in the bedroom but on the bed. To Ata, that's the kind of thing people do in movies, not in real life. Another little thing that made her warm to him. Audacity. And the way he rests his stiff hands, fingers down, on his big boney chest while lying like that, with his amazing Adam's apple poking, shockingly, out of his throat. It almost made his neck look broken.

She bounced onto the bed alongside him and he automatically raised his hands to protect his spectacles—this always made her laugh. She'd surprise and grab him from behind whenever she could, imitating his cowering while they laughed. She kissed him, lying on the floral bedspread, slowly. And the kiss tasted like the curly illustrations of childhood fairy-tale books. Traces of mint on his breath, the flavor she imagined those fields smelled like, sweetness and peppermint, candy-wet breath. Soft, bendy blooms touching skin, that perfect young skin on the glossy page. Knee bent just so, fingers joined, pixie ears, tousled hair and ringlets beautifully arranged. Swirls of delicate blossoms. Lying on grass without ants. Mischievous eyes sparkling love. Entrancing. The kiss smudged and melted into the humid morning air.

The phone rang then. Ata answered it and passed the nasal voice of Pierre's colleague and doctor-friend to him. She picked up her wrap from the chair and tied it on firmly, then loosened it a bit across her chest. Splashing her face in the bathroom, she heard Pierre's voice drop as she noticed the slight fungus-and-hotel-bleached-towel smell. She came out to register Pierre's face, a pallor of shock. He was hardly responding, hand worrying his mouth and—something Ata had never seen on him before—fear.

Pierre put the receiver down and sat shaking. He cried before talking, holding on to her as she gripped him waiting to find out—who? His mother? Who? Her heart pacing, racing, readying her.

At first, it didn't sound as bad as Ata imagined. Thirty percent function. That's what she didn't understand, at first. When Pierre said kidney failure—limited, irretrievable life didn't register. It must be fixable with surgery or drugs. Transplants. At least it's not an incurable disease or paralysis.

Sleep the lovely toxin wrapped itself around his heart, his lungs, his shrunken kidneys and liver, pulsing in its poisonous race. Mama D'leau slithered her mermaid tail and serpent hair. Tapping. Ticking . . . breaking and entering, forever. Sucking blood work. Tests. Transfusions.

The lady doctor-friend was as quiet and calm as Fraser in his coma. She came back out through the emergency room doors, spoke quietly to the nurse behind the counter, and approached Thomas. "I've called Helen, she's closest. She'll get in touch with his parents and . . ." She shook her head and touched Thomas's shoulder. "You couldn't have known. I don't know why he didn't see his doctor before—he must have been feeling ill."

She explained the details but Thomas's heart had turned to his own phone call to make—how could he explain or tell them?

"I will call Pierre," the doctor-friend said.

Thomas felt even more useless. Worse, as Helen arrived, saying Fraser's mother and father were on their way, glancing at Thomas as the doctor-friend explained, again. Useless. The gray hospital feeling every friend feels.

Sammy went home early that day after waiting awhile with Thomas. He picked up Future Mamee-in-law from her shift at Valsayn Hi-Lo Supermarket, as he did sometimes. He mind still wondering how a man could be good good one day and then next day—he almost gone. "Is not that we can't get lick down and dead anytime," he say aloud to Future Mamee, "but the thing is—all kind'a things could be going wrong inside a man, and he have no idea. That's the part that troubling me."

Mamee didn't mind Sammy thoughtful mood as they rolled down Central flat highway. She thought Sam is a good soul even though he black. She didn't see why Pappee had to get on so—the boy is a hardworking, decent fella even though he have a child already. She could see he is not no runabout. He responsible. He does look after he child and see about he mother. Is so he would look after they own Douli, if he could ever marry she. Mamee secretly wished she had a son so. She didn't even mind the chats.

Sammy quiet that day, though. He cruised the three o'clock lead-belly road, watching the old rice fields and cane fields. He didn't need to talk, he just glad for the day and the homebound feeling. Some things he couldn't understand but that's all right. Some things is better not to know too much about. Except maybe the physical health. He himself supposed to go for a checkup long now, will go this week coming, for sure. But things like this does make you think . . . what kind'a man Fraser is anyway? He have that gardener fella living by him—the one he always treating nice, when the man look like a damned criminal—them things Sam don't want to dig up in too much.

What he do know, is that is two years now he courting this lady daughter. Picking up Mamee from work sometimes to drop her home bound to increase the chances of getting through with Douli. On Saturdays too, if he have time, or sometimes he does make time, he takes Mamee to Chaguanas market and they buy things together—he shopping for he own mother and for the catering, and she taking she time selecting lil' vegetables for curry and so. Sam know is just a matter of time for Douli father to come around and agree for them to marry. He couldn't even ask the old tiger too often, due to he temper. Didn't want to rile him, by being there too much or at the wrong time. He could never understand the man moodiness neither he racialness. And if Future Pappee own wife couldn't understand him—who is Sam to try?

They passed the mosque, then the Hindu temple, the homes with jhandi flags and Moonan Hardware & Lumber, slowed down with the traffic lining up to go through Chaguanas City. Sammy could never participate in this racism thing. All these roads and fields is home to him. Black people live in Central too, side by side with Indians in some places, and is no big deal. That always been so, as far as Sam know. Don't mind them fellas in town tease him and say he have a weakness for coolie t'ing— they just kicksing. But Pappee serious as if he still living in Bagvad Gita day. He wife cool and nice, though, just like she sweet daughter. And anyway, is love that is the crux of the matter. One day he will get through with the rest. Sammy could see that wedding day ahead, decent fella that he is, courting all the way, carrying Future Mamee home. Life short, yes. But you have to have patience.

The glimpse of her partner's fragility stuck snapshot-clear in Ata's heart. Pierre bears his pain so different, she thought. More tortured and knotted than the source of pain. Fraser lay calm on the hospital bed between them.

"I think he can hear us, people can hear when they're in a coma . . . subconsciously," Ata said as her eyes traced the saline lines, blood, oxygen, monitoring machines.

Pierre scrunched up his shoulders even more and hugged himself, cringing. He literally crumpled in on himself.

She felt cruel because she wasn't about to cry then—that she could notice these details about Pierre while faced with her best friend's brush with death. She had cried. They cried together late last night when they got back home from Saint Lucia. They cried for their friend and maybe for all that was gone, sensing that nothing could be perfect again.

Fraser couldn't be frightening, he seemed at peace, and the doctors said his signs were stabilizing. As his blood detoxified with the transfusions and saline, he would come out of shock. But his kidneys would never recover. That took its time to sink in.

Ata looked again at Pierre and, for a second, he almost seemed a stranger in the hospital room. His hunching, worried form, a nuisance to her. She held Fraser's warm, dry hand, long beautiful fingers heavy and already, his skin relaxed to inactivity. His feet. She touched. How could skin betray its body and look so starved for feeling so quickly? Hospital feet. Even the little bit of soil under a nail, the crack of a heel, no longer seemed dirty. Everything suspended from the function and senses of life, isolated in white sheets and antiseptic air.

She picked up the lotion from the stand and poured some into her hand, rubbing palms together. "You look peaceful," she said.

"What are you doing?" Pierre asked.

She ignored him and began creaming Fraser's feet, massaging the slippery lubricant into his soles. He would never have asked her to cream his feet but she thought she would have if he did. They are lovely feet. Toes without corns. Clean, clipped toenails. She had always admired them in his Birkenstock sandals, the ones he was so proud of because they were comfortable, well engineered, German, and expensive. She pulled each toe out, her fingers slipping over knobbly joints, rubbing more cream into the slightly creased sides of his feet, where dark skin meets light sole. Fish-belly camouflage. She smoothed cream on his ankles, calves, rubbed harder on the hairy, rougher skin, and stopped at his knees. The hem of his gown and a private gap between his thighs made her pull the sheet back down a little.

She was still holding Fraser's feet in her hands when the door opened and his parents entered.

"Oh, it's . . . Ata and Pierre, right?" A tall, skinny woman, in front of her squat husband, who was holding a plastic bag. He handed it to his wife, sidestepped in, and shook Ata's hand, Pierre's. Ata turned to Fraser's mother, not knowing if to hug or shake hands with the lady who seemed occupied with the plastic bag.

"We, we're late 'cause we had to prepare, we brought sandwiches and a flask with some tea 'cause yesterday we were starving. You can't get anything around here when the cafeteria closes. I'll just rest it here . . ."

Dorothy Goodman turned to her son. His broad chest and

high belly made her seem even thinner. Her hands fidgeted with the sheet, fixing, patting, tucking. She tapped his chest lightly, scanned the wheezing machine. "They say they should be able to take him off the oxygen soon." She looked quickly at everyone for approval.

"That's good," Ata said.

The two men nodded agreement.

"Yes," Mrs. Goodman said.

Everyone solemnly nodded again, glad for something to feel better about. Hope as something separate. They looked at Mrs. Goodman's nervous fingers fluttering around the edge of her son's body. She uncovered his feet, touched them quickly, noticed the gleam, and darted a look at Ata.

"I creamed them," Ata said quickly, "they were dry."

Dorothy looked at her in some sort of surprise, just a little more than when they had entered. Ata moved to the balcony door, to give her room with her son. Her birdlike way made her husband seem very solid and calm but it was unsettling. Ata and Pierre had met them only once, a year ago, at their home for Sunday lunch, and Mrs. Goodman was only slightly less nervous then.

In her own kitchen, Mrs. Goodman was overwhelmed by the piles of food she was preparing. She spotted Fraser parking outside the yard and hopped out to greet them. "You reach! Oh gosh, I thought youall would never get here. How many times you do me that, eh?" Reaching out for Fraser's face. "Look at you, what happen?" Taking in his rumpled T-shirt and shorts.

Fraser automatically smoothed his T-shirt, sucked in his

belly, and tried to straighten up to the Sunday formality she expected.

She greeted Ata and Pierre perkily, glances darting at everything—Ata's white skirt, Pierre's long pants and closed shoes, their color and class—well suited, she thought, to Sunday lunch at her home in the green suburbs of Arima. Fraser had pointed out, tour-guide-style, the well-kept houses with pretty flower gardens and how this marked the neighborhood off from the roadside town and Carib capital of the island. It was a history he was proud of, in a different way to the middle class he mocked.

"Arima—a blend of all the races, including the last Amerindians, with an old-fashioned emphasis on good 'proper education,' faith, and hard work. People like my father, agriculturists, from humble backgrounds, came to set up field stations and food-processing plants. Those people worked, boy, they worked their way up to cushy class and respectability. In this case, with my mother's constant nagging and pushing, I don't know if it so cushy after all, nuh. She wasn't easy, boy. Still isn't. I love her but that woman can make you miserable!"

"Mothers," the Brit in Pierre had sympathized. "If only we could be born without them."

Then Mrs. Goodman was ushering Pierre to the front door, harassing her husband to get out here. Mrs. Goodman had instantly decided that Pierre was the most important guest from the time his mouth opened. The English accent did it. Upper-class, she thought, with a touch of French—it thrilled her no end and was clear to Ata, as was Fraser's embarrassment. She practically twittered around Pierre, to seat him, to find out where he lived in Port of Spain.

Mr. Goodman was quiet all the while. He didn't need to add much to his wife's chatter, which was filling up the already cluttered living and dining room. Every surface was crammed with porcelain and glass ornaments. Carpets and rugs, at different angles, covered any stretch of floor. A cream synthetic one even lay under the dining table and chairs. Little plants and wind chimes hung on the ironwork that enclosed a little veranda at the end of the room, and out there, plant pots, pedestals with urns and hanging ferns crowded the few garden chairs. Mr. Goodman seemed at odds with his own house, even after living in it for twenty years. Something Mrs. Goodman still didn't seem to take into account. Ata had noticed Fraser's reaction, almost a wince, as he stepped in. Maybe it had gotten more cluttered, maybe he never felt at home either.

The lunch was good middle-class Sunday best, with way too much food spread out like a feast for a dozen people. But they all made good with the occasion. They washed down as much of it as possible with one bottle of cheap rosé that Mrs. Goodman had flourished, then two good bottles of white that Pierre had brought. Fraser had reverted to the overly sensitive, tremulously unhappy small boy he claimed to have been in this house. Bit his tongue a few times, as the little signs of distrustful marriage slipped out every now and then from under the angled rugs. Ata helped Mrs. Goodman put away the loads of leftover macaroni pie, stewed chicken, roast beef, kidney beans, rice, curried duck, coleslaw.

"I know you like it!" Dorothy exclaimed when Fraser asked again why she had cooked so much, and curry too. "And you could take some home, I don't know what you eat in town. Alice came in and cooked most of it anyway, you know me."

The "top it off" trifle was more than great. By then even Pierre drank the sickly sweet sherry served in little cut-crystal glasses and matching decanter. They all did. To give the lunch a fitting end, as suggested by Mrs. Goodman. And in the warm afternoon, the stuffing took effect, stretching them out on wicker chairs in macajuel-snake syndrome. Mr. Goodman reclined in his special chair for retirees with tired bones and arthritis, the ones that old men sit and shrink slowly in, until they die. A chair too aging for such a strong, early-retired man. It seemed merely a pose, his gesture to his wife, about settling into forever. He sat in it now, broad, red, and comfortable in his pose, half listening to Mrs. Goodman still tweeting fitfully, unaware that his son had already told the secrets of his failed marriage to his guests.

Food is love. Sammy stay in the kitchen waiting for the food to finish. The big aluminum rice pot almost full to the brim with pilau. The trickiest part—when you have to keep checking to make sure it not sticking—although many a good pilau must get a lil' burn at the bottom. Some say that is the bestest part. Sam smell his fingernails. Raw chicken and seasoning. His hair must be burnt-sugar-browning flavor. *Cookeen* and salty red-butter sweat. "Is in yuh blood," his mother had tell him when he take over the pot and make it taste better, meltier . . . "Ain' no shame for a boy neither. Cooking food is how I put clothes on yuh back and build this house." This selfsame house Sammy loves, loves it just how he love his Moms and daughter. Douli love is different, red bird-pepper explosion. Hot hot in he head and heart, heating up blood and making him faster, finer, fantastical. Sometimes he does feel like he flying with Douli on a silky flow'a black glass and Caroni skin. Yes. Bird-pepper love like scarlet ibis in the swamp at sunset. Plentiful, fiery, and beautiful.

Sammy rise, take up the long-handle pot spoon, and force it

down through the sticky rice. The open window by the stove suck out the cooking air. That was one good thing with this kitchen, always cool 'cause it's at the back. Concrete attach on to the lil' wooden house, and the breeze like to lick through as it open to the yard. No sweaty baking box. From this kitchen, he and he mother feed a ton'a people already. All kind'a food. And the events they cooking for getting more varied now. He, knowing he brighter than he mother, introduced entrepreneur skills to what she been doing for years—food vending. Now they catering. At first for the police, and one or two government functions, then now they getting private and corporate functions. Sam even have to hire neighbors and friends to help, sometimes. But the trick is to keep it simple. Never hang your hat where you hand can't reach.

As Sam heave the wet rice, he watch his mother checking on the ducks outside. She bend right over the lil' fence and pick up the water pan to refresh it. He heave some more. How women able with this kind'a heavy turning and lifting, boy? Sam thinking that is why his Queen and them vendor ladies so strong. Iron-pot strength. Ladies does have to go through plenty more than men—where they find the patience from, he don't know.

Moms come through the door sniffing the air. When she do so Sam know she mean is good. She wipe her feet and start on the few wares—never stop cleaning or doing something with her hands. She pack away the plastic bowls, even though she know Sammy would do that. He works nice and clean in the kitchen. He learn good, from her.

"What that girl father saying now?" she ask, back to back in the small space.

"He ain' saying nuttin' . . . and I can't akse nuttin'."

"Most times, he does can't even look upon me. And like it getting worser and worserer"—Sam cover the pot and step back to his stool—"since they been having praise meetings by he house, with a set'a pundit and t'ing."

"Hemph." Moms didn't turn around from the sink. "I know you love dat girl, eh. But you buttin' up yuh head for nuttin'. Sometimes, the company a man keep."

"More like the babash! He drinking heavy too."

"Unh."

Douli's silky hair and skin, warm as this smell of sticky rice, stay with Sam. Douli my Douli. Chutney sweetness, sugar dumpling. Is only she stupid father can't see that, treating her like she is a blight. The man's bad company watching her like she is poison. Douli my Douli. My pepper love.

Fraser's parents, Ata, and Pierre entered the hospital waiting room and Mrs. Goodman stopped abruptly, eyeing Fraser's "bad taste of character," his gardener and "house boy," Vernon. Ata went over and hugged him. Vernon awkwardly patted her back, eyes bouncing off Mrs. Goodman as they settled to wait for the doctor.

Vernon tapped his suede Hush Puppies. He shifted his long gaberdined legs and slouched a little in the hard plastic seat. Fraser and Pierre used to laugh at Ata's imitation of Vernon's voice and manner of speech, an incomprehensible, deep rumble that rolled out as he looked everywhere but at you. His eyes were shuttered but smart and dark-street wise, when you got a glimpse of them. In his early twenties, tall and darker than Fraser, he had an invisibility about him, a way of wearing clothes so that you didn't notice his body. So when you saw him topless, with perfect abs and every muscle moving as he swept leaves, it was shocking. Like a stray dog used to being unnoticed, he could appear and disappear without a shadow, just slipping past the gate, down the steps, to his "grotto," as Fraser called it. His fleeting handsomeness was captured in a quick sketch by Fraser and it made you wonder how you could miss it. Or, could Fraser only see this for his attraction to him? His romantic attraction to ghettoness. Or artist's eye for beauty in the unusual. Mrs. Goodman had repeatedly warned Fraser about having Vernon "all inside" his house and about letting him drive his jeep. "You can't trust them," she insisted. And Fraser would hand Vernon his keys while looking her straight in the eye.

Mrs. Goodman glared at Vernon like he had no right to be at the hospital now. She sat there quivering her purple-tinted hair at him but then SC arrived together with Helen the Greek, Fraser's best friend. After hugging everyone firmly and somberly enough, SC had to break the silence. "Oh jeez, this is something else, eh? Who could'a guess? Youall had any idea . . . ?" She needed no answer but turned straight to Vernon, to feel some impact.

He squirmed, with more than his usual discomfort, in her full-on female presence.

"Thank God for Pierre's doctor-friend or else he could'a . . . knock out, right there on the couch."

Helen had sat quietly next to Mrs. Goodman, holding her hand and staring deep into her eyes. Her full, genuine features radiated all the goddess compassion and intelligence that Fraser worshipped.

"And poor Thomas, all now-so he must be still blaming heself . . . Jeez, man."

"The thing is, we all feel guilty," Helen said, looking at Mrs. Goodman. "It's natural we feel we didn't do enough."

Mr. Goodman was looking at Mrs. Goodman too, looking for the guilt. She glared at Vernon some more.

A clack of shoes approaching announced Dr. Turner, a tall female nephrologist with a slight stoop, ill-fitting ordinary clothes, and a medical preoccupation about her—the air of someone who cares more about their profession than their own health and appearance. Dr. Turner turned to the parents.

After the complicated report and answers about procedures were finished, Helen kept looking anxiously from Dr. Turner to Mrs. Goodman, again and again. Something else was bothering Helen. She pretended to usher Dr. Turner out, to get out of earshot. The details had already been softened by all the general predictions and preparatory medical explanations of renal failure but Fraser's parents both looked a little older and weaker. SC put an arm around Mrs. Goodman's narrow shoulders.

"We going in to see him," Mrs. Goodman said to Ata and Pierre. "When Helen comes back, tell her to meet us in there."

SC moved off slowly with them toward Fraser's room

"There's something more, that Helen's hiding," Ata whispered.

"I daresay," Pierre mumbled, hugging himself again.

Vernon was still seated across the room, studying his hands.

Pierre continued, "They had to test for HIV, of course. And that would change everything. It's highly likely."

Ata almost hit him in sheer anger. "Why didn't you tell me?"

"The results are only now ready! It's only a possibility . . . and I didn't want to worry you any more—"

"I should have thought of it anyway, of course it's a possibility. But . . . I don't like you hiding things from me."

Helen returned and Pierre demanded immediately, "He's positive, isn't he?"

Helen looked at him, startled, then she softened.

"Worse. It's advanced too. You know as well as I do that renal failure is sometimes the consequence of AIDS."

Ata's eyes welled as she turned away and held on to the aluminum window rim.

"But we don't have to tell his mother this—it would kill her!" Helen insisted. "It would kill him—to come out of a coma and find out that his mother knows, before he has a chance to . . ."

"The doctor wants, is obligated, to tell the parents but I asked her to give us some time."

"What? You plan not to inform his parents?" Pierre demanded again.

Ata turned back to them as Helen accused Pierre of not understanding Fraser's relationship with his parents.

"But they do have a right to the full picture of what's happening with their son. And how could we ask Dr. Turner to not do what she's legally and ethically bound to? We can't do that," Pierre said, as if he had the final say.

"At least give it a few days—give Fraser a chance to gain consciousness and tell his parents himself, or give permission to someone else to do so."

"And if something happens?"

"Like what?" Ata asked instantly.

They all became silent as the true implications crept through.

"They can't put him on hemodialysis because they only have two machines, and everyone has to use them," Helen whispered.

Wood-lash pain-cracking ribs and heartstrings twang. Breath feeding life falters, curdles, wringing soul salt. Ata crumpled into tears with Helen now, hugging. Over her shoulder she saw Vernon sitting across there, looking at them.

"I'll ask Dr. Turner again if she could put it off for a few days. It's asking a lot but I'll try."

Vernon watched all of this and no one knew how much he could hear, how much he wanted to hear or maybe knew already.

"IT SHOULD *CONSUME* YOU!" God of Design's voice rings steel-clear in the big old airplane hangar. Ata's shadow hops in ahead of her in the slanty sunlight, through the door cut out of the metal entrance, to work. Her eyes cool from the outside brightness.

"Imagine. Just imagine." His white T-shirt materializes in the dim center. Performers, dressed in black, group dark round him. He starts twisting up his body, contorting. "Let your mind crawl beyond your eyes. Let it move your body, push away limits. Let it breathe and expand. Fill up this whole space!" He flings out his arms and spins around.

Ata can see clearer now. Hanging his glary face forward, Slinger shrinks the dancers, pushing them back. Elfin ears red and trembling, blazing eyes skinning under a clean white skull, he pauses. None of the performers know where to look, unsure if they should stare back in his eyes, or freeze looking at a speck on the floor, or what. Dare not smile. A few new members glance around, fidgeting.

"IMAGINE!" So loud everyone jumps. It booms out like his

chest is an empty warehouse itself. "A parade in celebration of . . . a wedding! Cupid has been at work and Venus is at her peak. *Imagine.* Columbus is marrying Liberty. Saint Valentine has given his blessing, Eros a gift, and all the gods in heaven are watching—the Old World marries the New. The conqueror and the virgin. But oh!" He jumps aside and crouches.

Ata moves up next to the manager leaning on a crate, smoking a cigarette. She braces on the crate too, knowing it will take a while before she can talk to him.

"A virgin with such great virtues and *will*, Liberté! Imagine a wonderful christening of these islands. And Trinity"—he gathers up precious air in his fingers—"Trinity is receiving them now. Between the two cold continents—Europe and America—a tropical Eden for them to lie in, surrounded by miles of warm silk sea . . . the bridal train a froth of frangipani flowers floating . . . ," frillying his fingers, clasping hands tight, "an island, an island, an island . . . of FESTIVITY!" and cracking his mask at the lips, he starts the festival with a clap, plucking revelers out the air, swaying, as if pulled by invisible strings, music carrying him in a rhythm that only he can hear.

The performers listen hard. They hear it too. He calls them in. Rhythm growing.

The manager chuckles.

"Yuh see it? Yuh hear it?" Slinger shouts over his shoulder, leading away. "Oh God, look it have tassa drummers over so, and steelpan playing. Look Sugar Boy and Tantie wining, gyrating theyself Kitchener and Sparrow singing. Come, nuh. Moko Jumbies will fall in. Pierrot, Sailors, and Wild Indians coming too. Mind you don't dirty the bridesmaid dress. Tingaling, tingaling . . ." Wiggling an arm, they fall in behind him. "Tingaling, tingaling, chip, chip . . ."

"*Ring de bell,*" they chorus.

Now they chanting up more mas, chirping and whooping. A whistle echoing shrill jabs.

Slinger loops away from the train and comes to watch them with the manager and Ata. They are beautiful, these dancers and actors. A set of beautiful young Trinis, sexy and flexy with theyselves.

Slinger takes a pull from the manager's cigarette, slow, as if tasting the shiny bodies undulating in the soft light. "Allyou know the thing," he murmurs, his face clammy and drained. "But don't just stay there . . . stuck."

"I won't be able to come in this week because."

"I know. We heard. I'm sorry." The manager reaches out and holds Ata's hand.

Slinger turns to her with great effort. "Come here, girl." He hugs her, damp and heavy.

The dancers are still snaking and puppeting around. Slinger drops his arms, steps in, and stops them, too tired now for more imagination. He tells them to elaborate, that this could just be the beginning, they should come up with the performance piece for this year's band, Matrimony. Try. Something.

Two lead performers tower close over him, trying.

Slinger just exhales hard, collapses his shoulders, and walks off to the office, while they promise they'll come up with something, he can trust them.

The manager and Ata know that they will make up something. And the dancers know that halfway through rehearsing it, Slinger will come back with choreography better than theirs and make them start all over again. But they wouldn't complain. Not to his face.

The manager grimaces and turns to slouch off but catches the tremor in Ata's face. "He's HIV, isn't he?"

She shakes her head but walks into his embrace. His chest is warm and it purrs as he murmurs, "Shhh. It's okay, you can cry. We've lost so many. So many. Shhh."

Ata and Pierre help Fraser move from the warm guest room into the bright sun by the flashing pool.

"Sorry, we can't put it off any longer."

"I know, I know." His voice as stiff as his body tensing and clenching around the tube in his stomach.

Maybe the virus moves like the millipede that has fallen into the water, jerking and twisting in the jet stream. Crystals spark and blue light snakes as it dies. Then you can't even tell if it's dead, or if the water is still moving it. Whose job is it to tell?

Helen and Fraser's lawyer-friend arrive precisely on time and step across the blazing grass. Fraser watches them approach, reading the tightness, the grim squinting energy they hold. He sighs deeply and blanches for a second in the white daylight. "I'm ready," he says. "Let's talk about this. Not that any of the fuckers who have it ever do, but anyway . . ."

They all watch him sitting there, fresh and clean, dressed in soft comfortable clothes, with his eyes closed. They wait.

"Yes, go ahead," he says with his eyes still closed.

Ata looks at his feet, alive again and moist in his Birkenstocks.

"Fraser, you know as hard as it is, there is a moral responsibility with HIV, with AIDS . . ."

"And since when am I moral?"

". . . to contact those you may have exposed to . . ."

Fraser holds up his hand, eyes still closed. "Could someone help me to the room, please? I am not feeling well."

Helen and Pierre take him. He asks them to drop the bamboo blinds and leave him to rest. He says he's sorry.

"Won't the doctors or AIDS clinic contact Fraser's partners?" Ata asks.

Helen frowns, sitting on the edge of the bench, and Pierre spreads his fingers out on the teak tabletop. "I don't think they do that here," she murmurs, and Ericka, the lawyer-lady, agrees.

"They only provide testing and a little counseling. They don't have the right to contact other people . . ."

Pierre looks up quickly. "They do in some countries. There should be a routine of passing on his information to the public center so they could follow up."

"They don't here. They used to trace but it became a mess and the policies . . . the confidentiality thing too, especially in such a small place."

"Bloody human rights. I know, the U.N. caused that too but I don't agree with it."

"He can't even tell his mother." Helen shakes her head repeatedly, like Angelica's toy dog with its spring neck. "He should . . . the others. Or we could do it—if he gives us the names. But he can't even tell his mother. He's angry."

"He should be, at himself," Pierre slips in, and they all stare silently at him for saying it.

Knowledge—that the lovers are entitled to—sits like a shadow over them in broad daylight. Sorrow sleeps inside. In the room just past the philodendron vine, behind the bamboo blinds.

"He needs counseling."

"I could book two sessions a week for him," Helen says. "But he said he doesn't want it. I'll try to talk to him. He might open up to me easier than a stranger. Is just denial still, right now."

They all look at the room.

"They're entitled to know," Ata says. But if Fraser asks, which one of them would be prepared to break the news? To someone whom they know.

"Terence. Oh gosh, Terence." Helen holds her head and the lawyer-friend rests a hand on the small of her back.

"You remember him from your birthday, don't you?" Ata asks Pierre. She watches his face go back and escapes with him to that night. Pierre with his haircut fresh from London, clucking and blushing. She couldn't kiss him hard enough. Dinner out by this pool, with flambeaux waving lights around them. Thomas had filled beer bottles with kerosene, stuffed rag-wicks in, and stuck them in bamboo poles, fixed all fifty upright. Fraser had sent Vernon and all afternoon he was busy helping, rushing around the Savannah many times, to deliver fifty full balloons—cussing how they flying out escaping, excited with the silliness of it all. They cut the cake like it was their wedding. Fraser and Terence approving and solemn on the side, happy for them and slightly sad about something.

Just from sharing a few moments with Fraser and Terence, Ata could see how irresistible Terence's intelligence made him. He charmed his students with his professor-knowledge of Caribbean history and literature, as well as current music and film. He was creating an archive, spending his own money on first-edition books and tapes, videos and photos, which others had overlooked. He inspired his students with politics and theory from ancient to first world, to third world. And from the genuine timbre of his voice, and the care with which he chose his words and spoke, Ata sensed he charmed women easily as well. He never overdoes the flirting, Fraser swore—he is so decent, he deserves a perfect life.

That was what Terence was busy creating when Fraser met him. He had moved from Yale to the University of the West Indies in Trinidad, arriving with his beautiful wife, a lovely person and teacher too. With his mother's approval, Terence had courted and did the right thing by marrying. He was one of these people who worked hard all his life and the right things were his biggest reward. Doing right by his family, he supported his mother and put her upstairs in the brownstone house he bought with his first-world salary, proud that he could buy one at his age and be the right person for his lovely wife, her friends, his friends and colleagues, students, nieces and nephews. When they moved to Trinidad to start their own family, he reassured his wife that she would make friends easily and she did, falling more in love with her husband as they re-created a home full of books and paintings and souvenirs they had collected from their happy vacations all over the world. He'd tell stories about them always being the lone, perfect black couple, in those off-the-path tourist adventures. In Trinidad, the women were openly after this prize husband but his wife's good heart smiled at them— she trusted her husband. She had welcomed Fraser with black American food and jazz into their homey home. She deserves a true life too, Fraser had said.

Ata remembered Terence's smile, that birthday night. Out of his big gentle shape, a soft smile and gold wire-rimmed spectacles. He was simply and quietly there. Fraser's glance at him was melty, in that moment. Soft and strong love all around them. And more beauty from the piano. Long, gorgeous André stroked it, rippling out sounds it had never uttered before. Notes flowed through the open windows, past the dark leaves outside, streaming—rushing feelings together, like only piano music can, sinking them into the settees and love dreams of their own. Close friends. Family. Lovers.

"What about Vernon? Anybody spoken to him about it?"
"You think they have that kind of relationship?"

Three heads turn to look at Helen while minds stretch back again, to all the introductions and possibilities.

Now Ericka has to rush back to work and she gets up, chasing away the ghosts of men hovering around them. She promises that Fraser will come around, he really does care. And Helen goes in to check on him.

Ata's picture mind is still cruising the black smooth roads of Tobago, with Fraser, late at night.

Cruising is an art, Fraser had told Ata and Pierre. "You have no idea until you go out there at night and meet the jackals, run with them."

Ata had put the jackal talk down to his tendency to over-romanticize everything with foreign references. She was still getting to know him.

It was not long after she had met him and Pierre when Fraser turned up one night, blocking traffic in the narrow street outside her fretwork home. "Come, quick, we going right now." Hustling them into his old jeep. "Hurry—you don't need to change!" Excitement revving with him and the slipping clutch. Ata and Pierre had joined in the stupid grinning adventure with him and they headed to downtown Port of Spain at 11:00 p.m.

The image of cruising that Fraser had described, and what went on then, was the joke. No smooth drive, with a long arm draped out the window, sweet night breeze caressing and cool music lacing—only jerky bradam-bradam, in all potholes with the jeep coughing, Fraser sweating and craning through the dirty windscreen to see properly. He straightened the rearview mirror, glanced at Ata, then at Pierre. "What youall was doing, eh? Youall have it bad bad, sorry for the interruption but we going to see the life."

"Downtown at night is 'the life'? It's dead," Ata said.

"But the dead will bury the dead. Or raise them, you'll see. Is one life I have." His lines. The old shocks and jeep joints squeaked loud as they bounced their way onto empty Tragarete Road and Fraser started singing, "*Captain, this ship is sinking. Captain, these seas are rough . . . we have no electricity . . . the oil pressure reading low. Shall we abandon ship? Or shall we sit on it? And perish slow—we don't know, we don't know. Captain, you tell me what to do. Oye-yo . . .*"

The cow-heel soup center was shut up tight. Pierre crouched in his seat to see better, peering out at the empty pavements and big dark trees of Victoria Square. They swung onto Frederick Street and Fraser slipped the clutch again, ready for action.

"Okay, okay, Ata, put on that hat and slouch down in the seat." He scrambled around and threw some old socks at her. "Stuff them in your pants, look like a boy in the back there and make your chest look flat."

"Socks, Fraser? They clean? I not pushing your stinky—"

"They clean, hurry, look somebody! Make it bulge like you have something down there and keep your face in the dark."

Pierre's shoulders shaking, laughing.

"Shhh!"

They approached Woodford Square, the People's University, the homeless inside, sleeping. Shops opposite locked down with steel shutters and a vagrant going through the garbage.

"Don't laugh."

Tall iron spikes flickered past, guarding black bushes by streetlight. A man walked the pavement, slow, along the fence. He stopped as Fraser crawled the jeep along the curb. A flame sparked and the man lit a cigarette, cupping it close to his face.

Fraser stopped, slung one arm low outside his window. "Breds, yuh have a light?" Fraser's other hand, with an unlit cigarette between his fingers, jabbed at Pierre's leg. Pierre slumped lower to look while Ata tried to keep her head in the dark. The man bent to the window and all of Fraser's shoulders leaned over to meet him. Fraser's long fingers lifted his fresh cigarette slowly to his lips, cupped the man's fist, as the lighter scratched. The flame was long and the moment hung between them, a hand gently wrapping a strong fist, their eyes meeting, faces close in the flickering light. The cigarette flared on a deep pull and the flame went out.

Fraser let out the smoke, hissing softly. "Thank you, breds."

The man straightened up. He didn't step away.

"So, what going on? Where you heading?" Fraser's voice was self-conscious then; he pushed his head outside.

The man mumbled something and Ata and Pierre only heard Fraser saying that he has friends with him right now. He started rolling the jeep forward gradually, his arm still hung outside, cigarette smoldering on the steering wheel. "All right. We'll catch up. Take care." He took a deep pull and jerked them forward fast as he could, away from the pavement and the man. "I don't know him, I don't know the man at all! *'Captain, these seas are rough'* . . . Oh Lawd . . ." Whooping like he couldn't believe it himself. The fact that the man would have gone with him, the mad scare of it, zinging him even without the act. "Breds," he told them, is short for brethren, "it's like 'bro.' And the lighter signal is the thing. Phew, boy."

"But, Fraser . . ." Ata whispered, "wasn't it a friend of yours, found chopped up in his bed a few years ago? You have to be careful." Immediately she regretted saying it.

Fraser hunched forward and threw them round the corner, past the dark Red House.

Outside the Red House of Parliament, "the People's University" of Woodford Square is Sammy next favorite place in town. He was right there earlier this evening, killing time and learning all the while. You might as well, 'cause you never know when that knowledge might come in handy. In this crazy place anything could happen, anytime. And that is what two men on the lil' wall round the dry-up fountain was arguing about. In Trinidad, a man could do anything and get away with it.

"It only looking so, brother, don' worry with dat," the next man saying. "It have no hiding place from God eyes and His punishment. Every dog got he day."

It wasn't so late, and Sammy had decide to dawdle a little before looking for a late job to head home. The real active daytime limers and talkers gone home already and the square settling down to a regular dead, downtown night. Them tall trees tinkling up clear orange streetlight, disappear the urine, dry dust, and homeless smells. A few people had already bed down with they cardboard, some pedestrians still walking through the square on the pathways.

"I tell you a'ready," the one man said, "God don' interfere with Trini business. When you go realize dat? Where in history you ever see this kind'a thing, eh? Watch, for example, right in dat Red House, only here a madman could hold up a coup, stick up everybody, and ransom de government—dat is national kidnap, yuh know! Only in a place like this, he, a man like Abu Bakr, could do dat and then be walking round the place free! What de ass . . ."

"He will not escape God punishment, though," the Seventh Day insisted.

"Well, the man say is Allah tell him do it in de first place, so that is to tell you. That is what is de problem as well—too much'a damn different kind'a people thinging up all about. Too much'a chance to conduct they wicked ways. No unity. And don' talk about justice—dat is why . . ."

Sammy could see that the Seventh Day man was biding he time patiently, to come back with his rounds. Man like him-so does say the same thing over and over, whole night. Sam get up and cross over the dry orange grass, to more lively talk over so.

About five men was on the old bandstand steps with a lil' radio, talking politics of course. This one saying Manning is a ass making nigger people shame and that one admiring Panday, the gray-hair Silver Fox with he cunning, Indian, opposition ways. As they greet Sammy, the talk turn to who deserve to win the Calypso Monarch Crown this year, 'cause David Rudder song came on the air. And that make the men and them laugh and find it funny—funny that they was just talking politics and hear the song, about Hulsie X and "Manday." Sammy himself love the song about the feisty young Indian woman in the op-position party. He love it the minute it release, just like the rest of Trinidad. The high-pitched, nasal chorus *"Ah not moving!"* is the best part, making big man crack up and sing along, tapping they foot with the bass—*"Go down. Go down. Go down with the Hulsie X."* Sammy, small and petite as he is, did a lil' jiggle, chut-ney head-wag and snake-hand move, just to make them laugh more. All'a them know already—that is the dance and the song of the season. They appreciate it properly 'cause they know the newspaper's story, about Hulsie striking for water in Penal, with a set'a women and buckets in the middle'a the road, shouting, *"Ah not moving!"*

"Well, gentlemen, I heading down de road." Sammy's time to

kill is up. He leave them trying to figure out the words of the next song, and go to his car.

Them Syrian stores lock down with padlocks and chains, fluorescent lights in fabric shop windows. One'r two vendor stalls light up selling music, incense, and sweets. The shape of a rasta lean up in a doorway on Frederick Street, the main street. Is dead. Independence Square at night, silent, compared to day. Two coconut sellers guarding they vans, smoking cigarettes to pass the time. Sammy feel like he crawling past today's leftover garbage, looking for leftover people. A few'a them there, liming, on their way home or going somewhere. A man buying salted peanuts, the nuts cart pressure valve screaming steam and the sicky-sweet smell of hot nuts and brown paper hanging in the night air. Fast food glary signs calling leftover late-nighters in, to eat on them bright blue Formica tables. They have security at the door. The corner bar now full of dingy laughter, and the scratchy speakers playing drunken music for drunken men on the pavement. Sam didn't stop. Straight home he heading.

The sticky night greet Sammy as he get out'a his car at home. In Central, on the flats, the heat and staleness of Caroni Swamp trailing inland, in the dark. Much as he want to pass by Douli, he didn't. He restrain himself from calling her 'cause is lateish. And that always made matters worse unless they had arrange something first. His Queen was up but she wasn't watching TV, which was strange 'cause she didn't have no lights on neither. She was waiting for him, Sammy realize as he entered the house.

"Me son."

From the time she say "Me son" he know something, but he still had to ask what happen.

"Oh Lawd . . . she . . ."

"DOULI!" Sam scream and pelt out as she grab at him.

"Don't go, don' go there! Sammy!"

But he gone already, speeding his car the lil' distance to her house on the edge of the fields. "Douli, Douli, DOULI! I coming, I go take you away, out of that house, that . . ."

A crowd had gather up on the street outside Douli's house, a police car, a ambulance. And fear. Big, cold, and sweaty fear, box Sammy. Whuddup. Beat him again and again, on he head, chest, legs. Whuddup, whuddup. Two-by-four wooden blows, force him to crawl forward, push through people. "Where Mamee? Where Douli? DOULI!"

Bags. Bags with zips. What they doing? The ambulance empty.

People tried to stop Sammy but he rip through.

Blood. Blood. Plenty blood. Oh God, no. Where she? No. He . . . he . . . NO!

The whole room red. Stinking red. Dripping red. Slimey and thick as the hot air choking. Sucky fluid, air bubbles rattling in Sammy throat. Red marks clawing mashed-up furniture, the walls. And he, the devil' body, not covered yet. Not bleeding but covered in blood. Cutlass, Gramoxone poison, killer, bleed. BLEED. Blood.

Moms pull her son out'a the red room, away from the neighbors and wailing family. But he couldn't hear them anyway. She couldn't pull him away from the madness, a mad rush in him, raging red.

"Shhhhh." Moms hold him tight on her chest. "Shhhhh. Sit down here, come. Hush. Don't say nothing. Hold me. Here . . ."

The big stone was warm through Sam jeans. Skin hot. He touch it. Bury his face in his mother's soft stomach. Bread. Ghee. Roti-skin softness.

"He chopped them up . . . her and his wife . . . then he kill heself. You couldn'a know, Sammy, no."

No. No.

Fluorescent net and satin cover the table in the mas camp. Bright pink, green, orange. *"Ka-nee-val again, bacchanal in Port'a Spain. Whoa donkey. Whoa whoa donkey"*—riggadigging on the little radio—*"Whoa donkey. Whoa whoa donkey . . ."* The gofer boy steps in the sewing room, cocks out his bottom, and does the jockey dance with his imaginary reins.

"Dat blasted song so stupid!" the high-pitched, hot-mouthed Firerago exclaims. "Why de hell they can't sing sense no more? What is dat, eh? 'Whoa donkey' my ass."

The boy slaps his behind with his whip and gallops forward to the table, in rhythm. He has everybody laughing, except the supervisor and the shy Chinese guy at the sewing machine, who just smiles to himself and keeps sewing.

Ata had left off drawing cardboard patterns to help Firerago and three other women make fabric flowers for the bridesmaid hat prototype. She takes a strip of satin and pulls the loose stitching along one edge. Watching Firerago's hands, she follows, curling up the frill and punching it with plastic staples. One of the women winces and sucks her finger, burnt by hot glue. Firerago sucks her teeth and snatches the glue gun, admonishing her about how to glue the bases without burning herself.

Ata glances at the sewing guy. Three other machines around him are empty at this time of the evening. He had chosen to remain and work into the night.

"What yuh want, child?" Firerago brandishes the hot gun at the gofer. "Don' upset nothing on dat table, yuh hear?"

The boy is beating the donkey rhythm on the edge. "Slinger say he coming in a hour, to see de bridesmaid costume."

Firerago steups her teeth even louder and launches into an explicit tirade about Slinger unreasonable ass and the flicking impossibility of the flicking flowers and wretched straw hats. Why the brim have to be so wide? And who tell he it go be ready in a hour? "Look! You, move from here—out!"

Gofer shoots out the door and the flower-making pace picks up. Firerago stapling the blooming frou-frous onto the hat on the mannequin's head in a vengeance, shooting the Styrofoam face every now and then, just for so. She is vicious with those guns—plastic staples, glue sticks, and bad-bad cusswords her bullets, interspersing the hour and intricate handwork.

The manager enters and goes over to gently check on the sewer. Ata watches him double-checking carefully, to see if he's feeling well enough to stay on. The guy smiles and nods peacefully, without pausing the electric hum or taking his eyes off the piercing needle. Ata, like everyone else in the camp, knows that this worker, in the prime of his fashion design career, is dying of AIDS. He comes and goes quietly, to and from the busy mas camp, but mostly he stays, taking the shit longer than everyone else without a word of complaint. It is his choice, Ata reminds herself. His way of spending his last days.

"Can you put on the costume?" the manager asks Ata.

Her first thought is that she cannot be seen in one of those fluorescent spandex bodysuits. Skintight skinny legs and big feet—no! And, she objects, he could have asked one of their models or dancers.

When he assures her that the big netty skirt goes on as well— the *whole* costume, to show off the hat—she agrees.

"There," the manager says as Firerago nestles the extravagant hat on her curls. "La Belle Creole. You look like a Boscoe Holder painting."

"A blinding fluorescent one! Everybody can see still? Or youall need shades?" Ata looks around but there is no mirror.

Firerago tips her head, admiring. "Is nice, yuh know. You should see the effec'. But is A HUNDRED FUCKING FLOWERS! On that hat—one hundred blasted flowers, not to mention the freaking leaves and shoots!"

God of Design lopes through the door at that moment. He stops abruptly and drops his hands and bottom jaw. Theatrics again, just like how conversation drops to absolute silence whenever he walks in. "Oh . . . my . . . God. Good God. Isn't it perfect? The skirt, that is—look at it! Just the right amount of fullness, move a little please, and bounce, and unh . . . Where is the shoulder piece?"

"Right here." Someone loops the ruffle of flowers and net and spangly sequins over one breast and fastens it on Ata's shoulder.

"Wonderful! Magnificent! Isn't it?" He forces the others to agree. "Walk around, my child, move. You look lovely, by the way, quaintly old-fashioned." He takes the offered stool to the middle of the room. "But it's the hat . . . the hat . . ."

Firerago clenches.

"Why am I seeing patches of basketry?"

"Basketry?"

"Yes. That is bare patches of straw hat I'm seeing, isn't it?"

"Of course! You wanted bunches and height on it too, right?"

"Depth, yes. But we can't have bare patches of straw-colored *basketry*. The underside of the brim is bad enough. Ah—maybe we could cover that with satin! The flash of shine against beautiful faces in the sun would be the ultimate . . . once the whole hat is covered in those blooms and leaves and things." He isn't even looking at Firerago.

She has her hand with the gun on her hip, akimbo, breathing hard. "Slinger!" she shouts. Firerago is the only one who ever shouts at him, and everybody believes he accepts it because she is crazy and hysterical, but good at what she does. That is why he likes her, mad attracts mad. And she must be, to stick with him all these years and return after quitting upon the completion of each band. "Laws of attraction," she explained, her girlfriend who reads runes had told her, after the breakdown.

"How much of the freaking 'lovely blooms' you think there on de blooming hat? EH? Take a guess. ONE HUNDRED! One freaking hundred and now you looking at wanting to cover de whole entire hat? You can't *afford* to put more flowers on one hat. You can't afford to pay me . . ." She brandishes the gun again, gesticulating between Slinger and Ata.

He keeps leaning aside, to see round her.

"Impossible! Unh-unh, never! We could maybe spread them out instead of bunching them up—"

"No, no, that would lose the exotic shape you've created."

"Or we could cover the hat first with satin . . . then the weight . . ."

"That would look cheap—too much plain satin. It would only take a few more to fill in . . . maybe about thirty—"

Firerago starts hopping. "One hundred and thirty mad flowers?" she screams, banging the table with the gun. "NO, no way, NO!" Stamping her foot in time with the banging, fabric and tools bouncing on the table, she refuses point-blank.

Everybody stares, admiring her bold tantrum. While Design God chills on his stool, marveling at his creation—the shivering gold lamé leaves, pipe-cleaner tendrils, the flounce and textures, layers of net dangling a large sequin here and there. Sparkle, on top of shine, outdid the solid yellow spandex against dark skin. Alive—before his very eyes. Everybody could see he was imagining five hundred such bridesmaids.

After he leaves, Firerago breaks down in tears. Ata and the manager comfort and console her, assuring her of Slinger's lunacy. The manager promises to work out the costs and hours of labor, not only for this but for other impossible designs, and present it to Slinger the very next day.

"I not letting this band buss me," she sobs. "Even if it buss, it ain' go buss me, ah swear. You know how many hours I spend here already for today?"

Too many, they all agree. They should pack up now, even though they had prepared to work late into night. The sewer quietly insists they leave him there, he would like to continue.

Pierre strokes Ata's hip bone and pulls her closer to him in bed. He inhales the scent of her thick curls and sighs. "Mermaid's Brush"—her hair and vetiver. She feels him stir and slides her thigh against his warm flank. Neither of them likes getting up early, but as the morning warms, Ata's strength thickens and she listens to Pierre's arrogance and impatience fire up. As he gets ready for work he can't keep it in—the vacillation, the lack of responsibility, he thinks, is the problem with these people in the first place. It is simple.

It is not. Ata insists, "Nothing is black-and-white, you know that. And wishes must be respected. Give him time."

"Time for what? Other people have rights too and he made his choice. A week has passed and his friends are just pussyfooting around, like you." But as he kisses Ata goodbye for the day, he knows she was caught between worlds, between black and white. He can't say this, though. Or talk about his complex love for her, how it puzzled him and his logical, straightforward heart. "I love you," he says as he kisses her, and it will suffice. She must feel the reliability of his steely support. "Be strong," he tells her, pulling out of the garage.

"I am," she says.

Why does he have to fight me even now? she wonders. *Why do I have to be the strong one?* She could feel his love but also his fragility, when he looks at Fraser. Pierre couldn't spend time with him. He offers generosity in exchange for his "weakness." But why the fight? Why fight the soft and gray, when life is so harsh already? Oatmeal strength. Ata goes with her thick, lumpy feelings to bathe their friend.

Fraser is sitting up in bed, looking down at his second navel. The skin around the tube sticking out above his waistband is almost dry, scabby. "You'll be able to bathe completely soon," Ata says.

"I want to shower and feel the water beating on my skin like rain. How I long for that feeling—to be clean all over."

They cover the tube with a loose dressing and then wrap cling film around his waist. Pin and tuck the towel over the plastic with diaper pins like a sumo-wrestler baby.

"Ready?"

He nods and stands slowly. Still weak, he waddles straight-backed into the steamy peach bathroom. Dove soap and a wash-rag. Another washrag by the gleaming sink. Two towels ready, clean and soft, and a fresh mat on the floor.

Bracing on the corner of the tub, he lets her pour a bowl of water over his head. Warm water sheets over soft fuzz and fat flesh. He swipes his nose and jowls and groans, every time she pours a bowl. A round soft shoulder and upper arm, Ata cups the water under, into his shy hair there. She has washed the small bare armpits of her nieces and nephews but this intimacy feels illicit, with her hand disappearing in a slippery crevice.

"The other one." Soaping, sudsing the soft, baby smell. One bowl for a powerful calf, cup behind bent knees, more for arms, flipper-fingers draining, swirling white soap clouds. Neither of them has spoken again about Sammy's tragedy. But it tries to sneak into the soft bathroom with them. Ata pours again and they watch the bubbles stir the scented water.

"Smells nice," he says. "Safe."

They retreat right to diaper days of silky skin and powder-puff hygiene. A mother's sure grip on a slippery arm, her breath against your cheek, sweeter and hotter than the steamy air.

Fraser's legs tremble as he stands and steps out slowly, leans heavy on the hand basin. The air is peach vapor and Fraser's head sinks between towel-shoulders, a brown sheen in the misty mirror.

"You should lie down now. You can make it?"

He lets her help him, his voice too rusty to talk.

Ata silently dons the sterile gloves and connects his dialysis bag to a fresh nozzle, as she was shown. Taking care to preserve the sterility, she attaches the tube to his clean navel hose and Fraser tries not to tense against the cool, purifying solution filling his abdomen.

"It feels so strange cold," he whispers. "I don't think I could ever get used to this." Three cycles a day, for now. But that would reduce as he detoxified, the doctors had said.

There is a new coldness creeping out of Fraser, though, sliding around sometimes, like the cool fluid filling and draining from his insides. It saddens Ata but some of his older friends don't seem that surprised. He still refused counseling or any mention of the dreaded disease and, as much as he could, rejected the help they took turns providing. Ata had taken over most of it and felt privileged yet burdened with the responsibility. She had, with Pierre's logistical help, worked out Fraser's daily diet and care routine and pinned it up in the orderly kitchen.

"I could never get used to the cruelty." Tears slip out of his closed eyes. "Sammy's murder is just too . . . ask my secretary to send flowers, please. And a message from me for his loss."

"We already did, soon after we heard," Ata mumbles and his eyes open, his grief flickers. Was it that she was too presumptuous, or guilt for realizing his self-centeredness?

She excuses herself hurriedly. The lack of sympathy for a dying person, even for a second, feels worse than the first signs of his ugly side. "Maturity must be the acceptance of compromised beauty," Fraser had once said.

Pierre pulls into the UNDP parking spot he was so kindly allotted temporarily, going on two years ago now. The wanker's motorbike is there, the Harley the idiot so loved to show off, like how he flaunted his short-assed Italianness, overdoing his accent to charm the ladies. Like he is the only one who knows about good wine and art. The little wanker, with his pointed shoes and tight pants. Pierre is sure the Italian isn't any good at his UNICEF "Save the poor children" job, but thankfully he doesn't have much interaction with him. The poseur.

In the ratty elevator, Pierre looks down through the dirty glass at a car that is trying to fit into a space that is too small. Pierre stops on the central admin and UNAIDS floor to collect his mail himself, and once more notes how posh the office seems, compared to all the others. Too much money in HIV, he has always argued, distorting the true health picture and creating useless projects, organizations, and campaigns to spend it, while people can't even get critical primary care.

Dr. Khumalo, the South African secretary general, the "Queen" of UNAIDS, prances out of her richly decorated office to her secretary, where Pierre stands. "Nice shirt," she comments on his choice.

Pierre knows its baby-blue color suits his tan. The meek and mild middle-aged secretary signals him to give her a second, puts down the "In" pile, and goes for Dr. Khumalo's document. "Thank you," he replies.

"You know, I am making some headway ensuring we get a space in the new waterfront towers. It will be fantastic, eh? And I *will* get through, I know I will."

"I'm sure you will." Pierre takes in her elegant mauve stilettos, silk shirt, and black skirt, stretched tight over her high bum.

"And everyone will have me to thank." She stretches a lavish hand, overly manicured and full of expensive rings and gold bracelets, to her approaching secretary. "Thank you. Don't forget the MDG meeting this morning, Pierre. In the conference room. Nine-thirty."

As Pierre makes his way up the drab, soon-to-be-officially-dingy steps, to his UNDP floor, he is thinking—what fun, the Police, the minister of Works and some NGOs will be there. Lovely. And joint meetings are always so useful—by the time the five UN agencies finish their statements, developed in the last meeting, there's only time to set a date for the next meeting, which takes a while because everybody is always busy or off on travel duty. This is why, Pierre knows, he is not climbing the ranks past a P4 and keeps being moved around the world. The Trinidad country rep, from Bangladesh, didn't like Pierre's repetitive question—why are there so many U.N. offices in Trinidad in the first place? It doesn't qualify as a recipient country. With a GDP so high, Trinidad could even afford to be a donor country. Okay, the care systems and policies need sorting out but let them get on with it, for God's sake. At the very least, the U.N. should demand matching funds for its projects.

His new assistant secretary looks up from arranging the colorful, well-produced pamphlets and reports on the table as Pierre enters. She loves playing with them. The glossy rich photos are her daily reminder that she is working for the great United Nations. They make up for the disappointing cubbyhole and overwhelmingly demanding staff. She smiles uncertainly at Pierre and runs back to her desk. He has overheard her attempts at follow-up phone calls for the MDG public launch. And she has listened to him complaining about her incompetent language and brainlessness. She brings him the coffee he needs to stay awake through the bloody meeting and scampers away before he can go on about the terrible instant "fake coffee."

Everyone is well seated in the extra-air-conditioned conference room by the time Pierre rushes in. He has managed to miss the painfully formal greetings, breaking the protocol for the presence of a minister. Dr. Khumalo glares at him and he straightens his shirt under his blazer. All the men have on ties, some jackets, a few of the women hug themselves, unprepared for the cold.

". . . and the Millennium Development Goals, as established by the United Nations Millennium Declaration and adopted by world leaders in 2000, are very important to us in Trinidad and Tobago." The minister of Planning and Works drones on. "Indeed, the development of our very own Vision 2020 is in keeping with the MDGs. And as we speak, each key ministry is already preparing a plan of action to meet these goals . . ."

U.N. language really helps the civil servant waste precious

time. The little Italian poseur is nodding somberly, as if this was a new and brilliant idea, thought up by the minister himself. Dr. Khumalo and the country rep have on their very-intelligent fixed stare, encouraging the blithering idiot.

"Ahem . . . Under this present administration, we have been fortunate to have increased budgets and expenditure for areas of concern that have been challenging so far, such as: child protection, human rights, basic health and education, small business development and job creation, and the reduction of violence."

An Afrocentric women's activist glares at the potbellied speaker and he hastenes to add, "As well as violence against women, in particular, in fact. I take this opportunity to thank Dr. Patangali, UNIFEM and the joint U.N. committee, for facilitating this meeting and providing an excellent opportunity for collaboration between government and nongovernmental partners, on the MDGs and Vision 2020, which will ensure that Trinidad becomes world-class, in every way. I look forward to hearing the following presentations and updates. Thank you."

Thank God, Pierre thinks as he slips lower into his comfy seat. The polite clapping makes the minister beam. He has said absolutely nothing new.

"Next I would like to present Nzunghi Stuart, president of the National Organization of Women of Trinidad and Tobago, NOW-TT, who will update us on the progress of the response to CEDAW and the country report that is being prepared in conjunction with the Bureau of Women's Affairs." The do-it-all chairperson is, of course, Khumalo, beaming her flat South African smile at everyone.

The Trini activist, in her African dress, goes to the podium, prods the projector, and looks expectantly at the screen. Jesus, she has a presentation, Pierre realizes. *The Convention on the Elimination of All Forms of Discrimination Against Women*

(CEDAW)—An International Bill of Rights for Women and Trini-
dad and Tobago's Existing Policies.

Pierre's mind drifts off to his surprising love, and her strange mind and limbs. Atalanta, burning in the sun to darker shades of brown. Her moisture sometimes tastes of garlic and turmeric and sharp lemons mixed with salt. Hair, wiry like the springy questions she snaps. Skin, softest that slides around you, slips into your arms, heart, mouth . . .

Her mouth. Douli. Full lips. Bloodred. And brown. Pepper-skin burning. Chopping. Flesh. Douli. Hold me. Kiss me. Kill me. Douli.

Sammy, Sammy fighting the fever scalding him up from in-side. The fever only he and he mother can feel. She had make him stay in bed, tie a rag with Limacol on his forehead. Now he sitting up in the gallery. Friends keep coming and Moms had food spread out, as if the funeral and wake is at they house. The dead house, not far away. The dead inside Sammy. Who know what her family arranging? Sammy can't go. "They don't even talk to you . . . and you not well."

Neighbors and friends advise his Queen that is a curse the family pundit put on Sammy—maybe something the girl her-self had put in him—that's why he had get totoolbay. The rea-son for the tragedy, the dead-blight zone now on the edge of Chase Village, wasn't something anybody could figure out. The condolence-friends whisper, guessing that these things does al-ways happen in Trinidad, and who knows who it go be next. Right in your neighborhood. Death by chopping and Indian-tonic. Just so—and the poor girl didn't even do nothing wrong.

People finish off the little plates of food and cakes on the side table. Plenty cakes and cheese straws. Everybody loves cheese straws, they show a little class, and Sam' Queen likes to make them whenever she get a chance.

"These statistics are real. And dark and ugly. Because each number is a woman who had no choice, no one to turn to. There is no protection, no hiding place—not for the magnitude of Violence Against Women that we face in Trinidad and in Tobago. And so, ladies and gentlemen, I for one can't wait to see the policies changed, the measures put in place, *and* the actions taken to ensure that no more lives are lost at the hands of merciless and alcoholic men. The mothers and daughters of this land are bleeding and dying, they are under attack. And it is up to *all of us* to do something about it."

The clapping around the U-formation of tables is genuine. The activist's proud features suit her regal hairstyle, locks woven up into a stiff hive. A coffee break is announced and little savory plates snatched up. As usual there is too much food, but Pierre is always amazed to see how readily people stuff themselves. People who have fridges full of food at home and boast of trying to lose weight, ensuring they don't miss a morsel. He has even seen some taking wrapped plates away in their handbags at the end of an event, filching cheese straws in napkins. Awful cakes fill the sweet table.

After the break, the community police give an awkward presentation on child-gang members moving arms across the country and the dons controlling government road-repair contracts in their territories. The final presentation, the cheap white flour and commercial cheese straw thing of the wasted morning for Pierre, is from the minister of Social Development. He proudly announces that at last they are getting close to the final draft of their Plan of Action. He doesn't say it has taken five years so far. Soon, they will be able to give a date when it will be ready. When asked "What then?" the ministry will look into getting it printed, nicely—are there any suggestions for that, since the U.N. always has such nice-looking publications? And then, of course, it will be distributed and made available to the public. Then. And then, they will look into drafting the Implementation of the Plan of Action for Social Development in Trinidad and Tobago (PoASDTT).

Thomas steps into the kitchen, turns, and hustles back out when he sees Greek Goddess's face. She is more upset than Ata, who's measuring Helen's worry-crease furrowed deep between her brows. Helen reads the recipes and timetable on the cupboard doors. *She has seen them before*, Ata thinks, *she never took the time to read when I explained?* Greek Goddess stares at Ata, as if seeing her for the first time too.

"Sometimes it's really hard monitoring the foods people bring for him."

Helen nods but still doesn't uncrease her stare. "People?"

"Friends and family." Ata doesn't glance at the fruits resting on the counter that Helen has just brought, but opens the fridge to point out containers of macaroni pie, callaloo, pilau, Lucozade, Ribena. "Even Malta drinks—Lauren gave one to him directly, without even checking, and it's loaded with sugar."

"Maybe he asked for it, Ata." Her voice rises at the end.

"Maybe, but you know it won't help—to give him whatever he wants to eat. He hasn't taken in everything about his diet yet."

"I understand you *stopped* his mother from coming to see him." Helen's voice quiets to the pale cream of the countertops.

"I only asked her to put off her daily visit and said he wished to just sleep that day."

"And who are you, to stop a mother from seeing her son, Ata? *Who the hell do you think you are?*" The shouting jolts Ata to the kitchen door and she glances nervously to see if lawyer-friend and the others on the veranda have heard.

"You have any idea of the pain you may have caused that woman? You have no right—"

Ata cuts her off with the facts that Greek Goddess already knows but which create a conflict in her too—that Fraser still has not told his mother, nor accepted counseling, nor contacted anyone about HIV. And so where is the balance in respecting his wishes in some ways but not in others? "It's not as easy as food. He never was close to his mother before this, was very upset after her last visit. They quarreled and she seemed relieved not to have to visit, too."

"Yes, but what kind of person are you?" Caribbean Greek Goddess asks. "The most precious thing we have is family. If you were sick, wouldn't you want to be back in your parents' arms?"

"Not necessarily." The answer jumps out before Ata can stop it and wipes the crease clean off Helen's face.

"No?"

Ata finds herself explaining, almost to herself, that of course it's not automatic. If it was still a close relationship, then yes. But she would want those who understand and love her for who she is, the ones actually closest, to be there with her—and that's not always family. Ata reflects on her own points against Pierre's cold view—being able to choose friends, but you can't choose family. Tough. Helen's shocked reaction makes her feel British and foreign, while her father's voice reminds her of her free, green Caribbean childhood. *Your children are not your children. They are the sons and daughters of life's longing for itself.* Her mother's sisal-sweet spirit breath whispers "It's okay" in her ear.

Ata had left Fraser's room totally embarrassed for his father on one of his visits. Fraser had shrunk into his shell the minute his mother stepped out of the room and then slowly emerged again. His shuttered eyes took in his father's discomfort and he extended his neck a little further. His shell looked rougher and duller than normal, skin folds and creases appearing. He licked a dry tongue over sharp beak and his father looked down nervously.

"You always thought this would happen, didn't you? That I would die before you—"

"You not dying, son."

"Pay for my sins, and all that, eh? Ata, when my mother would be lambasting me for my 'nasty' ways and before that, trying to straighten me as a child, locking me in my room, whatever—this man, this spineless father of mine, would stand by and say nothing. You never really agreed with her but what?"

Mr. Goodman was melting into the dusk-pink floor and Fraser swung his head and turtle eyes round to Ata. Why humiliate his father like this now instead of standing up to his mother himself? He was Mrs. Goodman's pet rock a minute ago. When his neck levered back to his father like a compass, his eyes shrunk even smaller taking in Mr. Goodman's apologetic slouch. Ata had excused herself then. And as she left, heard "Now you have a chance to say what you think and make amends, before I die. So what you have to say?" Silence followed.

Marriette, the Egyptian sphinx of a woman, slinks into the kitchen. She has seen that Fraser's asleep, takes one look at Ata and Helen, and says, "Okay, I'll let youall get on with it." Goes to join the others on the veranda. A burst of laughter breaks the bright air out there. Helen's pain is gathered all in her Carib and European features as she stares, incredulously. She, more than anyone else, knows of Fraser's strange relationship with family. She has had many arguments with him about adopting too much from his oppressive education and about bullying his father like Fraser was bullied by his mother. But she has also seen the private torment, of him being himself in Trinidad.

The torment of choice lies bare between the two of them now, but it only makes Ata feel judged, by the friend of Fraser she respects the most. Extra aware of her own mixed-up values, way of doing things, and lack of religion—flaws that make her rootless. Gray.

"Father McBarnette is here!" Thomas announces cheerily at the door. "Fraser still sleeping?"

"*Ka-nee-val again, bacchanal in Port'a Spain, whoa donkey. Whoa whoa donkey!*" The Matrimony financial figures and the time left before Carnival didn't add up, and God of Design refused to accept it. The manager shut down the camp while they battled it out. But secretly, in the dim hangar, the core group of performers, key craftsmen, and the King and Queen of the band gather around the bolts of stretchy fluorescent fabric. A few have on the yellow and orange body suits, their limbs glowing, looking like skinny aliens sitting, standing on crates, around the strapping

King. "Look how much of the spandex left-back. And how much body suits done already—we could make this work."

"Whoa donkey. Whoa whoa donkey!" rattles again on the insistent radio. One of the luminous bodies springs up and starts jockeying around.

"Exactly! What I thinking 'bout is . . . the 'Donkey Rally'—hear me out! Serious, watch—we making heads and de tails . . ."

The Amazonian Queen of the Band looks at her subjects, handsome face aglow and amused, waiting for the outbreak.

"I is a ass! I is a damn jackass? To jump down de road on Carnival Monday, dress up like a ass!"

"For Slinger? You mad?"

Three out of the sitting four jump up, gesticulating, while the infectious song by the United Sisters rallies on.

"Dat is pure madness. Slinger would never agree to dat. Is a joke!"

"No, look, I run it by he right arm a'ready. Is to save the band. You know how many people done sign up? Thousands. And yes, is a joke but Kaneeval is about joke and at least everybody go have fun. I make a headpiece prototype . . ." The King, who has always been admired for his physique and skill at carrying the massive costumes, stalks into the office to retrieve his prototype.

The Queen smiles knowingly and the performers and craftsmen mumble, milling about. "Whoa donkey" fades into the monotone of the radio DJ and the King appears again quickly, wearing a brown stuffed donkey head with fluorescent net ears sticking up. The effect is even more comical on his spandexed oversized body, with a cloth tail swinging behind. The whole pack falls about rolling on the ground, kicking up and slapping each other like real asses. They laugh, they laugh, they laugh till they cry, and even the Queen joins in. The King is mad but he holds his ground. Till they cool down, spluttering and begging for the song to come back on the radio again. The Queen sniffs through her laughy-tears, "Allyou listen, man, is not a joke. He have a good idea here, oooh . . . a good idea. And allyou could help, try nuh."

The old wire-bender man, sitting in the darkest corner all this time, steups his teeth.

"Ah sure if Slinger mad enough to ketch de joke, he could design some real boss-ass head! If he want to."

"Yeah, right, I is Slinger ass a'ready. *Whoa whoa* . . . yuh think he go even listen? Jesus!"

Sam's Queen know the best way to get her son back on track is cooking. Even though he have no appetite and he not interested in nothing, she will get him back in the kitchen. The household quiet quiet. The grass and all in the neighborhood silent these days. The little drain, running from the backyard all the way 'long the edge of the empty field to the back of Douli murder house, choke up with water plants. But they not even sending out two purple flowers. Is a blight. Sam can feel it and she know it all along but what you go do?

"What you can do wit' these kind'a t'ings happening, eh? This is not no ordinary crime, yuh know. Crime'a passion? Is not dat neither."

"Is frustration."

The ole boys done seen the headlines and the rumshop talk come back around to that one—the most outstanding in weeks.

"What frustration? He frustrated with he daughter so he kill her, then why he kill heself *and* he wife?"

"You don' hear what I say? Frustration wit' life—dat is the only thing that would make a man get in a rage so."

"I hear the daughter had like a black man, and he didn' agree to that."

Big steups all round the rumshop. "Don' come with dat ole race talk."

"But what you saying, life more hard in Trinidad than other places, that's why we have so much'a these crimes so?"

"What stupidness you aksing, boy?"

The dingy rum belly of Port of Spain growls and grumbles, echoing the dark guts of the hills. Digesting the murders. Crude oil deep in the bones of the land.

The priest, the same tall, dark, handsome priest that Fraser had had fantasies about, and cursed, is at his bedside. Father McBarnette, the obstacle to his church project, the blocker. Fraser looks up through sleep-soft eyes now and sees a blesser. He makes up his mind to listen to the priest and not argue. Maybe he has come to use his priestly healing powers.

"Let me tell you a story, Fraser," he begins, and Fraser thinks he's right, it must be a miracle story coming. "I know you are a well-educated man and most probably know much of what I'm about to tell you, but bear with me . . .

"This land of the Holy Trinity has a particular history that runs through our veins. It is inescapable and . . . tainted, built on lies and deceit. The Amerindians first told tall tales of a city of gold to the Spanish, and Trinidad was set up to look for the third El Dorado, after Mexico and Peru.* But it never materialized. Piracy, murder, and mayhem founded the first capital here in Saint Joseph—you know that's where I'm from, right? That's why I have a special interest in this story. Requests were made for ships and men from Spain, for expeditions that never happened. Antonio de Berrio did try before that but then after the initial glimmer of gold Trinidad remained a backwater post, 'breeding disease, mixed-blood, and sin' for a few hundred years."

Fraser thinks this is a good setup for a miracle tale, but he is trying to figure out how much this black-power "man of the cloth" and slave descendant really accepts his colonial religion. He watches Father's sensuous mouth, set perfectly in thick black stubble, continue.

"It became 'the Ghost Province'[†] of El Dorado. Saint Joseph, or San José de Oruña, remained a 'ten-hut place.' French and English buccaneers, 'gangsters of the sea,' continued trading and raiding, taking Negroes, torturing Spaniards . . . The friendliness of the Arawacas Indians here, though, attracted missionaries. These missionaries worked hard despite the heat, for they were serving a greater King. They ruled that no Indian was to be called a 'piece,' they built settlements for some of the freed Indians, baptizing and instilling the practice of work for wages."

"Unh hunh, proper businessmen," Fraser muttered, but the priest droned on.

---

*John Newel Lewis, *Ajoupa: Architecture of the Caribbean, Trinidad's Heritage* (1983), p. 29.
[†]V. S. Naipaul, *The Loss of El Dorado: A Colonial History* (1969).

"The Indians became restless, and we're talking late seventeenth century here—Trinidad got its 'first Christian martyrs and its first miracle.'"

At last. Fraser wishes he could see the point, though. His toxic blood is putting him to sleep again. "Thanks for that, Father," he mumbles.

"But wait, I ain' tell you the story yet." Father McBarnette pulls up his chair closer to Fraser's bed. "They were building a new church one morning, and a monk told off two Indian laborers—the Indians killed all four monks and buried them in the foundations of the new church, burned down the mission. But you from Arima so you should know all about this. When the governor and his men came to investigate later, the Indians ambushed and killed them too. All of them died slow slow with the poisoned arrows." Father McBarnette pauses, excited like a boy in the middle of his comic book. It looks like Fraser has dozed off.

"Um humn!" Fraser breathes out and pulls himself up suddenly. "I missed the ending? Sorry—" A disappointing miracle.

"Well, that aside, the slaughter of Indians that went on and torture, plagues . . . My point is . . ."

He's lost it by now, surely. Fraser's eyes close but he can see Father McBarnette feeling around in the warm room.

"They even t'ief slaves from other islands and sold them here. My point is that, yes, we have a unique history of corruption. But out of that history also comes a ground that was and still is creative, among other things, and genius. Even in the architecture of the church."

Fraser's eyes open.

"Yes, I have taken over the research on architecture of the church in Trinidad that you started. I know now that Amerindian ajoupa building design remains in some of the churches of

Trinidad. Philip Reinagle—the two cathedrals here that blend Romanesque and Gothic forms. We shall live up to them. You know I used to question the links and facets you dug up— black history, influences. But I will continue them. You have inspired me."

"Me?" Fraser suddenly feels humble, small as a child in a huge bed, with a feared parent standing over him. A parent whose kind words he always waited for, now given but still without a hug. He wants to hug Father now but holds back. Just as his own father held back from hugging his little boy.

"Father, thank you . . ."

"No, thank *you*, Fraser. I will ensure that your church is built in Maloney. In the way you designed it. And I will give a sermon one day in its pulpit, or many, passing on its messages to the next generation. Thank *you*."

Fraser folds silently into tears, ashamed of his overwhelming gratitude. Father McBarnette excuses himself, offering "a chance to rest," squeezes his hand, and steps away.

"In Maloney, t'ings don' happen so. Is murder still. But not so." Sam's bestest friend thinks he consoling him. Sam had come to see him but wouldn't sit still. His friend thinks that when a person grieving, they should stay quiet and in one place.

Sammy look down from the small balcony of Mano' mom's apartment. A Nido milk tin, full of Mano's cigarette butts, resting on a pile of old newspapers in the corner. That's a lot'a nasty cigarettes. He look at the facing row of project buildings—no less depressing than the tin of butts. Sammy shifts against the rail and peer down to the shaded yard. "What you keeping dem stinking t'ings there for? It ain' making no difference if you throw them down there." He slide back closer to the ashtray, he flick through the corner of the newspaper pile, just enough to see the types—*Guardian, Express, Newsday,* one'r two *Bomb.* "Tha's good yuh Queen like to read them, mines don't. She say them headlines does make she sick and aggravated." He sit back down in the one plastic chair and lean forward, inspecting the legs.

"Is I does read them, breds."

"Eh heh?" Sam get up again. "But dat is a fire trap right there."

"Why you don' take some ress? Settle. You only moving up and down, driving all over de place—that ain' go help."

"These t'ings does attrac' rats too—old newspaper. You shouldn' keep them pack up so." He stare down, over the rail. The yard might be cooler, even though it uglier and full'a litter. No gang fellas liming by the old car, just right now. "Leh we go down there, nuh?"

Mano steups and start heading inside. Sammy follow him out the front door and down the tenement steps. "A fella had get kill right at the bottom here. Rememba dat? That is what I was telling you—is a different kind'a murder here. Black people don' kill-up theyself just so. Not they family. Hardly, compare to Indians. But is same difference, they kill one another. Children does get kill too, sometimes. It don' make sense. But is all about."

"I feel to drive," Sammy say, as they step past the bottom stairs.

"Rich or poor, everybody feeling it."

Outside the breezeblock stairwell, the yard depressing in true. "Leh we take a drive." Sam fish out his keys and start heading out.

Mano hesitate a second, then follow. He not sure 'bout this restless business. Supposing Sammy start to speed in a rage, and kill them both? He skip faster to catch up with his friend. "Awright. We could go by the river up in Saint Ann's, and chill out. It go be nice and quiet there."

"I just need to drive. I feel I go start back work, instead'a wasting gas. Eh heh. It better so. I go see yuh."

"Donkey WHAT?"

"Rally."

"Rally *who*? I can't believe what I'm hearing! Is this some sort of crude joke? Are youall conspiring to push me to the point of NO RETURN?" Slinger's whole head is red, and when he shouts the "no return" his voice drops down in his stomach to sound like he's dying, with his mouth horribly open. "All these years. All these painful, heartbreaking, wrenching, yes wrenching, 'cause youall drain every little, last drop of energy and creativity out of me. And *sanity!* That, that is sucked like an oyster out of its shell, leaving me, ME, empty! Completely and utterly empty. And devastated. Every year. Every goddamned year . . ."

The group of performers, King, and Queen, are not surprised. They wait.

"Then allyou want to call me CRAZY? *Mad*? I know what is said behind my back—'Slinger this, Slinger that'—but *this* is insanity! Who could've thought—no, I don't want to know whose brilliant idea this is because all'a youall *are* damn jackasses—who could've entertained the idea that I would, for a split second, be open to such ludicrousy?"

From anger to the point of tears and now they watch the corners of his mouth twitching intently.

Slinger stares back at them.

Will he laugh, will he cry? Does he want them to say something? They all hate when he does this, it out-tricks and makes them feel like the dumb pretending to be bright, when they know they are bright and normal.

The sounds coming from him are laughter. They aren't taking any chances, though, that could make it worse. They wait. The sounds carry on inside him but his face remains the same. Maybe it even looks like pain . . . getting worse. Maybe he's having a heart attack? Anything is possible.

He coughs. And chokes. Bends his head, holding his chest.

But before anybody can rush to him, Queen recognizes the shuddering of his shoulders and starts to laugh. She laughs her big ha-ha I-know-de-joke laugh, so all can get the message clear. By the time Slinger straightens up and raises his head howling at the ceiling, everyone is laughing, even King.

They laugh insincerely at first, guarded, because you can never be sure with Slinger. Then, like the good actors he has taught them to be, they get into it, feeling it belly-deep bubbling up, cracking open throat-holes, flaring nose-holes. They collapse on each other, on the floor, doing a good laugh—the biggest joke. They sweat and cry and dribble that joke while Slinger braces himself, doubled over on the manager's arm.

"This is the joke of my lifetime! Really. Allyou too funny, too . . . ach!" He starts again like a sneeze. And they can't stop, not until he's well finished and sobered up. They must outdo him at it, show him.

The old wire-bender, sitting on his crates in the corner all this time, watches the jackasses. When the lovely cleared silence returns, uninterrupted by a snort or a "O Goood," he sighs "Amen."

God of Design echoes it without missing a beat. Says it again. "Amen. Ah-men. That's it! Yes, Hallelujah, praise the Lord. Good God, that's it—Amen!"

"Make a joyful noise," someone says, keeping the beat. "Amen."

"Sing a lovely praise."

A church clap starts.

"Oh yes, Aye-men."

"Hallelujah—make a joyful noise."

"Aye-men."

"That's it. That is it! White. Plain and simple, black and white. Prints on T-shirts. Monday will be T-shirts and then—we can do this!" Slinger is blessed again, weaving and conjuring. His crew singing praise, clapping spiritual chorus.

No elaborate skirts and sewing. Just wraps of white cloth, however people want to tie it—on their heads, draped, swathed like the Holy Grail, sari, toga, sarong, kaftan, cloak—different weights of white with black strips for tying. Oh, why didn't he think of it before? So simple. Happy. Rejoicing. Slinger rushes up to the old man and snatches him off the crates. "Thank you! Linton, you saved my life, thank you."

"Yuh mean, is no wire-frame ass heads?"

Slinger hugs the man tight.

"We could put 'Ketch the Spirit' on de T-shirts," comes from the brave heartened bunch.

"Or . . ."

Slinger holds up his very white palm. "That would be offending. The church will come down on us onetime boop, with a name like that. We must be careful with this one."

"Is truc," they say, "that go be the problem right there."

It sets everybody thinking hard, like Slinger, problem solving and arguing.

Fraser sits out by the pool at 3:00 a.m., swaddled in his bedsheet. He lies down on the bench and stares up at the single heaven.

Stars are fantastic things. Even with the orange glow of the city they stand out from infinity, as only stars could. A particularly large one fixes its glory on Fraser. He knows when they were so big and non-twinkly, you could say it's a planet. But no one is around, so Fraser prefers to think of it as a guiding star. Orion's Belt and the incestuous cluster of sisters are pointing out themselves, waiting for him to name them too. Book knowledge—it gets in the way of his natural thinking, sometimes. Once his brain acknowledges the learning, though, he finds it hard to keep other names and things from surfacing. Zeus, Persephone, Cadmus, and Aphrodite, they stride this same heaven. Them and all the gods. His body, wrapped in white, feels like an offering. Sacrifice to the gods. Which gods?

Fraser tries to clear all thoughts but that in itself reminds him of TM techniques and Om. Suddenly he's aware of his huge rib cage, and feet sticking up, bones resting on the wooden planks, lined up straight and bound in cotton. His own pyre. Like the one he saw at the Hindu funeral by the Caroni River, Trinidad's own Ganges. He can feel the wood stacking around him, high, over him . . . until he has no glimpse of the stars or the night-river sky or the close hills. Only sucky, tugging, inky infinity and then . . . a crackling. Dry, greedy flames. Tinkling bones of pinewood. His bones. Crinkling them up, flaring on resin. And knots. Joints. The flames encase him, roaring a forest in his ears, all around, leaping into the air and licking at the magnificent heaven. A torch of amazing strength and power and fiery vitality—blazing away to kingdom come. Fire-shield armor gouging a path, a sword tip flying. Comet. Burning the sky. Burning out. Dark, lonely pain. Cold stars. Tinkling. He can see the pinpricks again. And feel his flesh caught in the stare of his guiding light, and the breath of the greedy hills waiting . . .

———

This is the day of the meeting. Ata and Pierre had agreed with Fraser that the caring business had to be taken in hand. Some sort of rules for respecting their home, and Fraser's wishes and peace of mind, had to be set up. Everybody, close friends, parents, agreed but they found the word "meeting" offensive. Just the tone of Helen's voice when she phoned her—the way she tasted the word—told Ata "too cold, too formal." Ata is not looking forward to the afternoon meeting but Fraser was gaining vigor and sided with Pierre, insisting that it was the only way to sort things out. His strength had improved as her nerves began to tingle. A weakness is loading in Ata's body. Electronic hourglass trickle while corrupt files multiply. She can feel the virus nestling in spaces she had kept clean and locked but she can't stop it. Her whole body is unsafe and unpredictable, ticking. Maybe it's hormones, lack of sleep, the evening glasses of wine she has with Pierre to help sleep? Toxins. In Dr. Turner's private clinic, Ata had marveled at the woman's strength—how she could treat patient after dying patient and keep losing them, yet remain so steadfast and bright.

Fraser had dragged his great feet from the cool car, up the few steps, to the baking porch and into the waiting room of the dialysis clinic. He pretended not to notice the heat. He and Ata said good morning and sat politely on the brown lino-and-steel chairs. The secretary, lost among filing cabinets behind the wooden half-wall, managed to find her way out and take Fraser's name. There were only a few people waiting—four. Normal-looking people, waiting patiently. No one reading the curling diabetes magazines or doing anything, just watching each other's hands and feet. Fraser crossed his ankles and clasped hands. Eventually, a man came out of the small corridor between what used to be bedrooms. The secretary looked up, nodded, and the lady with the umbrella went in. Dr. Turner came out, smiled at them abstractly, went back in, and the heat continued stacking under the peaked tin roof.

"It's easy, easy. So simple, you wouldn't believe how easy it could become. Just sit up there for me. One minute—just going to wash my hands." Dr. Turner made two steps to the next room and Ata looked for somewhere to fit, out of the way. With the tiny room divided in two by a flimsy partition, the homemade doctor's couch was only two feet from the cupboard-lined wall. More brown lino and sickly, meant-to-be-cheery yellow. Boxes were stacked up to the windowsill and a wire hanger hooked over the top of the partition. Bold sunlight pushed in, competing with the air-conditioning, winning gradually.

The doctor stepped back in briskly. "You want to lie down, Fraser? Yes, put your feet up."

Fraser shook off his Birkenstocks and they thumped down, taking up all the space on the floor. He rocked back stiffly in his shell armor but he was shrinking daily within it.

"You have to eat to stop losing pounds. Lots of protein. I'm just going to take your pressure, okay?" Hands doing things all the time. She was turning easy in the little half'a room, moving packets, a bowl, scissors on the counter, gauze on the bed. She patted Fraser's leg comfortably. "You like meat? Liver and beef, good things. This is okay. Let me just get a bag." She dug behind the partition, half her body on Ata's side of the room and the other still on Fraser's side. She grabbed hold of a bag of clear fluid like it was any old thing, rested it on the bed against Fraser's foot, and patted it. Fraser raised his head to look and flopped back down. His face glowed just before a dew of sweat appeared.

This was a lesson. Fraser needed to learn the procedure himself, but he just turned his face away and stared deadly at Ata. Her mixed feelings shone back at him. She couldn't control it, her disappointment, judgment, and sympathy, close and overwhelming as the warmth in the room. He cut her slap of a look and turned away. Dr. Turner reminded him gently, after his mini-tantrum and sullen swipe at her, that he was lucky to have friends so close to him. Ata felt grateful but transparent. The warmth dampened Ata's skin and slicked her armpits. She wondered if it wasn't too warm for storing the precious solution.

Dr. Turner didn't sweat a millidrop, while Fraser's brow popped beads. He kept complaining, saying that even the usually cooling fluid wasn't helping. Dr. Turner complimented him on his lovely feet. She was the coolest Queen of Saline and Ata couldn't stop admiring her—her sure dry hands, the comfort with her full figure despite her unmatched clothes. Her face held saline secrets deep in understanding eyes and a tentative smile. The fluid is called dialysate, she explained. She should be worshipped more than God of Design. But no one knew about this quiet hero. Only families of the lives she had preserved a little longer, at a reduced cost whenever possible. Sometimes she had to send them on to gory hemodialysis at the hospital. Ata could not imagine how she could keep grace while having to refuse a patient treatment because they couldn't afford it anymore. For years, this woman had dealt with her choice of speciality, saving dignity and souls instead of lives. If only everyone could find that grace when faced with sure death, or for a friend facing it. She looked at Dr. Turner closer.

The transparent viral feeling stays trapped in Ata on the day of the meeting, while Thomas is in cleaning heaven, polishing and prepping for the "event." He loves anything he can help prepare for, as long as it is planned, and Ata has even told him what she will serve. He reports how many ginger ales and mixers there are and suggests he give Fraser's bathroom an extra clean, because people will use that one. "We would need some more Ajax next time you go shopping, though," he says cheerfully.

When she asks how the two tins could be finished already, he claims that it works best for limescale and everything, and that is what he does use all the time on all them sinks and even toilet bowls.

As they all settle round the table and onto the settees in the living-dining room, Fraser's face and back are stiff as Ata's insides. She chooses the arm of the settee, between those on it and Fraser, Pierre, and Helen at the table. Lawyer-friend, doctor-friend, Indi-Portagee couple-friends who have taken to visiting regularly, cousin, secretary, SC, Vernon, Marriette and her brother, chat away easy as the afternoon light on soft cotton and warm terrazzo floor. They chinkle up talk nice as ice cubes melting in their glasses, cool-cool as the water droplets dripping past knuckles onto a knee. Rum and ginger with a piece of lime. Fitting. Even big mouth Marriette-brother's comments about the drink and SC's turkey laugh aren't too loud.

Fraser clears his throat, stretching his neck up as far as it can go. He has received the compliments on how well he is looking, with perfect grace. He ahems again, commanding attention just as God of Design could do. "I should say, before we begin, that we all have choices. I made mine, without regrets, and am fully aware of that. I am the one living with my choices and so you should be able to, to deal with yours, whatever they may be, without it being . . . stressful." He goes on to "publicly" thank Ata and Pierre for their hospitality and open home and all his friends for caring for him, in the most cold, meeting-like language. "But it *is* stressful—for me, for Ata and Pierre, to keep this up. The . . . bickering and demands . . . I have had enough."

Everybody freezes, staring at his straining face.

"I want a nurse. A nurse who will be there when I need her and help with the obvious."

They breathe a sigh of relief and all the different tones of relationships with him start blending again, babbling all at once. Relief—that what might have been a standoff difficult discussion is now agreeable terms—spreads, in Fraser's posture too, now that he has said his bit.

"And en't dat is what we been telling you all dis time, eh?"

Marriette boxes her brother lightly.

"Yuh brain so harden in yuh blasted skull, you never like to hear—but of course dat go be better for everybody, including you!" Talking as if he ever came to help with the obvious. He was one of the culprits who was always ready to start a lime by the pool, talking off whoever's ears he caught, while bawling about the lack of a flow of alcohol.

"It's not that we don't want to, or like, to look after you, yuh know, Fraser." Helen the Giver of Care has to try to counterbalance the crassness and make sure nothing remains harbored. "That is something I know each one of us in here feels is the least we could do to help."

Fraser stares just how Ata is looking at her—why's she speaking like he's a child? He hopes she won't go on to the helpless thing, the "how useless" his illness makes others feel in the face of it. Fraser widens his turtle eyes at Helen, she gets the message, and Pierre swiftly moves the talk along the agenda he had printed. Who is responsible for sourcing nurses, how to coordinate special food and medicine supplies, visiting, and house rules—all go smoothly. Helen and Pierre work well together and Ata sees a little glimmer of respect in her eye for him.

"Of course *everybody* finds it easier to follow rules. You just have to tell them and they do it, no problem, matter fix," SC contributes, and Marriette's brother agrees wholeheartedly.

It is true. The ones who bother to ask when would be convenient and what to bring aren't the problem. No framework was set up for those who never ask. And loud as Marriette's brother might be, he, like any big-skin person, really doesn't mind being told no, yes, not now. As long as there's a pattern. Black and white, simple and fine.

"Right, good, we done," Brother concludes the meeting. "Now a man could get a decent drink instead'a this watery stuff. Where de aged rum? Ata, ah feel yuh hiding de fifteen year El Dorado. Fraser boy, you looking well enough to tek a drink. If you know how glad I is to see dat!"

Vernon's chuckle breaks out through his nose like a horse sneeze. It was the only sound from him all this time. He knows where Ata keeps her old rum and is watching for her reaction. Fraser's amused too but Ata's mind is turning over his opening words about choices—how eloquently but bluntly he had put it. Who, in this friendsy afternoon room, knows what their choices are? Terence's absence was noted and exclusion of parents acknowledged without words as another choice.

"How Sammy doin'?" Brother asks, and the comfy chuckles stop.

"Oh gosh, I really feel it for him. That was a horrendous thing, eh?"

"You seen him since, Vernon?"

His head snaps up in surprise. "Me? Na, eh eh . . ." His voice and his face tuck back into a mumble. "I don' believe he reach back by the office yet but I don' really deal with he much . . ."

"Okay, that's enough darkness for now!" Fraser declares. Ata checks to see if he's serious but Thomas appears, to find out if they need more ice, and Fraser promptly blows him a kiss. He blushes and hurries away and the laughter resumes. Fraser hadn't really asked about the incident or called Sammy himself yet. Ata watches him holding court again.

"Thomas has been having a ball in the bathroom today with Ajax," he says. "'Ajax the Great,' son of Telamon and King of Salamis—he was the tallest and strongest of all the Achaeans, second only to Achilles."

"Wait nuh, 'salami' you say? Thomas and de King of Salami or, or Thomas, de Ajax fella *and* de biggest salami—inside de bathroom having a ball?"

Vernon gets this too.

"Yes, that would be the Trini version," Fraser continues through the noise, trying to keep a straight face and educate these people a little. "Ajax was never wounded in any of the battles of the *Iliad* and he killed many Trojan lords . . ."

"Oh Gad, Ajax kill Thomas in there with de salami!"

"Odysseus and Ajax tie in a competition for the ownership of magical armor forged on Mount Olympus. Ajax argues that because of his strength and service in battle for the Greeks, he deserves the armor. But Odysseus proves the more eloquent, and the council gives him the armor."

"Yuh mean, de Odyssey fella is a sweet-boy?"

"Hear the ending!" Fraser holds up a hand. "Ajax, 'unconquered' and furious, falls upon his own sword, 'conquered by his own sorrow.'"*

The friends indulge him and try to look impressed like they reading into the borrowed words. But smallee-Indi notes, when she finished guffawing quietly, "I find our friend here ain' truly, completely well. Because he still playing proper-proper around such a good joke."

*Roberto Calasso, *The Marriage of Cadmus and Harmony* (1993).

Fraser attempts to laugh off the comment and show his old witty self, with some comeback line, but he can't manage. Cloudy weariness washes over him. Politely, some start rising to go and Helen helps him to his room. The meeting is over. Air cleared. And evening approaching quick. No one else seems to have noticed Fraser's lack of care for anyone other than himself. But then Ata knows that you're not supposed to once someone's ill. All is excusable and forgiven. She feels worse now than before the meeting but at least a nurse was agreed on.

Ata drops Pierre off to work the next morning. Fraser's breakfast is ready, Thomas will see when he wakes, and SC has offered to come in, since she was off from work. As Ata drives, she realizes that she misses the working-morning routine, the feeling of knowing, as you dress, the workforce is dressing too. The solid, reassuring comfort of a lot of people doing the same thing with you. Riding out the door, into the car, the street, bus, going to work. Good, hearty industriousness. Pierre's shaven jaw, her shower-wet hair, that fresh facing-the-morning feeling can only compare, slightly, to the travel rush. No independent work at home can give you that.

They pass some little schoolchildren with their faces greased and shining, gazing away their sleepy freedom before the heat begins. Ata swerves off the Savannah and stops behind the line of cars dropping off teenage girls in blue-and-white uniforms. They step out, chatting and flinging hair and rucksacks about casually. They carry a confident ease of the bright and middle-class with them, into Bishops' conventlike compound. These are the ones who would soon be the sharp women parking their own cars and stepping, in high heels and tight skirts, into offices close by. No doubt about it, in the way they laugh with each other. They already own the morning. Ata always notices Pierre's reaction: he can't resist peering at them and smiling.

"Well, at least there's always a cheerful sight at this hour. More than I could say once I get inside the building. God, I don't know how some of the most sour-faced, civil-servant types get a job in there." He scrambles his bag from the backseat as Ata pulls up outside the U.N. building.

"They must be good at paperwork."

"Of course, no shortage of that!" He pecks her cheek, tells her not to worry herself 'cause he can see she's building up to something, and bundles himself off.

She smiles. Somehow, he has a way of carrying on with his strange gait and hunch, as if he's still in a cold country, battling a heavy coat and blizzard. His gray furry tail disappears through the doors and she drives off, getting the hint from the security guard who always behaves as if it's the Queen's palace he's guarding, with his special U.N. Security training orders.

Ata switches on the radio as she heads west against the traffic for her meeting with God of Design and the manager. The last bit of the day's brutal headlines hits her, then soca. Both too harsh. She turns off the radio and flows with the mindless, familiar hum of the traffic and the stream of caffeine-buzzed faces, gliding behind glass. She isn't feeling it this year. Like how some people don't feel Christmassy until the actual day, she isn't feeling the pre-Carnival vibes. Ata knows it's with good reason, with all that is going on, but she'd heard about some donkey foolishness, from the camp. No mind for nonsense now. Maybe it's time she quit, like everyone else, eventually.

The stupid man is weedy-whacking the whole flicking yard again as she walks in. He likes to annihilate every blade of grass, and slice up bare dust where there's none. He doesn't even stop when someone's passing 'cause he can't hear a thing with the racket. He and the robowhacker are one. And, like any other man with a machine, he loves feeling the power in his hands, vibrating, as he slowly creeps up to a fresh, unsuspecting bush. Covered in grass crumbs, he moves forward with relish, grinning when he catches sight of Ata scuttling into the hangar. Worse than bachac ants or locust.

"Slinger couldn't make it," the manager greets her, loud over the grass eater's din. "Let's go in the office."

It was true about the Donkey Rally business, but in Ata's mood the story isn't even funny. Pure nonsense. The manager asks how Fraser's doing and Ata says she has to get back home soon. *Amen* is right. Ata isn't fazed. She receives the concept description and sketches for T-shirt prints, makes her notes, and says nothing. Little bits of gravel spray the windowpane as the madman nears the building, and she stares at the manager's dull face. She can imagine the state of Design God's brain, he doesn't have to say any more.

"Scampishness! Scamps! All'a, or plenty'a we heroes is scamps— dat is what I telling you. Governor Chacon surrender Trinidad to the English *without a shot*! And furthermore, he play kiss- ass to the next scamp, Picton, yes, dat nastiness Kernel Picton, Governor Picton—ent yuh know Picton Street?"

Sammy's quick brain had start putting two and two together long before now, driving all about, as many hours and radio listening as possible. Programs sponsored by the library or university, or *We T'ing* hour. Anything to keep his brain occupy and busy. Now, in the rumshop on Independence Square, first time back after certain things had occur in his life, the ole boys hardly notice him 'cause they well into a piece'a ole talk.

"When you really check it, dat is it—we inherit scampishness. Picton, he receive half-pay as captain for twelve years, even when Abercromby leave him in Port'a Spain. And . . ."

Abercromby Street—downtown, vital, but dirty—has a few bars of course, but also goods shops, hardware, old strong buildings. Abercromby couldn't be so bad, Sammy thinks, is the Belmont taxi one-way route out of Independence Square. But, they say, maybe he bribe the coward Chacon. Sam amaze himself, that he could find similarities between the historical characters and places, streets, named after them. He would look into this further, check it out with Father McBarnette.

"Cipriani is the next one. He, they teach you in school, he set up de first Workingman's Association, say he was for de people—but he was on de white man side too."

Cipriani College and then the boulevard, broad and clean, came to Sam. He like how this thing playing out in his mind like a detective movie, enthrilling and guessy, giving him things to think about.

"Scamp. Dat wasn't Cipriani statue right here in de square?" another taxi driver ask.

"Yeah, boy. That's why Sparrow had to sing about it—'cause was more bacchanal before they take it down—'bout if they should keep it or not. People was only destroying it and breaking off hand and foot and t'ing."

Little, scrawny Oh Yes pipe up from the next table. He always tired and look like he can't raise heself, only to get in his car and move the gear stick, but hear him, "Oh yes, I is one'a them who break off de man hand, self!"

"You boy, Oh Yes?"

"Why not? Oh yes. Me self. One night, I lash it with a piece'a two-by-four, oh yes. Captain Arthur Cipriani—I give him licks, oh yes!"

Sammy have to laugh at how the man looking so proud and satisfy with heself. "But you not easy, Oh Yes!"

A next man clap him on his back and he grinning, settling back against the cool wall.

One of them start singing Sparrow song. *"I am made of steel and concrete, my address is downtown Frederick Street . . . Stand quiet and discreet, de sweetness of the oil drum round the street—that's where I am to be. Cipriani Statue in de heart of town . . ."*

"Where they take it and throw it?"

"Who knows? But de joke of it is dat now, they put up a statue'a Sparrow."

"Where?"

"Where?" One taxi man tap the next driver on his head— they realize he mean Lord Kitchener statue, recently erected in Saint James roundabout. "Don' get tie up, boy. Yuh too young."

Sammy young too but he know things, his brain making connections same as a professor—speed speed.

"That's de same thing Sparrow say, *'Schooling to make me a blughead mule . . . educate to make comedians, Humpty Dumpty sat on a wall . . . and Dan . . . is de man . . . in de van.'*"

"Ah wanna fall . . ." the others chorus, changing the lyrics one time:

"Mama look a boo-boo . . ."

"Sparrow is boss, yuh know."

"Dat ain' Sparrow."

"But Chalkie is de King'a political kaiso."

"I know but don' let we start on dat. I ain' finish with this scamps and scampishness story."

"Wynken, Blynken, and Nod, sailed off in a wooden shoe . . ."
They hush up the singer so the man can continue.
" 'De Deaf, de Dumb and de Blind'—Eric Williams . . ."
"Who sing dat? Chalkdust?"
"Gypsy?"
Two set off quarreling while the man continue. Sammy listening good, though, to build up his theary. This is a sign today—that talk, on top of driving, will bring him back normal.

"Well, is 'Eric de Ass,' 'Father of the Nation,' so they call him, 'Godfather of the Caribbean.' Chookolingo used to call him donkey, and draw him in de papers with big ears so, and them rest'a Caribbean prime ministers riding him, so . . ." He break down with all'a them doing the antics in the rumshop.

"I know de name Chookolingo . . . ," Young Fool say.

Everybody know about the owner of the *Bomb* newspaper, the same paper popular for sexy-porny photos of bullipscious local girls.

Sam don't approve of the papers himself, he like to leave that kind of staring deprivedness to them prisoners and unruly men.

"Was Seaga, Burnham, Gairy, and dem, in dem days, riding Eric de Ass, and he only giving out oil money, wild wild. Well, Eric Williams hold Chookolingo and throw him in jail for bad mouth. When Chooko release—two weeks later Williams name in de papers again. He say he exercising he freedom of rights and speech and t'ing."

"Tha's when them rest'a press say, that Eric say, 'Let the jackass bray.' Whoy!"

Table slamming, drinks downing, and the air in the rumshop roiling up good. Sammy like to see it so—in a racket. Who hooting, who braying, skinning up they lips like donkey smelling urine, and of course beating the donkey song percussion. Sammy not looking forward to this year Carnival at all. On top'a the usual madness, it go be one set'a foolishness. In the middle of the racket, he try to think of the Eric Williams Medical Complex, name after Trinidad's first prime minister.

How come more wasn't named after him? Sam can't ask 'cause they busy arguing about if Williams was a good man or a scamp or what. Then he remembers the papers, after the hospital was named—his daughter vex at the time 'cause her father had said he didn't want nothing name after him. Well, Sam reflect on the huge compound between the highway and Eastern Main Road—is a big hell of a thing, with the fanciest medical apparatus and "wings" of hospital spreading so and so. Was a big contract went down for it to get built. Something with some Canadian company and Moonan in the mix. A white elephant they call it now and is true, when you go in there, is big and foreign. Sam went once, and walk in the TV-style, cold waiting area. They even have a canteen nice like a restaurant, and coffee shop like in the malls, and plenty landscaping grounds. But when he peep at some of the wards with good-good signs pointing them out—no doctors or nurses or sick people about—chain and padlock on the doors. The image of Williams stamped in Sammy brain—the serious man in the dark glasses with a hearing-aid wire like a telephone cord dropping from one ear—is equally mysterious to him.

"Chambers! Chambers is a next one! Duncey Chambers."

"You ain' see how smart Gypsy sing dat? He say 'Chambers don' see'—duncey, yuh check it?"

"Gypsy didn'—"

"But allyou mixing up de order'a them. Wait nuh, I ain' finish with Williams. *Robinson,* now, was training under Williams but Robinson want to take over de place and he plan to do dat soon as Williams step on a plane. He go and see Williams off at de airport, not knowing he own wife, Patricia, deceased Patricia Robinson, was there. She had decide that her husband plan would bring trouble—so she wait till Robinson leave the airport, then she run quick and tell Williams. Some people say she was having affairs with Williams, me ain' know but anyway, is she that tell the man. So my boy Robinson, A.N.R. Robinson, Arthur Napoleon Raymond Robinson . . ."

"Napoleon?"

"Yes! Watch nuh, is so we used to laugh when we hear the name Napoleon, eh. Anyway, Robinson sit down in Williams office, well cock-up on de man desk, planning what he go do, now he can take over. When he look up, he see this bald-head man with dark glasses in the doorway—he almost faint!"

Big slamming and laughing, even though the ole boys know the story already.

"Williams say, 'All right, you want to run t'ings—go Tobago!' And he banish him to Tobago."

"That's right."

Sammy glad for the ole-talk core of this place. The way how people love talking things they know over and over—is a surety for Sam. It might sound the same but each time you learn something different. That you can count on. Everybody should have they ole boys and ole talk to turn to. That is what he wish. And he mind turn to Fraser. That man' kind'a company and they ole talk is a hard one to understand. Sammy tell himself he must go and check Fraser soon but he not in a rush to hear the sympathies and niceties and questions.

SC sits next to her old friend Fraser, realizing that she had never gotten anywhere near as close to him as Ata had, in all the long years she'd known him. Ata made her feel like she was strange, for not dropping everything to be there for him. That's only because her friend could now afford to do so herself, now that she's ensconced in the cushy life with Frenchie. Then she's going around behaving like she didn't ask for that life anyway. Idle bedside days biding strength has become the focus of Ata's time. She sits here, telling stories, listening, or "obeying the silence." Letting her mind go wandering in all directions, aimless as the minutes ticking by, searching under every philodendron leaf, like a lizard. She had grown distant, SC thought, preoccupied with Fraser and rapidly losing her sense of humor.

"Anyways, we have our differences and between you and me, I don't know when we grew apart so much, but it's not because of you, or anything to do with your sickness, sorry, illness."

Fraser looks at her. Perfectly matched brown leather heels and a tan skirt, swishy top and leather handbag—all melded with her smooth skin and plum lipstick. She even set off the horrid dusky-pink carpet. He smiles at her and she grimaces, absent-mindedly playing with her four rings. He doesn't have the energy yet, to tease her out of her darkish mood, and wonders if he ever will again.

"It's a shame, we were so close at one point." She keeps twisting her rings.

"Yes. A shame," he agrees.

"There's so much shit going on here—I don' mean you—distractions, people all up in yuh business, dramas. You could have a ton'a friends and none at the same time, really. Everybody so into theyself and all the stupidness, you could end up lonely and depress' wondering what is all about. Oh Laus, now I depressing you? Sorry, I . . ."

They hear the car arrive, door shut, and Ata steps in.

"You're back early."

Neither bother to feign surprise or ask why. The Donkey business had already spread across the land by hot-mouth wireless and Maco Daily.

Steups.

"And steups again, girl. You go be steupsing the whole way through Carnival this year." SC crosses a leg and stretches her neck. She never takes part in the messy, crowdy jump up and had already split up her holiday so she could take off, up the North Coast, when that time comes. Carnival had already come between the two of them. She could never understand how Ata could watch flabby, sweating, big-belly men and worse, women, with flesh hanging out everywhere, packing up on each other—and turn and say it's beautiful. "Real people," she called them and an "amazing range of bodies."

Ata watches her precious friend thinking about the stupidness again. She explains what little she knows of the Amen concept and Fraser takes an instant liking to it, ignoring her frustration.

"Yes, you *would* like it. 'How timely' is right. But don't even think you going anywhere near mas and play yuh-self!" SC is onto him and as soon as she says it, Ata can see Fraser's intentions walking across his sleepy face.

"No, no, no." He tries to pull his smirk in and get back to Ata's work. "But you have to make your decision, dahling. How long you been with him? Eight years off and on? In the four years I know you, you saying the same thing. The man's work is brilliant but he ain' go change."

They all know that the best of Trini's young visual artists have tried to work with God of Design. And not one of them has stayed on.

"The man is impossible!"

SC steupses.

"That's not even the sad part. It's the opportunity that is lost for other artists to carry this incredible thing on when he can't anymore." Ata wonders, though, if it really is an opportunity lost. Hasn't he contributed enough to the Carnival arts already? Imitations were already starting to pop up and his name had become "esqued" in style too. "Slingeresque."

"Well, thank God dat is not my worry. And is not yours neither, Ata, I don' know why you fighting-up with all dat."

"I'm not the only one. What about the Chinese guy who's dying and is working his last days away in the camp and just wasted them on costumes that would never be worn?" Ata knows SC's tightened lips are saying, "Well, who tell he to go and waste time in the first place," but she turns to Fraser, expecting some sympathy. He knows the guy too.

Fraser smiles. He's beginning to fade but can see Amen clearly. How fitting at this time in his life, his work with the church and Father McBarnette—this might be his "last Carnival." He'd be very happy to join thousands of people in plain white T-shirts with black print. "Hallelujah," he murmurs softly.

"Look you . . ." SC notices he's falling asleep and whispers to Ata that she has to go do some errands—this is her errands and "town" vacation week, before her escape holiday.

How could someone have an "errands vacation" and be so predictable? Ata doesn't object, even though she thought they were going to spend some time together today. She doesn't ask when they might have lunch either. Ata watches her town-friend look back at Fraser's sleeping face, then prance off purposefully to her sleek car.

Ata takes the notes and her unfinished feelings up to the study, changes, and stares at the sketches for a long time. A swim might clear her mind. Hot cream-synthetic-carpet smell, lingering upstairs. Blood stirring slow, turning in veins, cool in the room downstairs. As she walks through the house, Fraser, in his full glory, comes back to her, cavorting round the place as he used to. Running from the downstairs bathroom stark naked, long thighs chucking his bum, fleshy arms shuddering—splash. *Lovelay!* Ouffing and spouting belly-up in the pool, clacking his small-teeth grin.

The carpet stops at the door of the upstairs bathroom. The small white tiles are cool underfoot. Cooler than the plastic toilet seat. "I can see you from here," through the window. Gru-gru bef trees rasping the breeze and the big silk cotton, on the other hill, flying clouds of white puffs. Cotton magic puffs, sailing over the dust-dry town and the millpond shimmering hot sea. And on a glorious day like this, you sleeping a toxic dream downstairs. Ata likes the tiles in this bathroom. The way the black ones make a border round the edge and how some, just on the floor here, are crooked. It makes her think of someone laying each one carefully, with the white grouting powder on their hands and in their hair. Armitage Shanks. You washed your face here and you like this bathroom too.

A fan-palm breeze pats Fraser's cheek. Sleeping dreams of yesterday and nightmares of tomorrow.

Vernon walk into the ole boys rumshop. The whole town is his, seems like. All of Laventille, any part of the city—he could walk. Not like a big bravin' baddjohn or anything, just steely-silent. If you do notice him, you wouldn't look to trouble him. Vernon go cool-cool down inside the bar to the counter, and nobody don't pay him no mind. Except Jigga, who dancing and moving around in the corner. Sammy recognize Vernon straightaway but Vernon don't notice him.

At the counter, shiny Rosie come to serve him a drink. Jigga dangle over by him too, shaking heself, and he swell-up rum face, right up next to Vernon. Vernon don't take him on. Miss Rosie watch the stranger.

"Aye brudda-man, how you is today? Buy me a drink nuh?" Jigga splattering out the drunken words close close.

Vernon check his forearm resting on the counter, to make sure no stinking froth didn't fall on him. He ain' look at Jigga rample face yet but he can smell him, so he not turning.

Rosie ask what he drinking.

"Aye brudda-man, buy me a drink nuh?" Jigga rest he hand on Vernon shoulder and bring he slathering mouth closer.

In two twos, Vernon sling off the man hand and fling he back so, "Don' touch me!"

Sammy, from all the way by the door, could see hackles rise. All the ole fellas' talk stop. But drunky Jigga blind to that. He reel and smile, and come forward again.

"I ain' drinking dis hour'a the day," Vernon mutter to Miss Rosie. "Gimme a pack'a cigritte."

"Don' mind Jigga," she say, turning to reach for the small red packets on the shelf.

"Well, breds, a schmoke, a schmoke. Gimme a schmoke, nuh?"

Before he could land he hand on Vernon arm again, Vernon slam he up against the wall and rangle he up so.

"Oh Lawd Gad, e killing me!" Jigga bawl out. He head butt-up on the wall, how Vernon raff him, while he splattering and bawling, "He dead."

"Vernon!" Sammy shout out.

Vernon drop him one-time and he fall down on the ground laughing. "Yuh lucky," Vernon snarl, deep in he guttery throat. And he pay for he cigarettes, not minding how Rosie watching him scornful.

"Wha' happen to you man?" but he walk out without even watching Sammy yet.

Jigga jump back up on he antsy foot, shaking and dancing again. "Da is a vex man, bwoy . . ."

"That is not a man to trouble," them ole boys say.

"I know him," Sam say. "I always suspec' he is a troublemaker."

"Where he from? Aye-aye, he remind me'a Dr. Rat, but he taller than Rat. Yes, Dr. Rat, de informer for Kojak. Protected—a feared fella from Belmont. He used to be on de street insulting people and they couldn't touch him . . ." The scamps expert start up again and the rest like nothing better.

Sammy listening but he hope they would get back to great people names, so he could go driving around in he mind again, looking up where named after them. He looking forward to actually driving by these places, to find telling signs that match the character. But he have a feeling the talk heading to violence. It always comes back to that, somehow. Violence and corruption. If a person not in it, they talking about it. A lot'a talk.

". . . a time, Kojak realize Rat had two rum in he head and he slap him up in front'a people! Yes. Randolf *Kojak* Burrows, man, and he tatical squad."

"He wha?"

"De 'Flying Squad' they used to call them. If you see them coming out, with they black suit . . ."

"And NUFF come out too."

"Nuff what?"

"National Union of Freedom Fighters—they give Kojak a hard time in de seventies, but he was de first national police commissioner. After they run out de Englishman in independence."

"Kojak, eh?" The young fool will make this thing drag out.

"Yuh know Telly Savalez on TV?"

"How he go know dat?"

"Well, Burrows shave he head, keep on a dark glasses, and always have a lollipop in he mouth, just as Savalez. And he have a finney hand—was somebody he do wickedness to. And one day when Kojak walking alone—he uses to like to walk about in rough places without escort, to show he is man—well, de fella brackle him, break he arm, and push him in he car, wind up the window on he hand. Man, he drive him all'a about Port'a Spain with him so, before he let him go. Well, of course, dat was the *wrong* mistake he make—next day the Flying Squad search all over the country and find him and shoot him and put a gun in he hand. From then on everybody 'fraid Kojak and he shave he head and t'ing. Just used to kill off criminals as he ketch them."

"Duke sing about it. *'How many more must die . . .'*"

It don't look like they would get back around to finish off with the prime scamps countdown from Silver Fox Panday to present PM Manning. But Sammy can't think of much, offhand, that was named after them anyway. *Audrey Jeffers?* She have a lil' piece'a highway over so. Sam had hear on the radio she was a good woman who had work hard for poor people and like feeding them and things so, set up school lunches and de same Breakfast Shed down by the waterfront. Good food. Cheap. And cooling mauby drink. A good woman.

In his mind. In his mind, Sam driving again. So he decide he should leave. Them talky ole boys didn't even miss him when he gone. And Sam glad they don't know nothing about his private state a'ffairs.

FETE SOUNDS CLASH with the gentle Sunday afternoon. They had all had breakfast together out by the
pool, almost like how it used to be; Pierre crunching
toast and reading the papers, Fraser eating slowly, drinking in
the morning with his eyes; Ata shifting her focus between the
lines of Isabel Allende, Fraser's face, Pierre's distracted form,
and the facing hills.

The hills like to play mas with the fete noise. Sound-play is
their bacchanal. They bounce, smack, drum the rhythms back
and forth until they're a tangled mess. Now the insistent soca
bass marches its vibrations through the whole house and across
the lawn. The hills' mouths open wide and splatter it back out
on them, laughing. The MC screams at the crowd and a twangy
claw scratches the valley, slicing a cheek. There is no escape from
the echoing massacre of noise.

*"Take a jump, take a jump, take a jump right now—it's Ka-
nee-val . . ."* The hills swallow the words but Ata and Fraser know
the tune. They watch, from the birdeye perch of the garden wall,

down to the busy glitter of thousands of cars parking near the Oval cricket ground.

"And they're only just now starting up," Pierre laments.

Fraser takes the beating on his chest as the bands of sound come up the hill. His eyes gleam. "It's remarkable, it comes right up."

"Every bloody year. Every sound."

"The price you pay for the view. No obstruction and the hills behind us . . ." Ata turns to face them again and can feel the *boo-doom boo-doom*, bouncing off her chest, thumping her back.

The infernal Donkey tune starts and the horns blare up the racket louder. The DJ replays and replays the effect. Hill-teeth start gnashing and Fraser and Ata's eyes meet and fire up, she shaking her little skinny self on the wall and he riding his head round his neck . . . "*bacchanal in Port'a Spain, whoa whoa . . .*" A breeze wipes the words and raucousness away from the hills for a second, cleans their palate. Ata leaps off the wall and they head back across the lawn. You have to join in or run, and Pierre had tried to join once but was completely out of place. Pierre was not one to revel in the authenticity of a place and do like the locals do. He leaves that for the wankers he thinks are wannabes. He nurtures his aversion to loud noise and eye for everyday beauty instead.

"It's not so bad on the actual Carnival days when it's on the Savannah—it's the stupid fetes that lead up to it. Especially when there's one right below us in . . ."

"Boissiere Village or Stollmeyer's Castle."

"The windowpanes literally rattle."

"*Whoa whoa . . . godong godong . . . buddup buddup . . .*" Ata rollicks up and clowns around on the grass, for them to laugh—dangling limbs like a moko-jumbie stilt walker. Pierre is not amused.

"You better take him out, Ata. Don't feel youall have to stay—go," Fraser insists. "I have my lovely nurse now and Terence is coming later, to take me for a cru—a drive, a drive."

Thomas comes grinning out to meet them. "Is loud, eh? You could barely hear de TV!" Skinning teeth big, as if it's a God-given miracle, turning and admiring the hills as the echoes dribble around them.

Ata goes with Pierre, to the little beach house they rent some-times, in Blanchisseuse. He chose to drive, glad for the company and her decision. He thought she had wavered for a moment, but she chose peace over noise. They pass through the concrete-box suburbs that lie trapped, scorching in the valleys around the town. Squeezing through Maraval, up to the ridge where the housing stops, out, and winding over the hills of the North Coast. Pierre glances at Ata staring out the window.

She looks and tries to listen to her heart and mind, and what they could tell her about where she should be, what she should be doing, creating, making, mas, design, what? All she hears is landscape whispers. The road, curving, curving, heights control-ling. Green leaves close in then sweep away, down to Santa Cruz Valley. Closing in again, they carry you higher. Then Trinidad is revealing slips of her exotic dress. Lipstick-red slivers of chaco-nia and balisier, between wet green. Orangey-red immortelle. Pale heliconias, white spathiphyllum tongues in the dark shade. Twisting and flirting, the Northern Range dances the car along her spine. Fling and catch, in the dip of her waist. Clinging, holding on to moist mossy skin. Suddenly, way below, the shiny, silver-sea edge of a petticoat flashes. And up the back of her neck—banks of tree ferns dripping rain-dew, pull them into the intimacy of island plumage. The bamboo parts as they drive, slipping between quills. Against the skin of a peacock.

Further along the coast, she breathes in deeply and through the mountain-cool air, detects a distant, pungent cedar scent. The town ideas and worries have disappeared and she asks Pierre to stop for fresh cocoa flesh. The jewel pods have been catching the sun, warming sweet white pulp in their thick autumn-color cases. Pierre doesn't like the stuff. He watches her savoring it, but still she stays silent. A hip of the land lazes the sea: La Vache. Beaches pounding names, Maracas, Las Cuevas, Blanchisseuse. Vultures soar above mute villages. And Ata waits for her answers.

Fraser's new lightness of weight gives him spring and hope. Maybe he could live with this, the dialysis part. The expensive cocktail of drugs for HIV is another thing, but with more research, things would get better. They expect more years of life. He still hasn't contacted any of his past lovers and has only said to Helen, and therefore to the others, he will handle it. They watched closely, to see if there was any change in Terence when he visited, or any old friends suddenly appearing. None so far. Mother kept visiting, in her padded oblivion, and became almost a relief, some sort of embodiment of public normality for them all. His father kept his distance whenever he could but peace can be made when strength comes.

The nurse gives him a boost too. He loves her uniform and stockinged, white-shoe containment. The way her belt cinches her gabardine waist and her buttocks suggests an African shelf, but is smoothed over by the material, sealed in. Even her hair, stitched on, perfectly even short braids. Nothing out of place.

The strict routine she created worked better than any medicine. Charm and cheerfulness, appropriate disappearance just when it was needed, and supreme calm. A godsend, he calls her, and they all blessed doctor-friend for finding her. "Nurse Armor," they say when he shuts himself off with her, "Nurse Amour" when he waxes on.

Ata goes with Fraser and Vernon over to Fraser's apartment, for him to think about moving back home. This is just an initial visit, first time back since he had fallen ill two months ago. They sit on the veranda in the cool afternoon. The passion fruit vine has grown plentiful on the arbor and is bearing fruit and flowering at the same time. The yellow globes hang idyllic among the shiny leaves. Honeybees crawl lazily into the purple-and-white delicate cups. The white tiles, blue-striped canvas chairs, and clean walls—his little Mediterraneany bit of tropical paradise.

Fraser sighs and Ata goes to find the passion fruit juice Vernon had put in the fridge. Fraser had said that he was scared to move back but had missed home. She is as glad as he is, that this isn't sad or scary now but a gentle relief.

He sighs again as Ata gives him his glass with one of his artist-friend coasters. He admires the juice, the coaster's colors, the glorious vine on white rail, and the valley beyond, again. "I love Trinidad, yuh know. I really do."

"I hate it too. You was planning on going somewhere?"

The turtle is slow to answer, gazing away through squinty eyes. "Many times I left, before I began to build my practice here."

The times Ata knew about, he had disappeared off, gone gallivanting somewhere in the world doing God knows what, without contacting anyone, leaving his staff, clients cussing, staff smalling-up themselves.

"There's an ancient Greek argument, a long one, about those

who love boys and those who love women—who is better. You know I am not into boys, but get what I mean . . . Roberto Calasso looks at it in *The Marriage of Cadmus and Harmony*— you should read that one day, you'd like it. The question, since time immemorial: 'Which takes the erotic prize—love with boys or with women?' I, of course, always tell discerning persons that, like a good old clock, my pendulum swings both ways." He chuckles and Ata scoffs a laugh, knowing that his days of proclaiming love with a woman were long gone.

"And there's the scales—balanced with passion for both, at exactly the same height—Theomnestus. But the debate goes on, this one blinded for saying that women gain more pleasure from sex than men—Tiresias—that one torn apart, for declaring the superiority of love with boys—Orpheus . . ."

"I believe everyone is born bisexual," Ata states, and Fraser takes his eyes off the hills and turns to her with raised eyebrows. "Then through physiological, hormonal, emotional, psychological *occurrences*, they choose, or find, a comfortable preference or preferences. Sometimes in phases. One choice is not better than the other."

"Sometimes the preference ain't so comfortable, nuh." He turns back to the view. "But the fear of women and their . . . overwhelmingness, is written about back then too. The terror of the invasion of the Amazons, the women of Lemnos who slaughtered their men—there is a sheer, intangible power of women that I see at its peak in Carnival. The beads, the glitter and beauty, is terrifying sometimes. 'Sparkling with desire, laden with aromas, glorious.' There's a Pseudo-Lucian passage that describes 'a man climbing out of bed *saturated with femininity*, wanting to dive into cold water.'" Fraser sips his passion fruit juice.

"Calasso says 'the makeup and female smells combine to

generate a softness and beauty that bewitches and exhausts. Better for men the sweat and dust of the gymnasium."* Boys they looking at—give me men, though, not boys," he quickly adds.

"The 'gymnasiums,' eh, the 'primordial setting for desire' where the lover prowls, looking for the innocent or not so innocent beloved. Stalking, eyeing the boys working out in the dust, sneaking glances at the prints of their genitals in the sand, waiting until midday when the combination of oil, sweat, and sand blooms 'dew and down, as on the skin of a peach.'" Fraser takes another cool sip and Ata waits patiently for him to carry on.

"The 'gymnasiums' of London are the packed little streets of Soho, full of grimy and slick, hard-skinned or soft but grubby men—mostly dressed in black and dull colors like the pavements, the chrome stools, and old chairs that clutter up the cafés there. Cigarette smoke. Everyone smokes. And cold English rain. Gray drizzle and white skin stubbled with black hair, or a forearm covered in blond fuzz . . ."

Ata wishes she could write it down 'cause she can see it, she can feel it. Just how the written word seems so powerful and almighty to him—she is transported by words that roll out pictures and sounds and smells. A different side of the London she had glimpsed on her visits, but one she can imagine.

". . . here now, the 'gymnasiums' are Jouvert and Carnival, fetes. Even when a man is jamming on a woman's ass, there's a show of physicality and genitals, almost Olympian-like in its competition of ability and endurance. Have you seen some of the dancehall moves out there, I mean in a fete? Combined with soca antics—it's amazing. 'The primordial setting for desire,' ha! But anyway, I lost track of what I was trying to say. What is the point?"

*Roberto Calasso, *The Marriage of Cadmus and Harmony* (1993).

"The point?" Ata smiles. "The point is we're all just decent animals. *And* we have sex too."

"What!"

"People think animals are lower but it's the other way round—when we *like* sex, and the various forms of it, it doesn't mean we're debasing ourselves. The beastly-behavior part is when we dehumanize, for conformity's sake, power, religion, whatever—to the point of oppression or abuse . . ." She lost the point too. Wondering where honesty and dishonesty comes in with all of this, with one's self, with others . . .

Fraser always thought her brain was a little too loop de loop.

"Anyway, where all this Greek fascination comes from?"

"I was educated in the days where we *had* to learn Latin. In certain boys' schools and certainly for stellar, scholarly performance." He sniffs and raises his beak toward the *Passiflora edulis*. The flowers release no scent. He turns graciously to face the hills again. "I like home. I ready."

Sammy had bring Mrs. Goodman all the way from Arima because her husband busy. She in the guest room with Fraser now, trying to find fault with the nurse. Sam and Thomas can hear her from the garage.

"Da woman ain' easy, yuh know. She talk talk through de whole drive 'bout everyt'ing under de piping sun. Test me—is not a thing that go on in Trinidad she ain' touch on."

Thomas don't take up the challenge. He rest the wet spade against a post and take off his straw hat. This might be a long chat. Sammy must be feeling better. "That's how Moms is, sometimes.

You does have to let dem talk. I glad to see you back working, though, tha's good."

Now Sammy have to wait around, till Mrs. Goodman ready to leave. She never like him making turns when he waiting for her 'cause she might find errands to do, at any moment. Waiting is a thing.

Sam watch Thomas's comfortable slackness on he face, all the patience in he sluggish pose. Sam own phone not even ringing much these days, and he ain't start back football on a evening with them fellas, yet. His Queen had make a habit of cooking dinner regular for them now, and sitting and eating it with him when he reach home. She make sure she home round six and have a plateful set out for him nice and neat. If he bring his daughter home, better yet. His Queen know how to show love. Good cow-heel soup, peas'n rice and callaloo. Thick creole love. "She can't cook, yuh know, Fraser Queen."

Thomas squinting, embarrassed for she, and look down at a oil patch on the concrete. He thinking he must throw some Breeze soap powder on that stain.

"That is one thing she don' talk about—cooking."

Ajax might work better. Thomas keep his mouth shut.

"She come often? Since Fraser here? She does hardly call me."

"Regular enough . . . with Mr. Goodman."

"Okay."

"He does leave her here sometimes and come back for her. But she always quarreling that he never on time."

"Especially after she and Fraser fall out, right?"

Thomas don't answer.

"I never see a mother stress out a son so. I mean—"

The struggling sound of a old vehicle come up the driveway.

Vernon pull up and hop brisk out of Fraser's jeep. He grunt at them and heading toward Fraser's room.

"Aye, Boss Man," Thomas call out and Vernon stop. "He have company in dere."

Vernon not looking at them, he on pause like a athlete ready for business.

"Fraser Moms."

Vernon do an about turn and jump back in the jeep, slamming the door. He barely mungle out "Ah go come back." Gone, speed speed down the hill.

That set them off in the garage. Hearing Fraser calling out "Vernon?" they only laughing more.

Sammy go in with a straightish face to explain to Fraser—he come back out chuckling. "I never see Verns move so fast, boy, whey!"

"I should'a let he go ahead and butt-up with her in de room—then would'a be lightening!"

"And imagine he is a 'feared fella.'" Sammy thinking of the rumshop incident. "I meself never like him."

"Eh heh?" Thomas play surprise although he suspect that long time. "What he do you?"

"Nuthing, nuthing. My blood jus' ain' take he spirit. An' he like to play too much'a bad-boy attitude. I don' like how he chook up heself under Fraser. What is that, eh?"

"Vernon is a cool fella, man. I find he only looking so—he shy—dat is why he does play gruff. But once you talk to him, he okay."

"So Fraser tell me a'ready. But I don' trust him." Sam think of the times when Vernon would be lounging round Fraser office helping heself to coffee and brace back on chairs like he ain' working for Fraser but he is a friend come to check him. A good friend. Fraser self don't pull him up and even smiles and calls him Verns, watching each-another directly in the eyes. Sam don't like to think about these things. But this is what happens when you have to wait. Without good talk running, killing time is hard.

He watch Thomas quiet, slow self, keeping him company 'cause he is a nice fella and, for the first time, Sam see a softness in he manhood. Jesu Christ—that's why Fraser like him too.

"Fraser going home tomorrow," Thomas almost whisper.

"Yeah, I know." Sam wish he don' have to wait around no more.

That night on the North Coast, Ata felt a big, important thing had gone missing. After opening up the dank wooden cottage, they had sat out in the tender relief of wet salt air and wide sky. The unending sea below them turned lazily and steadily, rolling in breakers in its show of constancy, just as it did on all their visits. It was this they came for. The sturdy crashing and slap-rock sounds, the big and small feeling of staying still on the wooden deck, without the need to talk.

Ata had a rum and Coke from the rusting little fridge, Pierre a glass of wine from the bottle he had brought. And when night fell, they went to dinner across the road at the restaurant on the hill, as they always did. No need for much talk there either—about home, work, nothing. Only little comments about what was good on the menu, which hadn't changed, and how empty the restaurant always is. The waitress brought the steaming pumpkin soup and fresh white-bread rolls wrapped in a creole cloth that matched their napkins. These restaurants could be found all over the Caribbean—mostly empty, with a cheaply varnished bar and limited wine stock, mediocre food and hotel-packet butter. They ate and stared out at the fluorescent-lit car park, the treetops and rooftops, and could just hear the sea beyond.

Nothing was wrong, nothing the matter. But after they had made love and fell asleep, Ata woke. She stepped through the open doors onto the deck and sat there. They always take a chance, sleeping with the doors open, the sea quarreled. Why risk? the waves echoed, trying to hide their tumbling white smiles in the dark. But they knew why she came, was sitting there gazing, and maybe even what she could only feel was missing but couldn't name. The black hills behind her felt solid then, reassuring. Not to worry, things go missing all the time and new things wash in.

Ata sat there a long time, neither scared nor clear. She listened, unimpressed, to the sea banter. Eventually she crawled back into bed and snuggled up against Pierre's warm, dry back. She held him and he rested a paw across her arm. She nestled down in the hay-smell of his fur and was asleep before a strange kiss was placed on her nape. Something brushed a curl off her cheek and sat on the bed behind her.

Back in their home, the missing feeling had vanished with things to do. With everybody fussing, they moved Fraser back to his place and Thomas pottered around, trying to reestablish his old routine.

"Right, what about dinner at Veni Mangé?" Pierre suggests.

Neither of them want to seem too relieved to have their home to themselves again. But Ata agrees to eat at their favorite color-ful restaurant. A discreet celebration of some normalcy.

As Ata and Pierre drive off about six o'clock down the drive, suddenly footsteps, lots—running past Thomas in his room, into the kitchen. Thudding footsteps. Men's shoes. And voices. Thomas holds his breath, locks his door silently, and reaches for his cutlass. Two voices come back out of the house. Must be about four or five of them.

"Everybody gone."

Steps, closer to his room.

"Ah feel somebody in there . . ." A hand tries the door and Thomas leans all his weight against the inside. Sweat drips off his hands gripping the raised cutlass and he squeezes harder, wringing the wooden handle.

"Nah."

A shoulder thumps against his, on the outside, as the door handle rattles again. "Somebody in there." Kicks start. Then stop. They listening.

Thomas wonders how they can't hear his heart and blood thumping so loud. His breath in the pit of his gut, quivers like the blade in the air.

"Nah, boy. It ain' have nobody there."

Something hard hits the door. Then the footsteps leave and go back to the house.

Thomas stays behind the door. He dare not move or peep out as he listens to them talking and moving freely through the open house. They stay for hours and go upstairs, taking their time. While the minutes drip from Thomas to the sweaty floor. Pierre had talked about running a phone line into his room but Thomas claimed he hardly made calls. When everybody was busy clamoring for these mobile phones, he couldn't see the sense in one.

But like the t'iefs think these people wouldn't come back home?

Two hours pass. Then the footsteps again. Trekking up and

down, just outside his window. They carrying things—they must'a t'ief-out the whole house by now and . . .

Footsteps stop outside his door again. Thomas replenishes his cutlass grip.

Somebody still has a feeling he's in there—talking about kicking down the door, just to make sure.

Is he and them. First one that come through—he taking off they head. They better not . . .

Two kicks land, same time on the wood. A next two, and the putty between the cracks popping out.

His heart can't give up now, a next kick and they will come through.

Just so sudden though, they stop. Thank the Lord. And this time they don't stick around to hear his blood beating. They steups, give up, and leave.

At the end of their colorful meal, Pierre gets the call from their neighbor and they rush home. Thomas flapping and the police haven't arrived but the neighbor's security company is there flashing torchlights into the bushes.

"Are you okay, though. You okay, Thomas?" Ata taps his stiff shoulders as he splutters out the whole story, brave enough still to enter the house with them. The security had turned on all the lights and checked it out.

"The TV still there!" Thomas exclaims. "But the VCR gone . . . Watch what dese fellas do."

The fridge is wide open and some cupboards too.

"They was eating! And drinks too—all de alcohol gone."

The computers are still there but the camera, some British pounds, and all the small appliances—blender, toaster, down to hair dryer—taken. The police arrive, blink their siren lights about, point torches up the hill, and say they will be back in the morning to take fingerprints.

Upstairs, Ata walks past the bathroom to their bedroom, feeling the eyes of the men, who must have been watching from the hill, following these same movements, earlier. She goes back down the steps, just as she had then.

"Thank God Fraser wasn't here still."

"I say that too. And look how they cut the telephone cord—these fellas see how to do these things on TV." Thomas can't stop talking and repeating the story, no matter how much Pierre keeps saying it's okay, nothing much was lost and he wasn't harmed.

They lucky. Thomas lucky. But they should have more security measures, the guards told them. Too much risk. When Thomas protests that it was six o'clock in the evening, the place wasn't even dark yet—he would've locked upstairs and turned on lights at seven—what is wrong with this place? Nobody replies. Nobody could say what really had gone awry—what was taken or disappeared. Missing. Ata just feels more empty. Their bed foreign, room full of strangers, their home like trampled grass. The hills' ever-present stare and their betrayal lumps up, breathing down too close.

Next morning Ata hears Vernon's growl downstairs with Thomas. He came at first light, after hearing the news. How could Thomas have slept when she and Pierre hardly did, even in each other's arms?

"I couldn' close me eye at all las' night, boy." Adrenaline-shaky, Thomas waits for the police to arrive again. He had wanted to put things back in order but they told him not to, till they take the prints. "Watch how de place rample. They could'a do they wuk last night, that's what they *supposed* to do. If was overseas, first, they would'a come straightaway and next, they would'a do everything one time. Not here, boy, eh."

Vernon mumbles something but Thomas don't quite catch it. His voice just rumbles through the open garage, broad and reassuring. He glances secretly at Thomas's bloodshot eyes and looks down at the ground solemn, thinking he don't need to tell Thomas how assish the police really are, and not to bother with them. Vernon leans against the parked car. He spots the hill watching the back of the house, poui trees waving light, morning breeze all wet and happy, but keeps looking at Thomas furiously sweeping the drain.

The police arrive just as Pierre and Ata come down the stairs. Five of them, big and strapping, unfold from the police car. Vernon and Thomas watch them stepping out and looking around the place important-like. The inspector, the one with a little stick made just for police inspectors, walks up to them. "Where is the owner?"

"He coming jus' now," Thomas says without budging. "They pass from so, *up* de hill." He points, for the benefit of the officers stalking the corners of the yard and looking *down* the hill.

"Unh huh, we have a full report from last night." The inspector takes off his hat and tucks it under his arm, with the little stick.

Ata and Pierre appear in the kitchen doorway together. The inspector wipes his forehead and bald head with a kerchief and follows them into the house.

Vernon smiles, watching the man mopping his head even though the morning still cool. Them hats does give they heads some pressure. That's what must be making them bazodee and stupid so.

The officers make a big show of stamping shoes and wiping them on the doormats before stepping inside. Bits of wet cut lawn grass cling to their polished black boots. One bends down and wipes his off with a rag. Then they set about making a mess with their powder, all over the house. When they finish, and the inspector "concluded inspecting the crime scene," they head to their car, ready to squeeze back in.

"They not even going to look up de hill!" Thomas exclaims, incredulous. "Last night, they say they will go in the morning."

"Aren't youall going to see where they passed on the hill?" Ata asks the inspector.

He pauses, about to get in the front passenger seat, and looks up at the hill.

"If you go to the back now, you will see clearly where they passed to come down—"

"That's not necessary, ma'am. The grass is wet and I doubt we would find anything. We have the serial numbers of your stuff, so if we come across anything, we'll be in touch."

Vernon chokes a cough and Thomas's jaw drops. They all watch the car reverse, turn, and slide away down the drive.

"Ha! De grass wet! Yuh hear dat, Vernon? De grass wet, so they can't go up there."

"Can you believe this?" Ata turns on Pierre. "Their boots might get dirty, or their pants hems might get wet. God forbid, one of them might even slip and fall, because wet grass is dangerous." Ata raises her voice at Pierre's silence.

Pierre turns and goes back in the house.

"I know long time, dem fellas is jokers."

They all know the uselessness of the fingerprinting exercise, since the record of prints at the police stations is so limited compared to the number of criminals roaming about.

"Leh we go up there, Thomas. Bring yuh cutlass." Vernon heads to the jeep for his.

———

When they come back down, Pierre is greeting the security officer, to go over what system they could put in place, and Ata's on the mobile to the telephone company.

"They was eating and drinking up there on de hill, if you see juice box and t'ing—they had a party, a picnic! You could see clear-clear where they sit down and relax. And where dey come up from—Boissiere Village."

"At least you know now that they didn't come from one of the trails further up in these hills."

"T'ank de Lord for dat," Thomas breathes.

"Criminals hide out up there. Youall should really fence that side of the property too . . ."

Pierre instructs them to go ahead with all, no matter the cost. Secure the place, without making it look like a prison, and then they could try to live in peace. They all agree, brave-faced—you can't live in fear.

Thomas busies himself cleaning up at last and doesn't even want their help. Do like Sammy, keep busy and moving. Work it out.

Vernon hangs around Pierre and the security man in the yard, listening to fence options being discussed. "Tiger wire," he rasps.

"Yes, razor wire," the security man translates for Pierre.

"Dat will ketch any man tail."

"*I WANT A MAN come and ride me rhydem!*" Allison Hinds screams on the radio but the woman wining down to the ground, sandwiched between two men in the mas camp, shouting "*I want a man come and ride me belly . . .*"

Flat on the ground, juking and grinding in a heap, and the other workers start shouting encouragement. The manager says, enough. "Youall could keep that kind of energy for the fete, please, come on . . ."

"Yes, get allyou ramping backside back to work!" Queen of the Band shouts, more authoritatively than the manager ever could.

An artist who has just returned from Canada, and her volunteering girlfriend, look away sheepishly and turn back to the pieces of the Queen's costume.

Queen of the Band holds out her arms again, towering above and beyond the little group of the most talented around her. "Pull it tighter," she orders and two women cinch the laces across the back of her bodice. Her spine, set deep between gold muscles, flexes. The strapless whiteness of the almost bridal dress pops her bosom and broad shoulders out at the top, glowing and strong. Ata could almost see her dazzling on the huge Savannah stage already.

They lift the first fifteen-foot fabric wing and struggle to squeeze the fiberglass spine of it into the casing on the back of her bodice.

"Ah think allyou will have to loosen me again to get them things in." Queen places one arm across the bust of her dress to hold it up.

Fifteen feet are the shorter ones. It takes another forty-five minutes to fit the taller, feather-like wings and secure them.

Queen releases her bussom and breathes in deeply. Her flesh threatens to burst out but the laces hold. She bends forward from the waist and sweeps around and back up. The wings suddenly flicker alive and flag a most graceful arc.

"It works!" All the workers watching now as she tests and flexes the eight tremendous wings. The fluttering sight hushes them—an angel has sighed. When she spins, the soft fabric sings the sea and heavenly freedom of sails spinning by. The sound of swift bat wings, invisible in the night. They can see the Savannah breeze lifting them wings, bending and spreading them, in majestic flight.

"So, is more have to strap to my legs?" Queen's feet are planted wide under her skirt as she stretches her torso side to side.

She enjoys the sound of kites, a child's thrill in the paper-buzzed breeze, the tugging string.

"No, two more for your arms. And then the skirt frame and trail," the manager says.

She holds the imaginary wing wands and waves herself across the floor. They see horizontal wings transforming her from angel to star, with a blaze of frothing white surf sparkling behind.

"So where is them? I ready." They stay staring at her, admiring.

"Take me out of this thing, I tired." She slumps suddenly and the group hustles to start de-rigging.

Ata goes with the manager, over to where the wire-and-fiberglass outer skirt frame is being constructed. Upstairs in the sewing room, the huge ruffled train is still being cut. All man jack pick back up speed in their work, black spray stenciling outside, rags wrapping sponge over wire . . .

"Is only a few more days we have left, people. I need my costume finish on time!" Queen shouts, to no one in particular. "I ain' able with no dramas in this rounds."

The old wire-bender looks up from working on the Queen's skirt frame, takes out a cigarette from his pocket, lights it, and continues.

SC comes to check on her friend after the burglary only to find she is at the mas camp. She corners Pierre, who has just finished work, waiting for Ata's return. "So she still going and coming all hours after this t'ing happen? She going to play mas too?"

"I have no idea. You know her, I've spoken to her but . . ." Pierre shrugs.

SC sips her vodka tonic and waits. What was Ata waiting for? What really she looking for? "You don't find she restless?" SC doesn't need his answer. "What she looking to do *career*wise?"

"Ask her yourself. It doesn't work like that in the arts. You should know that."

"Yeah, right. I respec' real artists, eh, but a lot'a people with talent does just be wasting time. And spinning round from one thing to the next. Is time she know what she about."

Ata arrives home then, slightly surprised to see her friend sitting out with Pierre.

"It's not that simple," he murmurs. He goes to get Ata a drink and leaves them alone.

SC can't ask her the questions, though. This strain and strangeness between them shut up her frankness. She figured that the scary invasion would have shaken away that. Ata watches SC's sympathetic face and slowly tries to absorb the warmth of her effort. They try. But the small talk steers clear and safe away from the troublesome feelings. When it comes round to Carnival and design apprenticeship with the graphic artist that SC is jealous of, her face cools off. To her, this man had come with his higher standards and snooted upon all the other graphic artists in the town. Rightfully so 'cause he is good, but he made himself into a well-respected artist like a fine artist, with all his collecting of paintings and fraternizing. While they all now were only just seen to be doing graphics. Of course, Ata's apprenticeship was on hold.

The coolness reminds Ata of her friend's past words. Their glasses empty, sun gone, SC say no more, but the restless, bittersweet breath of the town sighs in Ata's ear.

Fete after fete, after fete, after fete . . . The last massive one before Carnival weekend and town can't talk 'bout nothing else. *Brass and Glow.* All them radio stations prime up and bussing airwaves. Steelpan finalists fine-tuning they last tune. Overseas family and visitors have the airport and Savannah vendors busy—everything well set. *Corpasetic,* Sammy like to call it— when things just so. But he himself, of course, not having any part in it this year. Fraser had take Sam advice and get Father McBarnette to bless his place, just after he move back home. Things good with him although Sammy suspect is more than the story with he kidneys going on. But even granted all that, he much better, talking about going to Tobago, and suchlike. Down to his Moms behaving peaceful, a little, 'cause she think Fraser taking God back in he heart. Every time she hear Father McBarnette was by him, she getting on bright, not knowing is church building and history and black people mysteries Fraser and he talking about. That Father McBarnette is a man and a half, Sammy thinking as he driving. McBarnette not joining sides in the papers, about Slinger Amen band and the blasphemy. He saying things, eh, but not directly like the bishop. And through and through, the way he put it, everything come out like it making sense both ways. That is a man to learn a thing or two from.

Sam on his way to pick up Ata and a lot'a mad drivers on the road tonight. His Queen thinks he working too much 'cause he not coming home to eat with her again. She hardly seeing him and he hardly seeing he daughter. Even though he try to ease she mind and tell her "is jus' for de season" and that after, he will build on a better bathroom for her, like he promise. Sam just not interested most'a the time now, with the catering orders. The driving more better than the cooking. Things drunken-wild on the road in the bacchanal season, though. "Be careful, me son," she say.

Ata had arrange for transport to and from the fete. That is always a good thing because Sam knows, from his days, that you can't really free up properly without drinking a good lil' bit, and then . . . She is a body that need a good free-up. The white man, sensible thing he is, had gone up by they lil' beach house, again. Sam himself had drop him up there while Ata was at the camp, but Pierre don't talk much, at least not to Sam. He only was looking out, and holding on to the dashboard, and the road plenty curvy so Sam was busy anyway.

"*In a party, with my baby, in a party with . . .*" Baron ole-time tune playing when Sammy reach the Oval with Ata, round 11:00 p.m. She looking fresh and nice in all-white and she have on a tight pants and makeup. She look more like a Trini girl now, sparkly, and Sam tell her so when he pick her up. He tell her she shouldn't be going in a fete looking sweet so without a man. She laugh and say she going to meet her friends from the camp. Sammy know she don't have much friends, due to her different kind'a way, which is why she and Fraser so close—but that's how some people are. Even though Sam know he does talk a lot, some things is not to talk about. Is a thing called privacy.

The car can't go faster on the crowdy street outside the East Oval wall. Everybody walking in wearing white—that is the *glow* part but Sammy don't know where they getting the *brass* part of the fete from. Wasn't no proper brass bands around again, only Roy Cape and he All Stars, and they in National Water and Sewage Authority fete tonight. The things they call "brass" nowadays, can't compare. This is a soca fete. Okay, granted David Rudder and Charlie's Roots will be playing, it go be the least wajang of the soca fetes but still . . . That's why—Sammy remind himself and Ata, whether she can hear him over the music or not—he stop jumping up and feting and such. Though he is a young fella, he know what things used to be like, and them soca instructions to *mash up* this, and *wave yuh flag, move to the left, move to the right*, spoiling everything. "As if people don' know how to move they own body."

"Yes, but people still have a good time."

"But they, and the singers-selves, only charging here and there like mad bull. Ever since Super Blue and then Machel

Montano come on the scene. Worse yet now, the stupid Donkey song." Sammy raise his voice. "Anyway, this is de safer fete— watch who going in—you see the security and the amount'a whitey and light-skin people?"

"And the music is the best, out of the lot."

"Ah know, ah know, I ain' saying is a bad t'ing—is good 'cause it safe, for you. I ain' mean you hoity-toity like them. That is a next reason why I don' go again, too much'a security factor. Gone is de days when a man could have a good-good jump up and enjoy heself, without a stabbing or a robbing or fighting. Remember last year somebody was juking people with a HIV needle?"

Ata remembers the scandal, and the "AIDS in Yuh Bam- Bam" song. She had experienced one or two fetes that were con- sidered working-class and rough. She had no trouble at all and had a good time, just like everybody else.

"Watch—that is a machine gun de security by the entrance have. Enjoy yuhself, girl. And call me when you ready, just call."

Ata and the white-clothes line stepping bouncy, some high al- ready, agitating to see inside. Sky clear and all the stars and the high old samaan trees even look excity, and ready to go through till daybreak.

The stage, set behind the cricket stands, sparkles loud, "*Sing Glory Hallelujah . . .*" David Rudder tries, with all his friendly face and charm, but the song is too goody-goody. The sea of white shuffles till it passes, and warms up with his next song. When the bass and tabla drums start beating "Hulsie X"— everybody bumping up. *This* is what they love this man for—he have it going on. Soul voice and "*lyrics to make a politician cringe and turn a woman's body into jelly, yeah . . . You could'a never refuse it Calypso, and when you shake like a shango drum . . . CALYPSO!*"

Tons of voices singing for him and raising him up, bouncing as one, *"CALYPSO-O-O-Oh . . ."*

In the middle of the fete, jumping with three Slingerites, Ata feels the mobile vibrating against her hip. She makes her way out to the edge of the crowd, struggling to get it out from her tight sweaty pocket. Fraser! Rum-and-Coke blaze, fete-sweat glazed, Ata calls back, hardly able to hear the ring on the other end. She covers her ear and starts pushing through to the entrance. "YOU WHERE? . . . OUT? . . ." She shows her orange wrist-tag and dashes outside. On the edge of people in the barricades still entering, Ata spots Fraser, with Vernon standing behind him.

From the itchy smile all over his face and the simple way he stands there, waiting to be swallowed, Ata can see that this isn't a time to buff him for venturing this far. She crashes into him hugging and forgetting his second navel, apologizing for her clumsiness, offering to get his ticket. She cut-eye at Vernon, for bringing Fraser, but both know there's no stopping him anyway. Back inside, Rudder heating steelpan *"thunderbolt tell me what going on, tell me, tell me where he gone . . ."* and the ringing scene hits Fraser bidip-bap.

"Oh, go-ooood!" He launches himself, pushing into the crowd, to feel the pounding better. *"Ah where de man with de hammer gone? Tell me, tell me where he gone . . ."*

Bottom grinding on bambazam. *"Aye!"*

Woman wining on man. *"Search under yuh bed, aye!"*

Woman and woman. *"All about yuh head, aye!"*

Even man and man jungle-up together, bumping. Everybody— Black, White, Chinee, even Syrian—tout bagai wining. Rudder raise his voice in vibrato . . . *"Tell me, tell me, ah want to knnowww . . ."*

He hush his people now, pointing up to the hills. *"One day up in Laventille, many years ago . . ."* Fraser's heaven, his favorite lyrics. Vernon standing still and strong, Guinness in hand, his birthplace celebrated in song. Ata looks at them both. She still isn't getting the feeling and tries to decipher, from the energy between them, in the middle of all these people—if Fraser had told Vernon. Or Vernon . . . ?

Now there's a drink in Fraser's hand. Ata sidles up to him and peeps in the cup—he says it's only one, winks both eyes at her, nodding—he's okay. Good. All the movement, skin and teeth shining, costume jewelry and silver glitter, is enough. With the sweat-slicking beat, was too much. Plenty to make you drunk before you even drink.

Allison Hinds is bringing on the soca glow of the fete and prances her heavyweight backside across the stage. Aerobic gymnastics in the place and the skin-up antics now start. Ata and Fraser are pushed back, to give way for two women and three men gone clear. The ragey-ness is building up like the volume and pitch onstage. Drinks sloshing, foot mashing. "*I want a man come un . . .*"

Ata suggests it's time they go, and Fraser pretends to be sorry but agrees quickly. They look around for Vernon and find him by the bar, well happy and brace up. They leave him there. Ata doesn't ask Fraser if he's worried about him driving home drunk, she figures it's something Vernon must do all the time. The breeze greets them cool outside and the barricade is empty. It looks like a corral now. For rutting cows and bulls. Fraser rests a palm against the wall, feeling the stampede vibrations through his whole body still, quivering his ears.

He gets into Sammy's car reluctantly. "I wish there was a gentler fete. I ain' ready to go home yet."

After Sam rants about what he doing out at this hour, and how his head hard and so and so, he concedes. "But allyou go in de wrong place to begin. Back in Times in the labor union place, on Wrightson Road, where it does have calypso tent—*dat* is where you will get de real sweet kaiso." And they swing down there, to check it out.

Alone in bed. In a damp, cheap little cottage, almost at the end of the North Coast Road, in Trinidad. Pierre stepped out naked in the night, onto the deck, and went cautiously down the wooden steps, to the little swimming platform. He sat on the edge as his eyes adjusted to the dark-sea tones, his skin to the tickle of wind. This is what he had thought he could have more of. He had dreamed of leaving this place. Thought of it, thinking he needs to. Living in a city without the benefits of a city was not for him. Not good for her either. She would gain more from the arts in London, or Europe somewhere. Pseudo city life is what Port of Spainians love and excel in, hurriedly erecting Miami-style town houses and air-conditioned condo towers, gated "communities." When everywhere else was trying to escape suburbia, these fools were rushing into it, boasting about how many security measures they have to take, how many hours spent in traffic, and how long ago it was since they made it to the beach. Mall life. While this . . .

Just a few men smoking cigarettes, and a woman selling sweets on the quiet pavement, outside the Back in Times fete. They can hear "Tiny Winey" whinging away in there and a couple come out leaning on each other. Her tight blue satin dress and his jacket and hat, slipping out into the streetlight—sweet reminders of the past. They step comfortably through the silo shadows to the bus terminal, in peace.

"What a sign, eh? Allyou going in?"

Ata looks at Fraser's profile from the backseat as he listens and stares longingly, lost for a moment. She has seen the inside of this venue in full oldie-goldie swing. Fraser has too, and was savoring his remnant memories of the silhouettes and figures like the Mighty Kitchener, stiff-limbed but agile on the dance floor; a man's hand spread on the small of a woman's back, guiding her round; big women squeezed into velvet and synthetic silk, cleavage powdered and hardworking feet pinched in heels. They would have tables in there, on the edge of the dance floor, where some mostly sit and eat heavy food with flimsy plastic forks. Ladies sip beer or Malta, men knock rum. Bumsies would be rolling but not frantically, no high-speed in there. Sweet, like the old voices and wicked lyrics of kaiso. Slow and tight in a fine-wine.

"Allyou going in, or wha'? Not to be rude or hustle you or anything, but if is jus' a drink you want at dis hour, I mean, just a chill-out before yuh head home 'cause you can't drink, Fraser—I know a place to take you."

They can see Fraser has relaxed and is tired but he insists he isn't, as they pull off. He shrinks down into his seat. Soon they're at the ole boys rumshop on Independence Square. The whole place brisk and lively, even at this hour, owing to the fact that this is like Christmas for Trinis. Sammy points out, "Some people does spend more money and be brokes-brokes after, more than Christmas. I mean to say, though, with the cost of fetes these days, and costumes all hundreds and thousands of dollars— what you expec'?"

They pick their way along the pavement toward the grungy rumshop.

"The bands nowadays have security, traveling toilet, AC lounge-room on de truck—you have to pay for all dat . . ."

Only a few of the ole boys there but well lubricated, so they make up in volume for the half-empty table. The overdone topic—Trini women is the best in the world—slurs, shouted over Roaring Lion's "Papa Choonks." They take no notice of Sam's new friends and Ata's glad for that as they hover, almost on the pavement.

The choonkuloonks powder-puff squeezy tune is the best, new but a classic already. Ata relaxes with her last drink, half listening to the conversation and playing cool in the town-night scene she rarely gets to see. Fraser is in his element, tired, but widened eyes and a tentative smile showing how much he's trying to absorb all he can. He sways a little, out of rhythm, and Sammy insists he sit. One ole boy swipes a stool for Fraser and almost falls off his.

Sammy sits too, shaking his head with Fraser—how these ole fellas so excity and enjoying theyself so much over rum and old songs. He glad the one who like to lash the table loud not here right now. The racket, eh—they clashing with the music playing. And the image of the big ugly horner-man, creeping, coming to commit adultery, the mother hushing him, and the child pointing, *Mama look a boo-boo*, had them good.

Fraser smiles serene.

Ata dancing slight by the door, gazing at a madwoman searching for something in the drain.

"But Bomber! Bomber come with the one, "Foolish People," with Ras and Choonkie. Yuh rememba? She charging for a kiss and giving he bow-wow to eat. Rememba?"

"*When he akse what is dat, she bawl, meow—he say what! From now I eating cat.*" They squeal and hoot, remembering well. Sammy and his friends don't know this one and the ole boys start talking all at once, clamoring to explain more of the song. Fresh, listening blood.

"Ah, but where does the name 'calypso' come from?" Fraser eventually dares ask. He knows there's no definitive answer.

The barrage of conflicting answers jumble out, just as one of his waves of tiredness sweeps over him, a strong one.

Carib *cariso* and French *carrousseaux*, Spanish/Venezuelan *caliso* and the various meanings of joyous song, drinking party, festivity, topical song. Each arguing, then admitting there wasn't one source, agreeing soundly that the West African *kaiso* is not to be disputed.

Fraser's impressed. And relieved, down to his soul, that he could find this and still be impressed.

Ata thinks, his Terence would enjoy this too. This is the stuff he and other returnees and intellectuals romanticize. They write theses about this, and would be tickled, and more attentive than Fraser is now, behaving like foreign researchers even though they're local. Anthropologists, sociologists, linguist, orthographist, philologist, and every other "-ist" kind of heaven here, especially around Carnival time.

The madwoman has moved to the other side of the street and is scouring along the curb there. Suddenly, a car lurches round the corner and swerves crazy. Green light shines from under the car, and scratchy treble noise, men's arms and faces, blare from it. A bottle pelts out from the car, aimed at the woman, misses, catching the pavement just by her foot. Laughter and red blinking lights on the rear spoiler, swoops and disappears.

". . . tha's why they end up calling a good calypso *kaiso*."

"Who tell you dat? You mad. I know it have good calypso, and it have good *kaiso*, and the both is the same t'ing."

"Shu' yuh mouth, nuh, boy."

"But allyou know the Greek meaning of calypso too?" Fraser intervenes.

"Of course, somet'ing with a island . . ."

Ata thinks they should be going, enough is enough. Fraser's looking weak but he is set. "The nymph, who imprisoned Odysseus on her island—"

"Da is Trinidad, de island."

"—to make him her immortal husband. Daughter of the Titan Atlas—"

"Ent' nymphs does have plenty sex?" Sammy wants to show off his learning too. "This man here have a lot'a knowledge about book things and religions, and so on," he boasts.

"Nymphymaniac, that is dem Trini women in true."

"Where? They only playing so, is only trick they tricking man, to mamaguy you. If you have money, they want to married."

Another rounds sets off, about Maestro's "Mr. Trinidadian" and how he love mamaguy, 'cause *"Trinis don' know what dey want . . ."*

Fraser gets up and joins Ata, chipping slowly side to side, *"I want a man, to hold on in de parrr-ty. Somebody to rub up . . . and everyt'ing will be irie, irie . . . shake yuh dingaling . . ."*

Just so—Fraser falling to the ground. Ata grabs him and Sam rush in like lightning but he reaches the pavement. Ata's heart's in her mouth as she calls his name, checking . . . eyes not opening but . . . a mumble, as all the ole boys helping to pull him up, and bundle him into Sammy's car.

They speed off to the private hospital. Ata on the mobile, to his doctor.

THIS IS THE BLOODY THING he couldn't understand. Why go through all of that, why bother, when it's just a show? Pierre had come in to work in the afternoon, after helping Ata and Helen take Fraser home from the hospital. It was a relapse from overdoing himself. His toxicity levels were a little high. Pierre guessed he must be eating whatever he felt like, now he's feeling better. What irresponsibility. And Ata and the damned jump-up nonsense.

The draft report of the MDG launch is on his desk for review and comments. The whole thing is a farce. This Trinidad office is a farce. He remembers thinking that this would be an easy post—the jokes by other new arrivals about what a piece of cake it is, to be in a place like this for a change. The beaches, sailing, no wars or hordes of starving children, a minuscule population. He used to like to ask about the numbers, in meetings, just to remind others of the scale that their percentages blow out of proportion. What a joke. And now, because of the evangelical U.S. embassy, IOM setting up office too. What trafficking?

Drugs, yes, but . . . even when there's outright corruption, can the U.N. do anything?

Pierre drops the stupid report back onto his desk. Mandated to work *with* governments. That is the part that eats him up and makes him become a smaller man, as technical adviser with UNDP. The bureau-pusher feeling, of dealing notes-for-the-record documents and reports, in exchange for "accountability." The well-educated Trinis had learned the language quick enough. Well-crafted proposals were flowing in, wheelers flocking to convince that they can take them to the promised land. *Yes, we are the new pirates,* Pierre thinks, *what the hell am I still doing in this job? The Millennium Development Goals, with the imaginary eight pillars of . . . must be the promised gold. Or is it the other way around? Them feeding us plans of action and visions, mapping the way to this fantasy millennium, and we pay the pirates in return.*

As Pierre leafs through the pages absentmindedly he knows, the sham of it all is ludicrous. The amount of guilt money actually filtering through to "direct beneficiaries" or real results in projects was negligible, in the face of what it cost to keep them all employed here. A shame. A trapped-in kind of shame, to realize, at this point in his career. A setup so very like this tragic-comic, dangerous island he's stuck on. A waste.

He looks out the window, to the back of the old Fernandez Hotel building. It was redone but they had tried to keep some semblance of the art deco style. It must have been lovely in its heyday, the social club of the Savannah. Tennis courts still there . . . The social chat among colleagues, when Pierre did go to functions, stayed focused on who had done what, where. Scuba diving, mountaineering, what air route they took to get to Belize, Chile, Laos. What hotel was the starting point. This was the "almost diplomats" measure, trying to make their "travel duty" glamorous. Their worldliness gave them the edge and authority to advise, as experts. The more hectic the schedule, to fly for two days for a three-hour meeting, the more important you are made to feel, the higher your salary and the bigger your perks. The perks. Oh, how these wannabe diplomats, wannabe Doctors Without Borders, without the medicine, love to compare perks. They conspire and help each other to get better deals, to be sent by high orders from HQ in Geneva on this mission before the other, so they can apply for the right post. The internal HR and job-speculation system is actually the biggest secret, handled carefully with governments and external ads, when necessary. CVs were banked and circulated but the unwritten recommendations were the classified files. Personal likes and dislikes make all the difference. Help draw the line between local and international staff.

Pierre had seen so many local recruits cast aside their civil servant or medical suits and decide to cross the line. They made themselves international, gradually. First, by getting comfortable with the endless stream of conferences, meetings, and workshops to attend out there, actually believing the jargon. Then short-term projects, then two- to three-year positions, far away from home. He saw the celebration of the Internationals and the adrenaline of the upwardly mobile race begin to wear thin, too late—as with himself now. After years of flying about, deciphering and presenting documents and spreadsheets and reading, reading, writing, writing, writing . . . too late and too close, to a plush retirement. Pierre can see the tattered edges of the Internationals, underneath the glamorous wealth, clearer now. Yes, the kids get to go to the best schools and posh properties abound. But simple peace of mind can never be regained. Information overload takes its toll. Never enough time, if you care at all. Why bother? Some don't and they do well.

The way Trinis take to the U.N. mafia makes him wonder about himself . . . and think about his childhood . . . the South of France. Ata enjoys their visits there. She changes and becomes calmer, like the old landscape, reading all the time and tasting new foods and fruits. Pierre loves finding exquisite foods for her to guess at, little obscure restaurants with gourmet but gutsy, almost peasant food. She goes on about the range of seafood, the quality and tradition of it. And she articulated these things about his birthplace in a way that woke a new love and longing in him. He remembers Ata near the canal in Eyguières. The church bell striking, slowly.

The stupid assistant secretary knocks timidly on the door and barely peeps round the frame when he answers. "Mrs. Singh want to know if youall will still need to meet on Friday . . . 'cause she wouldn't be coming in."

"What, why not?"

"I don' know, sir."

"Friday isn't a holiday, it's Monday and Tuesday's the Carnival holidays, isn't that enough?"

"Is only the Monday is the public holiday . . . actually. But alot'a people would be taking that Friday off, sir. And sometimes the Wednesday too."

"Right, I forgot, the whole of bloody next week is useless too. Wonderful."

From the resigned note in his voice, Moussey gets the impression he likes the idea of getting some time off as well. She waits, a little less afraid, for his answer.

Fraser foreign artist-friend arriving at the airport now and Sammy there to pick him up. This one is a case, with he deep-deep expensive English accent. It have cheap English accent, where they speak through they nose and keep checking to see if you understand, asking "Know wha' I mean?" every two minutes—and then it have the expensive ones, sounding like them radio programs, movie actors, James Bond and t'ing. This artist-friend think he is the ultimate. He have a way of saying whatever he like and laughing deep while he smoking, like is funny. Sammy know them two had a lot'a wild days in England, and that's why Mrs. Goodman never like he skin and can't stand the man.

"I can't believe I'm back, and in time for Carnival," he rumble in Sam's backseat. "It's Sammy, isn't it? Yes, I remember you . . ."

As if is a privilege Sam should feel, to be remembered. That's how this man is, just turning everything his own way, owning it, with he lavish voice. Sammy not feeling inclined to talk to him, and in his experience you don't need to anyway 'cause the man have things to say. If you do talk it just make you feel poor, anyway.

"This place hasn't changed *that* much, more cars, yes, but . . . my dear, mad Fraser."

"He home now, should be resting."

"Yes, I know."

Of course. But surprising, he didn't talk again all the way there.

"Why, why?" Fraser says aloud, to let Ata know he's awake again. His face is less puffy after his medicated sleep.

Ata has rested too and is leafing through the colors of the Barragan book, on the settee. Wiped out after the all-night action and drama, she had fallen asleep before Pierre left for work. She had lain there, listening to the conversation on the veranda about how careless Fraser is by nature, or rather how *carefree*, Helen insisted. The repetitious worry and blocks they face with him were well put by lawyer-friend and confirmed by doctor-friend. Ata had said all she had to say—they all had—but she still felt guilty as a negligent mother whose baby had hurt himself. She should have stopped him. She should have seen the signs. Sleep took her gratefully away for a little while.

Over his bed now, with the others gone and nurse checking his vitals, Ata can see again why she had leaned with him into excess. To fully live, for a moment, that's all. It is the only reason for Carnival. For living in Trinidad.

He is crying. Hating and moaning, mouth open dry and painful, gasping, "Why? Why?" Her tears fall on his hand clutching hers and she can't answer or console. "I just want my last days to be normal."

"You're not dying."

"Yes I am. I will, Ata. I tired of being sick. I don' . . ."

"You will be better, gradually." The nurse came back, Ata nods and she leaves them alone again. "It just takes time and healing is—"

"No, no. You know I can't heal. No amount of pills, I can't . . . I can't live like this."

Neither of them can acknowledge the killer-word "AIDS." None of us know how we would face an ugly end of our life, none. *How would I?* she wonders. *How could I ever empathize enough?*

"Don't cry with me, silly. You supposed to keep saying reassuring things."

But those words were hiding all up in the ceiling corners of the room. Watery cobwebs hanging there, useless. "Well, crying helps, sometimes," Ata sniffs.

Fraser looks at Ata's tremulous face and sees the shadow of the missing thing. "You not okay, are you?" he whispers. "You and Pierre?"

Yes, no. She doesn't know.

He watches the flicker on her. "I know . . . ," he wheezes, smoothing the blue sheets on the other side of him, ". . . the origin of your name."

Ata climbs in and settles herself against him, gently resting a cheek on his shoulder, an arm across his high chest.

"Tell me a story of your childhood and I will tell you a version of your name-story your mother never told you."

Sam bringing Alan, the next artist-friend, over the Lady Young hills into town. The sun now going down over the West peninsula and Alan make Sam stop at the lookout. He get out and light a cigarette, standing above the city. The smoke light blue against pink clouds and gold sea. And the land darkening quick now to black. Dragon Mouth rocks. The Bocas. Sparkling diamond lights coming on along the coast bringing brightness, climbing Central Bank twin towers, twinkling up Port of Spain and skirting round the dark green Savannah. Sam know the view without looking. He watch this white man smoking and taking it in, breathing blue flames and raising he big nostrils up to the sky. He snort and stamp on the cigarette butt, returns to the car, and they begin the descent.

It was a brief love story Ata told Fraser as the light faded. One her mother had written about her birth and used to read aloud to her. She had given Ata the written text when she turned eighteen.

"Poetry," Fraser called it, groaning deeply and rubbing her arm before beginning his tale about her namesake. "And you, my dear, have a strange destiny . . ."

The dusky room becomes an Arcadian forest. Ata watches Iasus climb the wooded slope, steadily, to a clearing on the hill. He rests the baby girl down on the cool grass, and the long poplar shadows lean closer. He walks away and doesn't look back. She is not the boy he wanted.

The earth rumbles under her arm, a throttled breath between ribs. A bear. In the thick and furry inky night, a she-bear melts to the baby's cry. Padded claws and milk-warm breath, Ata suckles a leathery breast.

"In the forest den she grew with the bears, until hunters found her and raised her with their own, until she became a woman. But as a woman Atalanta became known for her skills in male activities. A headstrong huntress, an athlete, a warrior, she was the only female Argonaut in the quest for the Golden Fleece. And she outdid the lust-filled Meleager and other men in the Calydonian Boar Hunt. Her strong sexual aura created havoc, but the fame of her prowess reunited her with her father. He was the one who wanted her to marry.

"This woman"—Fraser pauses, breathes slowly, and wets his

lips—"this woman had killed the centaurs who tried to rape her. She could outrun any man. Angered by the fools who were struck by her beauty, she declared she would only marry the man who could beat her in a footrace—but she would kill the suitor if she won. A good few men died . . .

"Melanion fell in love, deep love, with her. But knew he could not win a fair race. He asked Aphrodite . . ."

The familiar race, with the three golden apples forcing curious Atalanta to pick them up and lose, flashes by. *Galloping hearts and thumping veins magnify the scent of crushed grass and the fragrance of pommecythere. The mouthwatering sharp, juicy smell blends with green essence of chadon beni.*

Fraser had stopped. Ata raises her head off his shoulder and he smiles sideways at her. "You know it."

"Of course I do. But not like this."

The thin air in the temple, completely still between the columns and alabaster gods, tingles. White, compared with the darkness of this room— clear thin white light. Atalanta feels her body heat spreading like the red stain on the floor, drawing Melanion onto her, warm and cloying, into her. The cold immortal stare of marble eyes traps them.

"Sex, in the temple of Zeus. Right under Aphrodite's perfect nose. Melanion, stroking, suggested that Atalanta's breasts could be compared to hers—no wonder she turned them both into lions. And in those days, maybe even now, lions could not mate with each other, only with leopards . . . destined to a frustrating life, sounds like to me—if you can't mate with your mate." He pulls a big flipper onto her shoulder. "What were your parents thinking?"

"Well," Ata draws in her breath and sits up, "I never liked the idea of my parents giving me a Greek name, to begin with. It's a good story, though—"

"Some say they had a son, who knows?"

"People expect stories to have a specific meaning, don't they? A reason why. Once the characters are true to themselves and the action, each reader journeys with their own map. I mean their own knowledge, so every interpretation is different. Anyway, when in life do we know the full meaning or reason—as the thing unfolds?"

"You telling me? Who the hell knows. Hear this one, 'The question is the story itself, and whether or not it means something is not for the story to tell.'"*

"I like that one!" Ata switches on the table lamp. "You're feeling better, aren't you?" She inspects his lively eyes and they hear the noisy arrival of Alan, the next artist-friend.

"You bloody well be feeling better!" he booms, bouncing into the room and into Fraser's embrace. "You better get your arse up and . . . it's Carnival, for God's sake!"

"You got here," Fraser croaks through the tight bear hug.

"Finally, yes. Did you think you could keep me away? Idiot. Atalanta, my dear, what *have* you been doing to this *poor* man?"

Alan's Sussex accent reminds Ata of rich England too.

"She's been raping me in temples and working local spells."

Alan rattles his big self-assured laugh in the small room. "I have no doubt there's an obeah cure. What is it, charcoal, aloes, and lime?" He shakes his chesty sounds out again, coughing, and Ata leaves them to call Pierre and see if Sam is still outside.

The air had changed. Alan had walked in with all his smoke-tinged-male, cold-weather, airplane, and stale-cologne scents. They lingered comfortably in the apartment.

*Paul Auster, *City of Glass* (1985).

TINGALING, aling, aling, ling—bram bram bram! The rhythm section set off three hundred steel drums, shaking and glittering Panorama night alive. Silver metallic notes clutter and hustle the crowd. Herds of wheeled band frames, thousands of feet and hands pushing, down the street-corral to the Savannah stage. This Saturday night finals is the biggest, the excitest, mixest set of people and action. More important than Carnival Monday or Tuesday itself, this is the people's core of the bacchanal.

Ata and Pierre met Vernon, Fraser, and Alan among the parked cars. Helen and the others are arriving too. They step from the red glow of dust and parking lights, into the stream of people flowing to the little food stalls enclosing the corral. Fraser's gait is loose, awkward, with his shrinking size, his long arms flapping at his sides. Alan bumbles along close by, broader now than his friend. He almost stumbles forward to touch and feel Trinidad again.

This is the exception for Pierre, and for many others who don't partake in the madness. Young and old, visitors, country, town—all kinds come to see, and play in the bands. Despers—the strongest, from wajang Laventille, holds the legacy tuned and tight, pinging and pounding traditions high on their hill all night.

The oil-drum segments crawl like a massive centipede, electric black and shiny. Ripples of floating legs slide it forward, adrenaline anticipates the bite. Hair raising.

The small group of friends fall in with the chipping, *buddoom boom bam, buddoom boom bam . . . melody, it's only a melody . . .* Renegades, Catelli All Stars, Exodus, Invaders, Solo Harmonites, Carib Tokyo, and Phase II Pan Groove—the big bands and little straggler Panberi tuning and rehearsing in the queue.

Ata, Fraser, and Alan push up between the canopied frames of Despers, inching closer to the iron section.

The others stay on the edge, moving along with the band.

In a break, when only the shuffling of feet and the muted jangling of empty drums fall on their steel-deafened ears, they get right up to the rhythm section.

Rum and heat stoke this engine of men and old steel. Car rims and angle iron, metal-rod drumsticks in gnarled hands, wait. Sweat drips from crow's-feet, soaking headties, pouring salt drops into their drinks. And they tapping. The happiest, sweetest, start-up count . . .

Alan pretends he's carried away by it all, but is here to see his friend in his home element, for the last time. There would be no other time like this, not at the rate he's losing weight. He secretly watches Fraser gripping the pole close to the iron man, bobbing in time with everyone pressed close, stamping the heralding beat. Tenor pans join in, lightly, then the mass of chafing drums crash into action. The onslaught of rhythm always made Alan marvel at the perfect synchronicity and power of this music, played without a written score. The conviction of a self-furnaced orchestra, tire-tube rubber tips on steel.

He had tried to capture all this in photos and paintings—a young girl's braids lashing like whips as she snaps between six drums; three boys bouncing in unison, heads back and hands flying identically; old rasta bending, crimping himself over his pan, squeezing it out; a Chinese woman, straightbacked and solemnly ruling a bass. This was the kind of richness Alan knew Fraser missed, when he had been in England. A mixed-up, crashing sound in his heart. It travels now, from his grip on the rail, through his weakening bones, jarring his very core.

They didn't stay to see Despers onto the stage. Two hours was plenty and the crowds jammed up down there. From a distance, they had seen the blue and red of Catelli All Stars ramping up, clawing wildly, and raising the head of the centipede to the floodlit sky. Banners waving mad, flag-girls frenzy—Ata could feel the board bleachers of North Stand bouncing as she watched it shake and thunder.

Sammy was coming round the Queen's Park Savannah when he hear North Stand roar. His boys in there, making theyself hoarse with they whistles and thing. The ole fellas always on one side and the football fellas, with one'r two of they girls, down below on the next side, closer to the stage. They go have they coolers and drinks and pot'a pilau. He used to bring goat roti to start them off, 'cause they there since early o'clock.

This is the part now when the soloist bring down the volume, reining everybody listening tight. People, closing they eyes, ketching the scale. And that master climbing higher, higher, heights—up! Up, everybody standing, jumping, pitching screams as the rest'a the band buss loose. Creshendo in yuh skin. Sam swing into the parking lot with a flourish, in time.

———

"It's a wonder more people don't get injured. That stand is just waiting for a stampede, or to collapse or something."

"Don't say that, nuh."

Vernon had melted away in the crowd. Alan would take Fraser home. Helen was staying on and Ata was headed for the mas camp. They wait with her for Sammy, in the safety of cars and light on the edge of the old horse-racing track.

"Be careful, please." Pierre holds Ata close as he kisses her.

"I wouldn't be able to sleep at home anyway."

"And you think I will?" He closes Sammy's car door after her.

"I go take care'a she, don' worry," Sam says.

Pierre glances out at the dark, at the raping and mugging center of the park.

"Ah go safeguard she," Sam repeats, as they drive off and Ata looks back, to see Pierre get into their car.

Sam turns back up the radio volume. The Panorama commentator shouts the score above the racket, and then Renegades start up. The tinny version of the steel orchestra screeches along with them till Ata feels she's riding inside an incessant cicada. There is no way of recording pan on this scale, and nothing does it justice. She can't ask Sam to turn it down.

Sam listening carefully, a Renegades man himself for years. He already had speechify to her, long before now, about Despers being a "government band," 'cause anything they play they win, even one year when they come with electric pan. Even though now they are very good pan beatist. And about how he respect Exodus, from the day Jit Sameroo direct them to win and Rudder say is time for the East, with "Dust in Yuh Face." Sam can't talk now, for a change. Serious in his Renegades red-and-gold T-shirt, ears cock, almost trembling, he driving with the screeching.

———

Fraser sits in the jeep, and asks Alan not to start the engine for a moment. "I'm okay." He exhales hard, realizing he was unconsciously holding his breath with the start-up of the next band in the background. He sits, still shaking inside, and Alan lights up a Silkcut Mild. "Give me one of those, please."

His friend hesitates for a second, then hands him the pack. "You said 'please.'"

Fraser drags gratefully on the long filter. He groans, releasing the smoke, and again before taking the next pull.

"Fucking Christ, don't start that up again."

"I groan whenever I like now. I'm allowed. And besides, it's supposed to be therapeutic."

"Jesus."

A couple walked up to the car opposite them, deep in argument. Instead of getting in, the woman goes over and pushes the man's chest hard, cussing his nasty backside. She keeps flicking her wrists back onto her thick waist, punctuating. The lights of the cars on the road behind flash between them like a music video set.

"These mild ones are too mild," Fraser complains, sucking harder on the filter and dragging air through his teeth like it's weed.

"My gesture to doctor's orders, for my cough," Alan drawls.

Two policewomen stroll past on the pavement, noticing but ignoring the lovers' fight.

"Yuh bitch!" the woman screams and slams the man back against the car. "You fuck she, yuh lying, fucking *bitch*!" She hits the car and the man stiffens and grabs her face.

"We better get going, Alan, let's go."

Alan turns on the headlights but that only makes the man bellow at them. As they hustle out of the car park, Fraser tries to at least inform the officers.

"We know," they say. "We see dem. Is a lovers' t'ing, nuh."

Fraser starts questioning them, but Alan drives off. "I thought, living here, you'd know by now when you're wasting your time."

At the mas camp, there are only a few people working on the Queen costume.

"What happen to everybody?" Ata demands of the dog-tired manager.

"As usual, they can't miss the finals, and then they never come back."

"So why say they'll be here? I took a taxi to come here and . . ."

The old wire-bender moves his little transistor closer to him on the bench and continues wrapping the elaborate headpiece. The table, where Ata was supposed to join the team to finish the men's pants, is loaded and waiting. She snatches up the stupid cutout gold shapes and starts stapling them onto the flared legs of white sailor pants. The piles on the table were just a start—bags of pants for the entire section were under the table too. Steups. Ten workers. Workers, not volunteers, supposed to see this through. This is what drove Firerago away. And if she can't take it, who is Ata, or any newcomer for that matter?

Ata looks over at the manager fussing round the free-standing Queen costume. The artist-returnee girl, her foreign friend, and two British designers, friends of God of Design who came every year, were the only ones working on the thing. In the far corners of the hangar, at a table here or between stacks there, one or two local faithfuls were still at it. But these are the ones, Ata presumes, who have no interest in the crowdy part of all of this, only in doing their little part, then going home and watching the parade on TV. There would be no theatrical performance, preceding and enhancing the band, this year.

"What a t'ing." One of the performers' favorite expressions. The Queen was out of words to threaten everybody with. She had gone to the semifinals stage with a costume, she knew, wasn't near done. But the waiting fans and judges didn't have a clue. When she swept up there with her bare white wings, wands, and long-long dress, headtie instead of headpiece, "Amen" resounded, as if people were in a church. Queen rippled and soaked in the praise with the soft rhythm of the song, until every bit of vex blood and anxiousness flew out of the very tips of her sails. She became pure and shining, and beamed that angel form at them with her biggest smile. Waltzed off easy into the finals. Tomorrow. Dimanche Gras, the Kings and Queens and Calypso Monarch competition. The beginning of the end, of this mas camp life.

The artist-girl pulls out one of the feather-wings from the backpack frame, lays it on the long table nearby, and considers it carefully.

The manager comes up behind her and stares at it like mad. The way this man would be worrying and growing beard and losing weight every year—Ata doesn't know how he doesn't just break down like the financial figures he could never balance. The actors were always ready to tell her why a foreign nobody like him could take it, but they weren't here tonight.

The manager and the girl keep glancing nervously at the small sketch on the wall. Then, in a flurry, the girl opens a set of paints. She splatters plain water onto the wing and the others move closer to the table now.

Gently, Zenly, she picks up a brush, dips it in red, and touches the fabric.

The one paint stroke spreads quickly through watery threads, running red edges to palest pink.

The girl poises again like a praying mantis, a god-horse. She reaches out and places a spot of yellow. Then violet. Tangerine.

Ata goes over to look closer as the colors seep into each other.

They formed paintings of their own, the colors. As another wing was laid down for her, and another, the girl wet them and studied them, then touched a particular spot. The paintings float like a dream, lifting slowly. Off the walls of a gallery in London, Toronto, New York. Begonias, close up, and irises. Georgia O'Keeffe curling up to high cool ceilings, soothing Ata. She inhales the still, timeless air. And sits for a moment in that room, in the Tate Modern, opposite the painting. Noiseless, pale, and scentless strangers pass circuitously, pausing to pray or feed on each image. Stations of an invisible cross. The transparent people look through the ghost of Ata—she is glad for that. Alone alone, she enters the artist's flowers and Palmer-flecked English, and blue French fields; slashed bodies, nightmare portraits; or a line, a square, a streak of contemporary freedom.

This girl, painting here, has gone through scholarship training in the best cold-weather kingdoms, for years. There she was among select international students and teachers, like God of Design. In that strange creativity of warped time, these artists grew inside-out things and ways, to show for it. Ata had tried to appreciate the white skinhead girls, plain-naked, twisting up and contorting themselves on a silent stage, sometimes in a sheet. They skinned-up their faces, stretched-out pierced tongues at people, and kept doing alien sign language for bowel movement, over and over again. When that didn't work, they tried to fling off their heads, or get rid of their own arms. The music or noises they chose for performances—which willing people like Ata paid good pounds to attend—was even more curious. A twang here, a holler there. Recycled garbage as instruments.

Borrowed ethnic recordings and sometimes a real person from Borneo, the Amazon, a Hutu tribe—some equally underused sound.

The thing Ata noticed is that this honing and training of creativity had *become* the traditional art of these places. The products that came out of these unique fiefdoms were the artists. Institutional cultural industries. What about such schools in a place like Cuba? How does the third world choose what to use from the first world? Or are the means of study so adopted that there is no choice anyway? Writers, poets, scholarships, still going out . . .

Ata watches the morpho butterflies, the delicate poui, hearts of bromeliads and hummingbirds, slide and samba together as they appear from the trained, skinny hand of the god-horse.

When Ata crawls into bed next to Pierre at dawn, she keeps some of the quiet paintings in her chest. She covers them up in the sheets and sticks some of the large petals under her pillow. She would need them soon enough, when Pierre was gone to the North Coast till Wednesday. She would need them to carry her through the dingolay. She finds it helps, to bring something like the undersides of island hills into herself, for when she couldn't see them. She would miss him, Pierre. They should talk instead of ignoring the growing distance.

Fraser turns in Alan's arms and the nurses change shifts discreetly. He snores ever so softly. The perfect nurse had found two young nurses whom she supervised. They had come together, early, and Vernon had let them in. They make suitable noises outside the bedroom, prepping to enter for his morning ritual. As Fraser lets them in with a grunt, they do their best not to look directly at Alan. Perfect had said they work best as one.

One nurse touches Fraser's arm with warm fingers before putting on her gloves, the other whispers, "Morning, it's time."

He groans, but rolls flat onto his back and whispers in return, "Morning," without opening his eyes.

Dark could be day, dialysis filters light into night. Alan stirs, opens his eyes, and sees latex hands swabbing metal and stomach skin. He rises and goes out onto the veranda and lights up, still in the rumpled clothes he arrived in. Fraser listens to Alan's racking cough and catches a brief whiff of smoke. He breathes in deeply. The four-handed caregiver is connecting, hooking, smoothing. Cool, the chilling fluids flowing, turning dark into day clear as a glass night. Vanishing dreams and floating memories, the detail of a motmot tail feather, star sharp.

Fan and spread. "A 'Light in the Dark.' All things pure and beautiful—uplifting! Make a joyful noise for . . . *Heaven*, Qu-e-e-n . . . of the band . . . *Ay-e-men!*" The MC's ringmaster voice echoes her up into the thundering arena. He doesn't need to point and raise the audience to their feet. As the colored tips of her wings ramp into the sky, people clamor like children at a circus pushing to peep.

The gaudiness gone before her had crackled and popped onstage, and left its litter floating restlessly between the stands. Queens covered in tinsel, beads, and feathers had dragged stiff frames on wheels along to overbearing explanations by the MC.

The kings to follow would include some imitation of Slinger's massive creations, fireworks, smoke bombs, bodybuilder power, and more shine. But now, the sparkler-waving children sigh as heaven billows before them. They stay still, sticky faces and eyes glued, as the field of flowers on wings floats their candy-floss hearts up into the cooling sky.

David Rudder and Charlie's Roots truck, the manager, the artists, performers, Slingerites, and Ata, creep apace alongside the stage. Some people sing for moments, or stop mid-clap, to sail with heaven. Freedom flighting. In the night. Into the night. In her arms, his arms. Fan and spread. Souls flutter petals taller. Tail of a kite in the clouds, tall. Fall. Womb-shrinking ovation, heart-shaking elation. Dilation . . . dialyzing river, coursing past organs. Washing poisoned bones and liver-bed clear.

Jab-jab devils, crawling out from homes, from ghetto holes and inky air, gather on street corners with biscuit tins. Mothers wake their young ones, teenagers out already and drunk, armed with black oil and whistles. Jouvert morning is here.

Fete-finished feet change into old sneakers. Hands pull ragged T-shirts and shorts from car trunks. Ripping. Baby oil slathering, skin greasing. Women tuck hair under caps, men fix wigs, before waves of footsteps tramp through sleeping side streets. And the bands of vagabonds, pagans, and cursed are gathering, at 4:00 a.m.

They laugh loud and share bottles of spirits. Liquor fires voices and the last few asleep wake and stare. Independence Square is the deadly magnet, pulling trucks full of steelpan, sound systems, hoarse singers, and the hordes of devils—mud, cocoa, paint-covered bodies, and lost souls. Jab Molassie. Crude-oil rhythm. A guttural, primal scream is building, coming from pavement cracks, the bellies of rats, the white-rum spittle of the madwoman, from the city itself and its demons.

Ata goes with Fraser, Vernon, and Alan to the edge of the cauldron. They park by the empty Savannah and walk through residential Woodbrook, to the Slingerite Jouvert band starting point. Ata's same vagrant square. Ghosts of the homeless are there in the crowd now, alive like the throbbing truck, volume on the huge speakers turning up, louder.

"You should have joined," Fraser says to her.

Ata takes a swig from the bottle Vernon hands her, coughs, and shakes her head. The metallic mixture scours her insides, opens her nostrils.

Vernon's eyes are red as he looks at the blend of bisexuals, gays, lesbians, heteros, smearing black paint onto each other. He laughs. "Da' is a batty-boy band."

She chokes and shakes her head again, handing the bottle back to him.

"So, I guess it's not for you, then, is it?" Fraser holds Vernon's red gaze. "At least not in public," he adds and watches Vernon check Ata quickly.

She turns away as Vernon mutters, "I gone, yuh-see."

"I need some of that paint." Ata looks at Fraser lighting a cigarette for Alan as Vernon slips away. She crosses the road to get daubed.

"I need one too." Ata signals when she returns.

Fraser backs away from her stench and she tries to gauge his glittering eyes. She rubs the black slime across her bare stomach, wipes her face with it, and stamps, opening up her hip bones to the rhythm.

Her legs, like all the others', start champing and chafing as the truck moves off, dragging them slowly down the street.

Fraser's feet shuffle him along too. Alan walks, just behind, his marijuana veil shutting him out. Like Fraser, he couldn't take the halfways. As artists, it was their right to be extreme. Fraser couldn't join in so he wouldn't dance just a little, he walks. And he asks himself, why even walk and watch, when it's just a shell of myself moving?

Vernon heads down Frederick Street to the boiling depths of Independence Square, searching for his fellas wrapped in chains, trailing the heavy lengths behind them.

In the thick of it, no skin bare of jab oil. Mouths dribbling red. Ropes cinching waists, roiling, convulsing on the slick asphalt. Hard hats and sunglasses, coiling tails and pitchforks, rods and whips. Bras squash onto glistening hard chests. Shower caps and granny's nightie ripping and dripping Huile Diablo.

The lash of a chain on the street or a barricaded shop front, a broken chair frame dragging along, are the cruel, chinkly-metal slave sounds, clearing a path for Vernon and the jabs.

Ata chips along on the side of the band, tobacco rush giving more head. Bottle and spoon *ring ting ting ting. Bram bram . . .* Tin-lash, bat-screech echo . . . *bram bram.* Miles, yards of road, writhing snakes to the beat *chip chip . . .* to the shuffle and shrill. Unavoidable marching orders.

Ata curls back to Fraser and Alan when they stop. She stays on without them, when they insist.

Sam holds he daughter against him, sitting low on a bucket, in the yard in Belmont. The child-mother standing at the gate in she big old duster, a do-rag on she head. He could see her bam-bam rolling under the loose clothes, bumping just a little, when she flex her toes in time to the music. Face peeping, hands holding on to the gate—wouldn't give you no sign she was dancing, otherwise. This mother, eh. Sam hold his baby closer.

Them boys on the corner had wake her up, with they warming-up and daubing-up racket. And then them jab-jabs start passing, and the drunken neighbor step out in he Bat suit. Every year since Sam small heself, this man making up he own black wings and cloaking up heself all over—coming out, well high and drunken, to play Bat for the whole Carnival. And the next neighbor, on the corner there, blasting music right through the three days. Sam know about what does go on in this street. That is why he come to hold his daughter. As a boy, same size as she, his mother used to hold him, and his grandfather would raise him, to see. This is where he bruk out as a boy too, and start to play heself. This must be what they call old now—Sam here holding he lil' girl and worrying.

Now Ata and the rum-pickled serpents surge on, shedding, becoming insects. Afro-combs rasp graters, crickets calling dawn—day breaking. They stare at each other's strange, muddy features. Tiny feet burning, marching still. Dry paint cracking, rattling. Morning releasing full day. Carnival Monday. And they keep chipping, jagged and colorless as a predawn sea, splashing at the foot of the hills.

Sammy baby's lil' heart cool back down now. And the sweet-biscuit she nibbling making her smell even more baby again. She three-year tiny foot looking so new, and fitting the pink slippers so neat. Look at this—she bumping too. Comfortable now in morning light, she bumping her little self and saying, in time, "Haw." The damn Donkey song pound so much till she know it. "The donkey hee, the donkey haw, the donkey eat with a knife and fork. Whoa . . ." The mother come bumping to her child, and he see it again, the lil' dancing. Baby leave him sitting there and she bouncing and stamping. Watch t'ing. His child. And just now she go be wining waist. And then what he go do?

A syncing crotch nestles up behind Ata's rolling ass. She slides down and back up, and it follows sweetly. She leans back onto the wet stomach and matching thighs. Gluey with the Donkey laugh, she looks over her shoulder and the girl's perfect teeth grin at her.

The band bunches up for their last ole-mas jump. The stands and bare stage sprawl open and wide for them, day-hot. They mount. And the hills clap. Applauding no one but their soaked-up, nasty selves, stretching a tongue, a foot in the air, stamping and prancing and dancing on that big stage. "*Gone clear.*"

One on top another, on top another, pumping. "*Juxtaposition.*" Thong in a man's crease, buttocks quivering,

They trickle down the exit ramp, sated. Stained up and spent but beaming, with the broad daylight and hills. Heat-ripple thirst wavering, seeking water.

"HOW I LONG TO SWIM," Fraser says to Alan.

The clear morning sparkles his tiles bluer than the Tobago sea. "What I would give just to float . . ."

"I could take you to the beach, it'd be empty now."

"And do what—sit and watch? Dip my feet? The doctor says I'll be able to swim again in a few months' time."

The nurses has gone, Fraser had asked them to leave early. Instead of breakfast now, he sits puffing smoke on the veranda with Alan. The faint sounds of the end of Jouvert barely make their way into the green valley.

"I could cook, so when Helen and that lot come by, we have a lime, like we used to."

Fraser turns his appetite-less eyes on Alan and he shuts up. They are huge now, his eyes. Clear at this moment but far as the little clouds in the distance. His fingers are longer too. Fraser admires his own slender hand dangling the cigarette and notices how straight the smoke rises. Not a breath, on his veranda. Nor a strand of will to deal with the counseling, the contacts, the fuckers . . . Alan hasn't said anything even though he must know.

A light lick is waving the trees out there . . . his house phone rings.

It is his mother, calling to check that he hadn't gone to Jouvert and that he's eating, and if the nurses had come already, lah-de-dah. She still could never tell when he was lying. Her shrill singsong voice chirps away without listening and even though he manages to cut it short, the call takes away some daylight. It tinges the edges of his vision with a little tiredness.

The trees out there keep waving an ocean green. "Remember Back Bay, in Tobago, Al?"

Alan nods. He had painted him as a turtle too, emerging and disappearing in the lip of the sea.

The rough sea crashes Fraser onto the beach and slams a grunt out of him. It shunts him sideways, drags him back into its clutch, and growls. Fraser gives himself up to the greediness, and lets it beat and wallop him about.

Alan watches him, overturned and round, sticking on the sand. Boboli Gardens, Florence—the fat man riding a turtle . . .

Fraser's cell phone rings, and Alan gets it. Helen's mud-covered voice is all croaky and sad-happy. "No, it's not a good idea right now," he replies. "He's fine, just quiet. Okay."

"Let's just do nothing and watch movies and vegetate all day," Fraser suggests.

Alan finds some wine and snacks and doesn't say much. And they stay in, cocooned and slowly blinded by the blue screen and white glare. Night swimming, in mute light.

Macaripe Bay, the beach closest to town, is where the thirsty head. Ata slips into the cool blue-green arms and shivers. Bubble fingertips run up her back and she dives under, wriggling into the open lung of water.

Deep green—this bay is always dim, even on a bright day. The sun is quiet, listening to the overhanging cliffs of black rocks, and a man is perched there, fishing. He turns his back to the ragged Jouvert stragglers stumbling down the steps and into the sea. Their hollow shrieks about cold water are soon swallowed by the bay. It strews their empty bodies on the sand when it's finished with them. And they begin falling asleep in the sun. Safe.

Ata lies facedown and the Trini girl from New York looks up at the sky. Ata can see that it's Calvin Klein men's-style underwear on her now, gray from all the paint. They serve well as a swimsuit on her muscular body. She could most probably walk down the street anytime in that underwear and look and feel comfortable—that's how brazen and friendly she is.

The girl keeps smiling and not saying much, only, "I want you."

Ata places her ear on the wet sand and she hears a heavy pulse, a brown heartbeat, drumming. She pushes aside the stranger's eyes and closes hers.

In the chest of her bed. Her bedroom. Clean and airy in soft afternoon light, the pretty mas town beat washes her asleep. Something warm and heavy rests on her. Its head against the small of her back. Ata feels a male throat pressing her buttocks, lungs between her thighs. It breathes, deeply. Arms along the length of her legs, weighing her down, clamping her in thick, moist earth. She stirs. Soft puffs of breath against her waist, halt. And the weight rises, hovering over her back. She can feel its heat bearing down. A bite.

Gnawing her nape, it raises the tail of her spine up. A large hand swipes her hair and the mouth drawls down licking, tasting, holding her hips like a cup and drinking.

Ata pushes back without looking. She welcomes the throbbing flight. Night.

Day, light, and longing.

Pierre wakes early that Tuesday on the North Coast. Early for him because he likes to think he's a night person and could sleep late at any opportunity. Not a chance here, the way the sun comes straight through the open doors onto the bed. He steps out into the blinding morning, squints at the sea, and goes back in to make his strong coffee. His body is stiff and achy.

He finishes his jam and toast at the table on the veranda, reading the U.K. newspapers that Alan brought, without wondering about the things that haunted him last night. This is good, he realizes, since he hadn't a clue where those things were taking him or, indeed, what they were. His phone rings and the clear electronic bleat sounds out of place in this seaside peace. It would be Ata.

Her voice is rested, soft, and . . . lonely, it seems.

"I miss you too," travels from Pierre to Ata's perch above the town.

She stares out at the calm gulf, the derelict ships and seized Venezuelan vessel. "It's quiet for now, early yet, just the birds and me, by the pool. It's almost like a normal morning, except you're not here and soon the noise will start. I can see the cars beginning to gather down there."

She rambles on, about Alan looking after Fraser, and Jouvert, not attempting to describe things he doesn't care about.

Still, it brings back everything he cannot understand. His wine-colored dreams of Provence were distorted last night. After he had stumbled into bed, it felt like the sea was crashing on him. Something strong had rolled and tumbled him and left big dents in the lavender field. A storm, perhaps. The cigales were deafening. And there is something unsaid in Ata's voice. "I don't feel to go and meet the band today," she says.

"Then don't. You're finished with them anyway."

"It's not that . . . I'd like to see the end result but I wish it were over. You only see the individual bits, up until this one day."

"Well, go. You don't know what you want."

She pauses, watching the Savannah dust beginning to rise, feeling the dry heat pulling it up. The sky a clear glass bowl over the town.

Pierre looks out at the blistering, endless blue . . . so beautiful but untouchable.

Ata gazes at the artificial pool of water, the lovely landscaped yard and privileged home, and doesn't know what to think anymore. What does she want? What is happening inside her? "You okay?" she asks.

"I'll see you soon."

"Okay, my love, soon."

Thomas came to stand beside her on the garden wall. "How come you ain' down there?"

"I don't know, I'm just exhausted."

"The body getting old, girl!" He finds that funny. He chuckles, spreads his feet a little, and crosses his arms on his chubby chest. "Is like me, it does reach a point when the body can't take it no more." Thomas is well away from fifty but eagerly embraces a good old age, from the time they started setting up this perfect nest. That's what "nest" means to him.

The town reverberates with the booming, show-off part of Carnival. Flamming. So happy with itself, bouncy and socarizing, it embraces everything that moves. The poor old houses, like her gingerbread ex-home, rattle their windowpane dentures and jalousie teeth, shaking, till the very putty between boards cracks as the trucks and bands crowd past. Even the hills, the sour guardians of the swamp port, are rejoicing now. It tempts Ata to jump in the jeep and get down there, force her way through to the stage, to see Amen crossing, plain white and black simple glory. But she doesn't feel like celebrating. With thousands of blessed revelers. With the heat, the dust, and braying frenzy.

"Can you believe, eh . . . that de whole show going to be innadoors, just now. When they build the new building. They say they designing a t'ing to replace the Grand Stand and North Stand and stage, and make everything under one roof, so when rain fall or anything, is no disruption. I guess it go have to be air-condition too."

"Can you believe?" Ata steupses and sits down on the wall.

"They going ahead and tarmac that piece'a de Savannah. Heh. Manning dreams, nuh. If you see the design in de papers, it look like a sci-fi t'ing. That go be so jokey, eh. Heh."

World-class, Ata thinks but she doesn't say. Thomas can fill up the whole afternoon with talk, easy, if you give him a chance. The best tactic is not to respond much.

"Is then people go say even more, Trinidad is de Big Apple'a the Caribbean."

They stay looking out and listening for a long while, without talking.

Ata sails out with the dry-season leaves. She spirals up on hot-air notes, high over the confusion of color. Way above the bass flow drumming aground, she coasts, eagle soar and wide. Head swivel, wingtip angle. She flies, for some time, searching.

"Slinger band must'e crossing now."

From the wall, they hear the faint tune of Amen and the chant of three thousand players.

Thomas follows her back into the house. She glances at her phone on the table—three missed calls and a message. Fraser's number.

Ata enters the cool air of the hospital. A soundproof bubble trapped in the final Carnival afternoon. Silence. She walks past Vernon, slumped in the corner of the waiting room. His acrid rum-fumes blend with the faint medicinal scent. Inside, by Fraser's bedside, Alan doesn't even look distraught. It is an infection this time. A fever had suddenly run up so they had to bring him in. Terence kisses her cheek and positions himself, worried as always, by the door.

Fraser's face is peaceful. But his eyes have changed. Mean and hard, while his mouth tries to smile, a flicker. His anger defies hers, as she stands before him. The clinical air crackles and Alan gets up and stands on the other side of Fraser's bed. He shoves his hands in his pockets, and Ata just stares. Fraser stares back. What the fuck is she angry about, anyway? He is the one stuck inside this room, in this incubator, a heartless vacuum in the tattered flesh of this town.

Outside, tired revelers would be dragging themselves home, discarding pieces of their costume, peeling off mashed-up shoes from swollen feet. Fraser can smell the fettered but liberated spirits. He knows the type, too, who would now be coming out fresh, to join the costumed leftovers, heading to Saint James for

Las' Lap. But he can't hear them. Locked in this sterile soul-cage, he can't feel anymore. And so what is the point?

This is what Alan argues with Ata and with Helen and his doctor, back at his flat. What is the point of him trying to be someone he is not? How could a sanitized, cautious, controlled, and routine version of Fraser ever make him whole again? Anyone who knows him must know the answer to this. And Fraser lay, silent and still the whole time, stiff and terrifyingly haughty, a hard glitter in his antibiotic eyes.

They stay up late with him, he couldn't sleep easily. As the Las' Lap steel-bands jangle around Roxy Roundabout, crashing and clanging, ringing out and lamenting the end of mas. Happy, tired people, who can't feel their legs anymore, raise arms to the sky. And the steel notes fling their souls up like glitter confetti in the streetlight. The last sparkle, before all clatters back down to a standstill.

THANK GOD for the peace of it. Thank God, the hills repeat. Is normalness again, Sammy almost say aloud to himself, driving past Sea Lots into town. He figure Father McBarnette should be busy, as it's Ash Wednesday, but mostly alot'a people go to Tobago and Maracas beach, Down de Islands and Toco, instead'a going to church these days. And now, he hear on the radio, it even have Carnival Cool Down fete and Las', Las' Lap jam, on these same beaches. On this ashy Wednesday. He himself not business with the Jesus burn up, Lent or whatever Christian reasons—all'a that have something to do with the bacchanal in the first place.

Sam check the tone of the traffic, predictable—some decent citizens taking they children to school and going to work, goods trucks, buying-and-selling people going about they way. Noticeably quiet, and less movement than normal, of course, for the rest of the week. Even those who can't afford, losing they job to sleep and ketch-up theyself. To think he, Sammy, uses to be in the thick of it, eh? Times really change.

On Wrightson Road, he pull into the new version of the

Breakfast Shed. What they call it now? In a fancy silver, curly writing—*Femmes Du Chalet*. What that mean? They say is French for Breakfast Shed. Not even French-Creole, yuh know, French. Is still De Breakfast Shed to him and everybody. But Sam feel to scope out the new design, firsthand. He go up to one of the food stalls and wait he turn. Is not bad, it airy. Nothing like the old darky warehouse before, with everything black up and sweaty in the corners from all them ladies years'a cooking. This nice. Sam like it. He like how it have modern tiles in the cooking stalls, don't mind is cheap ones and them ladies will scratch up and break them in no time with they heavy hand and big pot. And he find the meshy designish thing they use instead of window in each concrete stall nice, 'cause is more breeze and it making the place bright, even though that cooking grease will black and clog it up just now. Is details does tell you things, you know. When is his turn by the counter, he spot the lil' house sink, with house-pipe handle and all, already giving trouble. These people ain' go look after nothing like is they own.

"Ah go take a large mauby." He watch the bake and buljol they have in the glass case and leave it right there. It can't compare to his Queen own so what he going to pay money for something like that for?

Yes, it nice in the *Chalet Femme La*. Sam step around a woman spread out on a bench, between all she basket of provision peeling fresh stuff. Maggie, the seasoning and packet soup, sponsor everybody yellow and red, aprons, hats, and menu board. And that, of course, is to make the place look more bright, together with the high roof and open front, or back, if you want to watch it that way, open onto the sea. Imagine you could actually sit down *inside* De Breakfast Shed, and watch the sea, through a good chain-link fence. Nice and secure, well bar-off.

Is only a few of the holiday visitors in the place, mixed with mostly people like himself, and office workers, picking up something "to go." It *uses* to be mostly cargo sailors, port authority, and stevedores eating in the ole shed. Now is a lot'a public people enjoying the food. Sam leave with his mauby.

Trust Maggie, eh. Them chicken-flavor cubes and seasoning salt good in some things but not in everything so. Is like when he invite he friends by him, and try to introduce them to some new foods—pasta with spaghetti sauce and vegetables like green pepper and thing, cook up plain on the side, even a little Chinese sometimes, a sweet-and-sour something—them fellas don't like it much. They say it don't have enough taste for them, meaning over-salty Maggie seasoning. But that is because they have a creole mouth for creole food only. When he and he Queen cater these things for certain functions, people say how the food lovely. She does tell them, "Is me son know how to cook dese fancy new things, he's the one."

Sam pull out onto Wrightson Road. Some of the construction workers out, big cranes moving. Soon all this place here will be the International Waterfront. And all them big-shot offices go rush to move into them fancy skyscrapers. Is skyscrapers he have to call them 'cause that is what they going to be, taller than the ones already marking town, twenty-six stories, they say. They go add more shiny glass and glitter for sure, more cityness. Sam don't know how the traffic going to work but he thinking now, design is a helluva thing. It could change things one-time, forever. So easy. Waterfront, walkway with café, and what they say again? "Outdoor cultural amphitheater" and "communal space to enjoy the vast views." It go be well light-up and patrol too. Town, eh. Is what really does make town a city? 'Cause is the *city* of Port'a Spain.

Right now, though, looping back to go to Independence Square, people clearing up the leftovers of the madness that had ramsack these same roads for two days running. Painting over ole-oil mess and taking down shop-front barricades. Just so Sam feel. This must be how it does be, when you putting back things in order after a hurricane or a war.

Pierre finds Moussey at her U.N. desk when he pops in to pick up some documents. She jumps, as if caught eating crumbs.

"How come you're here today? The place is empty."

She blushes and ducks from the big compliment. "Everybody is not like one another, yuh know, Mr. Lacroix."

"I'm not staying," he says.

In his office, he picks up a folder with his notes from the last meeting and remembers the big distraction at the end of it—progress on the new plans for Port of Spain. As he leaves the building, he looks for the name of the street, the sign. But this signpost is empty. All the streets and major road signs were to be redone in two languages, English and Spanish. Not because of a desire to do business with Venezuela or Latin America, but because any world-class city must have bilingual signage. A high-speed ferry from San Fernando to the city, and a monorail, would move them from developing country to developed. Some were looking forward and everyone agrees these are at least some of the better plans.

The time was coming to renew his contract—or not. Pierre thinks about this as he drives. The Savannah is a sea of quickly disappearing litter. The municipal authorities are pretty good at clearing up immediately. By afternoon every speck will be gone and then they'll start dismantling the stalls and the treacherous North Stand. A worker lifts a large net-and-feather back piece and throws it into the chewing dump truck. He remembers Ata always answering his questions with more questions. Who has the space to keep the costume remnants, anyway? And what if half of this effort could be channeled into less waste, more necessary things? But wasn't this temporariness and constant change the very essence of this island's history and culture?

Pierre had seen the blueprint for the Academy for the Performing Arts to be built right on the square of green near the museum. "Copulating slugs," Slinger had aptly described the heavy representation of the national chaconia flower. State of the art and seating for fifteen hundred. Everything was set to become "state of the art"—lighting, acoustics, accommodation. And the Carnival and Entertainment Centre for the Savannah, to seat fifteen to eighteen thousand. What wealth. It was to be completed without any consultation with the performing artists themselves. And for all the U.N.'s "participatory approach" and "good governance" support, they were as ineffective as the uncoordinated small protests from the artist community. Why bother, Pierre asks himself, when—he was constantly reminded and knew for himself that this was not his battle—he is a white foreigner? Dear old Fraser himself had washed his hands of the Vision 2020 plans. He was horrified and then a little pleased when he discovered that after rejecting his proposal they had used some of his elements in the new Breakfast Shed building. "The t'iefing fools can only bastardize things," he grumbled.

But at the same time he had begun to suspect his own fine art was better than his architectural design. His sketches for the waterfront development were more than impressions, they were wonderful inky pieces on their own. Fraser's way with a brush or marker was a thing of great talent. It was a type of talent he, Pierre, could understand and respect.

That was the last good conversation he had had with Fraser, before this deterioration. They had gone down to see the refitting work on the tiny basement flat and he had opened up then. Quietly, knowing that Pierre truly appreciated, and always remarked on, his sketches more than others. He had confessed his doubts about becoming a great architect. It wasn't just the weariness of battling with the planners or convincing clients to stretch their vision. He thought that, maybe, he could be happy living cheaply in his own little grotto, just painting and drawing. He could survive off the rent of the rest of the place. He had seriously wondered if he wouldn't find more peace from doing that, and freedom, than fighting up with the burden of his practice and the restrictions of design. He had asked Pierre, though, never to mention it to anyone else. It would damage his reputation as the most distinctive and promising contemporary architect and scare off prospective big clients. That's why it was a confession—he couldn't dare acknowledge it even to himself.

Pierre had encouraged him then to think about it some more, as mad as it might seem, to put aside old expectations and any disappointments and maybe . . . The brevity of his life now had cut them off. It put aside that brief illuminating conversation, folded it like a piece of a sad letter, and placed it under a brick being laid in the wall. Fraser wasn't even attempting to sketch, since his first hospital days.

At home, Pierre finds Ata sitting in the shade by the pool, looking out. She looks so small and frail and displaced. He sits next to her, puts an arm around her shoulder, but doesn't know what to say. The same as with Fraser. And sometimes Pierre thinks Fraser understands, that he feels his empathy, but other times it looks like he was hurt by it. Pierre tries to reassure himself that because of Fraser's understanding of British ways, he knows he is there for him from a distance. Ata sometimes helps him to remember this.

Her discomfort flitters like the light bouncing off the water on her skin. Unreachable nonfragrance of the yellow false-poui. She touches his leg and says thanks with her eyes. Her eyes also say she wants to sit there some more, alone with the lostness.

THE INSIGNIFICANT FRUIT catches blight on the tree. And all sugar apple trees are full of black biting ants. But the measly trees bear bountifully, and the birds, bats, rats, children—and a few adults—enjoy sugar apples. Fraser is one of these adults, and Ata shares the little joy with him, late morning. Trying hard to be in his true form, he couldn't just like sugar apples, he claims he *loves* them.

"You see that is exactly it," Fraser launches off, breaking open his sugar apple over the plate on his lap. "That's the difference between tropical and temperate, the wild and exuberant exotic and the controlled and logical North."

"Too messy and too many seeds. Too sweet," Pierre had said when Ata introduced him to the fruit. He didn't like the bumpy, crusty skin either.

Ata eases off a piece of the soft apple-sized fruit and sucks off the flesh-covered seeds. The fingernail-sized segments of crust fall apart in her hand. Fraser tries scooping the white flesh into his fingers to avoid the disintegration mid-lifting action. The juicy blebs slip out of his fingers smooth as tadpoles.

Ata watches his fingers try again. The bare seeds do look like tadpoles. She slips a few jet-black pips out of her lips into her palm. They stream silky but make little reassuring seed-clacking sounds as they land together. She clinks them onto her plate. "Even this is wrong."

"What is? What could be wrong with—"

"Not you. Eating them like this, with plates and paper napkins."

His mouth halts, then his eyes light up. "Oh, oh no . . . you're a purist!"

"You should only eat them outdoors, leaning forward slightly, your feet apart, so it can drip down, free. And then lick your fingers clean, after."

Fraser chuckles and starts his groaning, about warm nectar and sugar heavens of childhood. He runs a finger along the inside of an empty crust and sucks off the grainy cream that clings there. "Unh, that's why adults don't like it, the messiness. But it sweet."

People want convenient sweetness, she thinks. In a packet, preferably. Even partners must come as a neat, pretty package, with the full works. Fraser's state had not really improved and Ata had not initiated a talk with Pierre.

They continued eating the sugar apples in a silence interspersed with Fraser's contented grunts.

"Is true, what I was saying," he picks up. "That's the difference, the extremes. Temperate fruit are more manageable—one big seed or edible seeds, or small avoidable, conveniently placed seeds, like an apple. Look at a nectarine, a plum, peaches, grapes. Neat. But mango, now—not only overly sweet sometimes, but mess. Watermelon—wash yuh face in it and spit out the seeds. Pineapple—you know how to handle and peel one?"

"Pomegranate."

"Good one."

"Or the best one—genip, or chenet you call it here, skin-up, whatever—the relative of litchi."

The last of the sticky traces taste better as they laugh. "They hate that one! Especially when the flesh stainy and stick-up in yuh teeth."

People roll the seeds in their mouths for hours like cows. "Once we saw a lady driving, doing so—like when monkey want to kiss—was chenet in she front teeth! Pierre won't touch them."

"At least they look pretty."

Ata remembers showing uninterested Pierre how to taste before buying chenets. He had watched her take one from the vendor's filthy hand, crack the skin between her teeth, and plop the fleshy seed into her mouth, without her lips touching the skin.

Her taste buds spring fresh saliva at the thought of the sharp flavor. Ata thinks of Western travelers, like *some* French, who go overboard about everything wonderfully local and new to them. The ones who get to know more about the foods and fruits than the locals themselves. And then those temperates who have a taste for other extremes all over the world—going after animals and the highest mountaintops, glaciers, and caves, the most minute plant forms and species, diving down where man have no business interfering. The biggest, the deepest, fastest, slowest—never pursued by tropicals. Or else they're documented as exotic themselves. She mulls this over, playing with the tadpoles in her mouth.

Fraser had dozed off. Ata removes the plateful of sugar apple seeds and skins from his sticky fingers and sits back down with the messy unpolished feeling. The same as when she eats these fruits opposite Pierre, at a table—him with his silver knife and fork and linen napkin. She'd sometimes push aside her cutlery or table setting and come with her unmatching plate and paper napkins to eat the fruit of the season enjoyably. His reactions varied, according to the visual pleasingness of the fruit. Star apple, cut in half, with its glistening white star core set in purple flesh, never failed to please. Even its slitty seeds, dark slanted eyes shining on the porcelain. When she pointed the details out, he had already noticed. They both enjoyed it that way. And she used to love that he would notice the same color or shape she did, at the same time. But he hates the smell of passion fruit. Passion fruit, the queen of fruit essence. He only praised its unscented, sea-anemone flowers and the color of its juice.

No matter how fine Ata was with their differences some-times—when she ate a fruit that couldn't be cut conveniently or scooped with a spoon, or when she chose to suck and savor familiar flavors from her fingers, she felt unsophisticated, crude. Sometimes, she tried to pass it off as sensual or sensory, a complete culinary experience, but it just felt awkward and, if she dared let herself feel the full derisive state, apelike. Then her hackles would rise.

Ata had consulted the respected, intellectual Terence about this tropic/temperate dilemma and he took a long time to get it. Her language and how she "constructed" it climbed round and round in circles. He tried to decipher and eventually understood. And they laughed.

They laughed when he figured that was why many middle-class adults don't eat these messy fruits. They laughed at the fancy recipes: carambola crumble, mango soufflé, and pommecythere compote. At the drizzle of sorrel reduction and . . . watermelon soup.

"Dehumanization, objectification, and inherent loathing of

the 'other'—as well as attraction—goes way back to . . . ," and he started going into the politics of racial history.

He left Ata thinking of her Afrocentric friends who would never have a white partner and celebrated all local foods, who had withdrawn from her since she started living with Pierre. It couldn't come down to race, she thought.

All the same, if she couldn't speak about these oozy details, could she write them? If she ever could write, these are the things she'd want to write about, not just the brightly beautiful. The thought feels almost the same as her floating feeling, away from the in-betweens. More than an observer for a reason.

Pierre enters the quiet sugar apple room, sniffing the warm and sickly smell.

"He's sleeping," Ata whispers.

He nods and peers at Fraser, almost fearfully. "I see that." She stands up with the plates in her hands. As they leave, she whispers, "He enjoyed these."

"Yes, yes. I'd imagine so."

They were all summoned the next day, by Alan on behalf of Fraser.

"What on earth is T.G.I. Friday's? And there's another one, Ruby Tuesday. What is happening here?" Alan exclaims as if he is the first to notice.

Ata never liked how he demands people's attention with his breathless way. BBC reporters have the same tactic when they open their horse mouths and bray out ordinary news all in a puffy rush. She leaves Pierre with Alan on the veranda and enters Fraser's apartment. Helen is in the living room with him, and they look up expectantly. The doctor should arrive any minute now.

The worry crease between Goddess's eyebrows is deeper than Ata has ever seen it, and her earnest focus pins Fraser tightly to the settee. Ata joins the wait.

"I've invited Mother and the others this afternoon too," Fraser says in a faraway voice.

Helen scowls and picks up his hand. He gently removes it from her concerned grip and continues staring out blankly.

"You know, if you'd just try to deal—"

"Shh." Fraser silences her with the small sound without even turning his head. A long minute stretches by. "Let's just wait for the doctor, shall we?"

They overhear Alan and Pierre and it sounded like Pierre's voice had changed a little, to suit Alan's Britishness.

"Did that new Thai place survive?"

"Absolutely, it's packed with eager yuppies all the time. They thrive on the new and trendy—"

"I know. The food was awful, though."

"I still go to Oliver's. He's done really well for himself over the years."

"He has. You know, I used to eat there once or twice a week at one point, one of their favorite customers, as usual, and then I guess I just got a bit bored. It was okay. But there's this fabulous little Italian . . ."

Yes, his accent had definitely gotten more British in their cheery and confident London conversation. On Ata's visits to London, the restaurant talk would shrink her into a minute world where subtle details ruled—how the waiters tied their black-skirt aprons on, where they hooked or hid their wine opener, silence swirling in a chilled glass of white wine competing with clattering plates and cutlery, which plate sounds came from the kitchen and not the restaurant, and the origin of twirpy decibels in the glass aviary.

"And there's so much choice now, you can't keep up . . . ," Alan reports.

Fraser suddenly twitches and unhooks himself. He tries to clear his throat but starts coughing. Helen springs onto him. Finally disentangled, Fraser's face drains and he tells them he will invite the priest to come this week. Clear-eyed, he says he needs to ask the doctor some questions, but basically he's decided he has had enough. Straight up. Both hands firmly in the air, he silences the court. "She will arrive soon."

They wait.

The doctor arrives and Vernon ushers her in sheepishly, looking around for an obscure seat. Pierre and Alan come inside and immediately strike up conversation with the lovely lady about her clinic, how does she deal with the hospital inefficiencies, etc.

She politely replies and quiets them down, taking in Fraser's somber silence while gently checking his pulse and pressure.

"How long would I last, Doc, if I stopped the dialysis?" His question jumps out, slashing through the goodwill words that were dancing about, trying to pretty up the air. The broken letters clatter to the ground loudly as the doctor answers.

In a neutral tone, she says it's hard to tell—it could take a week, to about three, depending on diet—but it is really not a pleasant way to go.

Helen cringes, squeezing the shards in her stomach, Vernon winces, and Ata just stares at the doctor's open-toe shoes, and then at every detail she can find.

"Explain to me, please, the different stages I would have to look out for, what really would happen."

Doc explains the physiological deterioration in measured, medically undressed terms. And Pierre sniffs and shoves his glasses higher on his snout, up against his pale, narrowed eyes.

Fraser's turtle shell is his home, now collecting the deadly descriptions, tucking them neat, like old gazettes pushed up inside a tin roof, in the crevice of a shingled wall to stop the leaks. His eyes marble over, but not from the toxins. The macabre picture he is collecting polishes his eyes, stoking little blazes and making them smaller, harder, shinier, until Doc finishes. A flat, waddish note. It sticks in Fraser's craw, choking. And Helen is too crippled, too wrecked, to help.

Doc pats his back and he swallows. Ata swallows, painfully. Smarting tears and a shudder.

"You do understand I cannot agree to this, don't you?"

Alan is the least surprised, and most composed, as they all watch the enormous words Fraser begs to release slide around on the floor like wet slugs—the request for a nicer ending, from someone other than himself, perhaps even the doctor. Departure. Euthanasia.

"You cannot be my patient if you choose that. Euthanasia is not something that is accepted here. And in any case, it is only ever considered by physicians *illegally*, when there is no choice or no possible treatment to prolong life."

Vernon finishes examining all the nicks on his hands and fingers, fingernails. He looks up at Fraser, long and hard.

"Euthanasia." Fraser tastes the term. The doctor had made it light instead of ugly. An airy, ticklish feel to it. He keeps it in his right cheek for a while. "Vernon, I'm ready for my bed."

Vernon snaps to attention and leaps to his side. He almost lifts Fraser the short distance as everyone shuffles their eyes and shame and hurt. Fraser's whole weight leans on Vernon, then

they hear his dismissal. As he slinks out of the bedroom they try
to decide who should go in.

"But what you not satisfied with now?"

God of Design raises his head with great effort to look at the
artiste, and shrugs. "It's nothing." Perfectly at home in his home,
Slinger settles better into the hanging chair and leans against
one side of the bent cane. He swings his legs just short of a foot-
stool and the artist-girl kindly rises, to push it to him. "No, no,
no, don't . . . ," he objects, waving her back, but she's already
done it. "Youall mustn't . . ." He sighs instead of finishing the
sentence. And then, still tipping his head onto the inside of
his basket egg, he flexes off his black rubber slippers and slowly
rests one foot on the stool, the other across his ankle. Everyone
gazes at his white long toes. He wriggles them, glances at their
waiting faces, then wriggles them energetically. "Come on, people,
it's nothing, it's just me. Youall should be celebrating all-now."

The band was a success, everyone agreed, and one of the
dancers, who has some of Firerago's blood in her, yelps, "Yes!
Oh Gawd, what allyou waiting for? I for one want somet'ing to
drink." And she carries the manager off to see what the kitchen
has in store for them.

The chatter and remember-talk, remember-laughs, filter nicely
through the orchids in the veranda. Slinger adores his plants and
home so much he becomes soft and swollen in it, like a succulent
plectranthus leaf himself. He knew he had to "cheers" with them
although he didn't feel like drinking anything, and that they
were genuinely pleased with the saving-grace band and how
it had turned out. He was too. Despite the impromptu finale

215

performance that no one had told him anything about, and the almost waste of a design theme that could have been completely amazing, they did come away with Band of the Year and the Queen of Carnival title.

"So yuh know what would'a be going on if I had a costume"—King of the Band beats his broad chest—"would'a be more licks! Every year now—licks in they skin. They . . ."

The delicious rumble of the best actor wraps Slinger gently in his perch. The man walks over and rests his arm on the top of the womb-chair. He chucks his chin at Slinger, meaning "You okay, Sling?"

Slinger blinks both eyes like a baby and nods silently that he's okay, nothing to fuss about.

They all know Ata is leaving them, but no one has said anything to her yet. She watches Slinger exchange a glance with the beautiful man, the tenderness between two people of the same sex that speaks of unspeakable intimacies shared, kept secret forever. The only other glance that came tender close was a father looking at his delicate child. Protective loving.

God of Design catches Ata's eye. "It's a shame you have to go," he offers with a wilty expression. She smiles and acknowledges the gesture. They had spoken well, better than Ata thought it would have gone. And of course he understood that she had to move on to something that is more her own. He, of all people, knew about the creative process and what one must do—to find the thing you do best, with passion. In theory at least, for he had always been driven without hesitation to the point now where he feels used and limp.

Slinger had stopped himself from speaking about his secrets and divine ways. It would sound vain and mad, unless they were versed in flowing metaphoric speeches and public statements. Ata recognized Slinger's way with untouchable words from the first time she saw him on TV. He became a different person, controlled by some hidden ventriloquist. The voice rolled out of a serious, scathing, or sad expression perfectly. So convincing, you forgot to look for a flaw. As the rich voice rolled out intricate layers and explanations, a tapestry of mas and its history with cultural and universal references, rich and deep as the sea— listeners and viewers swam with him. Some saw things they could never have imagined. Some drowned. Some steupsed and turned away, settling to the cloudy bottom grumbling that this man liked to use them big words but he could "real talk." And the adorer-fish gawped and adored. Occasional theatrical gestures at the interviewer or camera were all part of the magical act of delivery, so well timed you could see them punctuating Slinger's words in print. But at the end, with a quirk of his mouth, a twinkle of his eye, you see he knows—that you could swim in the waves of his words but not be able to touch them. No one could rearrange a shade or a speckle of his mirage. The sea was ethereal. As intangible and immortal as he, the ventriloquist, would like to be. This is how Ata would like to write.

Firerago's daughtress had had some drinks and her laugh cackles sparky red, ending in a little smoky cough. "Allyuh is head, nuh. I ain' able."

The manager looks at her, tolerant and fond. He and Slinger's eyes meet above the scattered bursts around her. An outsider's lovingly patient look, one they shared occasionally whenever one of the exasperating reasons for staying in this place presented itself in fine form.

"Gyurl, we will miss yuh. You going overseas?" Daughtress swings her flushed face round to Ata, then hawks some more phlegm.

Cigarette smoke had laced itself into the mas postmortem

garden. Ata looks around for the heavy alabaster ashtray for her stub. "No. Not for now at least. I will miss youall too."

Leaf eyes and flower tongues lick at her. Does she have a clue of what she's going on to search for? Does she have it in her?

Alan stuck the quote onto the wall with a vengeance. He stamped the side of his fist on the masking-tape bulges and smoothed the sheet several times with his palm.

"IS THERE NO RESPECT OF PLACE, PERSONS, NOR TIME IN YOU?" W. SHAKESPEARE, TWELFTH NIGHT.

He struck up another cigarette and stormed out onto the veranda, leaving the trail of smoke to comfort Fraser. "What the fuck else would you expect from a Catholic mother!"

There was no one for him to rage to and he had had to rein himself in all day, for Fraser's sake. Fraser had asked Alan specifically, before his parents had arrived, to hold it in this time. Fraser had held up through the pivotal day until then, despite the tantrums of his impossibly selfish and narrow-minded friends. Can you imagine cursing a dying man for being selfish! Alan let it out through his nostrils.

When the idiot parents arrived, Alan had tried to kindly withdraw and not intrude, as planned. But she was just ridiculous. Absolutely unbearable, with her whining and fussing and flittering. As Alan sat there in solid support, he was well aware of what he looked like to Mrs. Goodman. He knew her type. He was even charmed by some of them at first, in his early Trinidad days. The lovely high-color ladies, tweeting away into graceful old age. Good-looking old people, he'd give them that, with their matching cheeks of silk and light blush dresses. No sallow, super-creased Aryan skin and cracked crimson lipstick, these ladies and old gents were the antique lace of the town in every sense. From their tasteful leather shoes and Mercedes, to bridge, Trivial Pursuit, and tennis, some of the real ones had all the sophisticated charm of an undocumented time gone by, and their groundbreaking colored-blood participation in it. A time of flying fighter jets, luxury ocean liners, and Venice vacations, working alongside Afro-doctors like themselves in Africa who had never heard of their island. They didn't need to brag these stories loudly but dropped names like Mick Jagger and Alvin Ailey with the scones being served with tea or ice-cube-swirling whisky. The real ones have style, suave like the ripples of Nat King Cole's hair and Dorothy Dandridge's smile, to carry off their brilliant minds and pasts.

Mrs. Goodness was one who aspired and pretended to be real, Alan had decided long ago. One who passed off as genuine to begin with, then unfortunately sold out herself as she spoke. She was positively quivering then as she sat on the edge of the settee next to her son, glaring at Alan. He positioned himself to better portray the devil he knew she saw—an ugly white anti-Christ nastiness who had blatantly corrupted her son and then rubbed it in people's faces all over Trinidad and Tobago. Even in this difficult moment, he could find no sympathy for her. Alan spread his nasty legs a little wider apart and leaned back in the metal chair.

"I will not come to see you while you are committing suicide!" Mrs. Goodman eventually screamed, jumping upright. "Charles, let's go! You will not see either of us until you stop this nonsense and cruelty—CHARLES!" Like a bird hitting glass, screeching for her husband to pick her up and escape with her.

Fraser sat still with tears streaming silently, not even attempting to change her mind. His tears had started when she swung into a panic-sermon about going against God's will. Not once pleading her love for him, but instead carried away in mad flight, in fear, of God. *Who the fuck gives a shit about God!*

"Do something, Charles, do something!" she shouted. As if Charles could just take all of his clumsy fathering and crack it on Fraser's head like an egg, cook it up, and somehow make his son whole again. Fraser looked through tears at his father's eternal fear of his mother that even now didn't dare diminish.

Alan doesn't know if it was the memory of childhood nightmares or the lack of his mother's real connection to him that started Fraser's tears. Or of course, the full fact finally sinking in, that he is beginning to die.

Fraser looks out from his bed, feeling himself falling deeper, down. *I don't want to know, don't feel, don't sleep. Please. No persons, no time. Place is a throbbing head and eyeball pain, again. Belief smokes tobacco, shaman, fly—with me, to me. Sickly. Place.*

He closes his eyes against the glare. *Black and Green. Red and Green make Black. Come back. Receive me, retrieve. Purple eyelid patterns, curtain flap, flashing light. Gray, a square, dissolving . . . I blink lightning bolts, dissolving gaseous pink. Black. Top-lip skin relaxing, sagging. Flap. Slap.*

As he slips, he feels his guddupy heart rushaling. Tingaling, in his veins. Nostril hair filtering air, through a dry throat. Hot, tired, breath. Aqualungs thud, with a basketball locked bouncing, hurting, rattling inside. Bouncing. Bone shoes with pink and black laces and rubber toes.

ATA KNEW, the moment she decided she would write, that this is what she was meant to do with her hands— write. Lying next to Fraser, her arm across his frail chest, leg along his now skinny leg, it came to her as he slept. A ghost of a whisper, with the scent of his sharp medicinal breath— she should write. She will write. About this, and Fraser . . . and an immense guilt, pushed her, hard.

She eased herself from his bed, so afraid to wake him. What kind of person is she? She rushed to the bathroom mirror and looked at herself. Returned to his bedside and stared at his sleeping face and dying body, for a long while. Until she felt like the ghost of a whisper, wrong and inside out but so close . . . somehow breathing in him, feeling the drugs fading in his veins, his pulse beating in her temples. She understood why he made his choice.

As Sammy drives her out to Blanchisseuse now, she has the same feeling, and no idea where she'd start. "Writing is a good idea. I'm sure you'd be good at it," Pierre had encouraged. As distant as he'd been recently, he would not go back on his stalwart promises to support her creative career. "You need to try it. You know I always thought that Carnival work wouldn't get you very far. Take some time, you need it, from Fraser too—get a little rest at least." They were all bracing themselves with Fraser. In turns.

Sammy was quiet all the way, he had his moments these days.

"You sure you'll be aw'right—you alone?" Sammy checks again, as he drops her off at the gate of the seaside cottage. "Leh me go and check everything, okay?"

He enters ahead of her and Ata watches his quick little movements, checking that the doors and windows were not tampered with. Everything in order. "Yuh know anything, you could call me. Even though I far away—I will reach here pronto. I don' make joke."

"Thank you, Sammy." Suddenly thankful for his unspoken understanding and caring.

Everything in order in the small neat space. She opens all the doors to the veranda and the wet salt air rushes in, lifting her hair and running its hand up her bare leg. A full moon is due and the ripe evening forces its way into her chest, quickening her heart. Three pelicans skim the glinting sea and her eyes follow, cruising against gold surf and pink clouds, reflections of a sun she can't see, setting behind the house. The battered, broken-bone feeling inside eases a little.

Ata doesn't bother to unpack her small bag but pulls out a tracksuit top and mixes herself a rum and Coke. She steps back out onto the open deck, to face the open sky and freedom again. Bare wood, paper, salt wind, and fire-liquid—these things caress her as the red moon rises slowly. The celestial disc slips day into night in her.

The book in her hands remains unopened, Naipaul's *Loss of El Dorado*. She won't turn on the lights anyway. The wet breeze licks her cheek and she pulls her top around her neck. The sea-breath slips cool round the back of her waist as the moon pales to gold. She moves to the corner of the deck so she can see both setting sun and rising moon. A surge of sharing breaks in her. Someone is there with her, she feels it—but it is not a threatening presence. Cautiously, she lies back to share the magnificent sky with him. The twin globes mirror dusky-dawny clouds between them and the evening star is steady and bright. "I am not afraid," she says aloud. Of you, of life. Of the straight line of a dying ray.

The sea-moon sparkle starts a silver dance that runs from the dark horizon straight to her gut, and Ata sits up to face it.

His arm, strong, solid-muscled, and a big hand, wraps around her shoulders and pulls her closer. His warmth seeps through jersey layers, through her ribs, and spreads with her heart.

For a moment she is afraid to look for a face, and just holds on. His other arm encloses her and his breast beats, slow as the climbing moon, against her back. She stays there and listens—to his breath against her ear, sweet against salt, syncing heart-surf rolling. She is sure she can feel the floor shaking beneath her, the slap of the tide vibrating up through black rocks and damp wood. She hears him.

> *The stars are aligning, waves rising,*
> *random rainbows conspiring.*
> *What kind of light to bathe in? Wash face with?*
> *To warm earth's pot, feed hungry souls . . .*
> *Tonight. Tonight.*

Ata stretches a hand to his features—a silky thick neck, small ears, proud cheekbones. She feels sleep take her. In her bed. Fumbling with her notebook and pen, waking for moments—1:00 a.m., 2:00 a.m., sweating against pillows, dew-points between breasts. When she can't sleep, she writes. All she remembers is his words.

It will soon be dawn, with fire-stoked horses thundering
to the humming sky of crickets.
I will see you run. And I will run with you.

That morning, while Ata ate a dripping mango over the sink, she felt him come up behind her and touch the small of her back, light as a current of air. He kissed the side of her neck, inhaled the steam of bitter cocoa, boiling with bay leaves, cinnamon, and nutmeg, and said it reminded him of his childhood.

"You are from the islands," she said. But then he was gone.

She sits waiting on the deck, again with her notebook and pen, blinded by the morning light bouncing off the sea. As the sun soars, she watches and writes. A reef protects the little cove below and the skirt of waves changes the direction of smaller waves within it. Leopard-spot shadows of clouds shift on the wider ocean, always changing. What would happen if the sea stopped swirling?

Ata looks for the elders in the sky she has heard about, Taino and the African ancients she had glimpsed at sunrise. The bent nose of an elder cloud's face changes to an open-mouth laugh. They, the pink-rimmed shift-shaping seers glide. Temporary, they say. Everything is only for a while. *Seems, is what you see in the sky, in beauty and ugly, when no one else knows why. Morning's dew is drunk by the greedy sun, which started off stroking the day so gently. Dissipate. Re-create. What fate is fixed by new minutes slicking, time dripping by?*

When she closes her eyes against the startling white page—green and red mixes with black, the slimy paint of Camp Swampy. She gets up and goes inside for a towel and water, starts down the wooden steps along the rock-face, to the little jetty below.

The wind feels so good on her bare breasts and the rush of it up against the cliff, under each foot, as she descends. The height, the thrill—that you could fall onto sharp rocks far below—is that what Fraser will feel, before he falls into a deadly sleep?

Now the shudder of water against wood under her feet is real. She casts off her bikini bottom and stretches naked on the edge of the jetty. Glancing around to check for fishermen or whelk hunters on the rocks, she realizes she should always do this before stripping. Shrugging off the second of caution, she dives in, parting pencil fish that float like blades of cut grass on the surface.

She doubles back to the air bubbles popping where she entered. Warm patch, cold patch. She flips and paddles through them, never letting her feet touch the seaweedy ground. Choppy waves push and pull her. A gentle current sucks slowly outward, beyond the reef.

He glides around her, a bulk against her back guiding them to warmer, softer water, near the deck. So easy, her arms float round him, lips of salt and sweet. Easy fluid love, nudging. Sea swell pushing, pulling—he enters her. Fire and ice. She hangs on to the edge of the jetty, twisting and spinning with him. A water-drumbeat in her belly, snaking ripples through them.

"Let's take flight," he whispers.

She sighs and sinks . . .

SLEEP, THE LOVELY TOXIN, wins more often. Fraser feels it fighting with the viperous poisons, clamoring for his blood. He feels every viral cell breeding, slowly. And when he can't bear it he asks for painkillers.

The nurse has them ready and passes them to Ata. She places the white pills on her friend's limp tongue and guides the water to his lips. He squeezes his eyes as he swallows and waits for them to settle in his stomach.

Scrolls of architectural drawings and sketches of the church lie around Fraser, on his bed. "It is so slow. Dr. Turner says it should take about two weeks, two whole weeks. I have much to do though, while I can."

He wouldn't change his mind. Ata had passed Greek Goddess on her way out as she was coming in. The crease in her brow now permanent, her eyes puffy, and she shook her head. His mother has insisted that she won't visit him, nor will his father, not while he chooses to kill himself. She had kept to it for the few days so far. Marriette had come and shouted at him again, about his selfish, spoiled, and extreme ways. Alan's sign didn't help. The drugs would get better, his lifestyle could change, he could live an "almost normal" life—he had heard it all and said he never lived a "normal" life so why would he want to live "almost normal"?

The painkillers are starting to dissolve and Fraser opens his eyes. Ata is still standing there. She looks darker to him. A waterproof sheen on her skin and sparks in her wild hair. "Tell me."

"I started to write."

"Good. What are you writing about?"

"I met someone, Fraser, the most beautiful man and I . . . I made love with him."

"What!" Fraser struggles to pull himself up on the bed. "You okay? Someone broke in, rape . . . you okay?"

"No, no, shh, not like that. I'm okay. I guess I must have let him in . . ."

"You crazy! I always know you crazy!" But he relaxes back down.

"He has the most beautiful heart, and gentle soul. Instinctively I knew he wouldn't hurt me."

"Tell me." Fraser sighs.

Ata sits and leans close, holding his hand between her palms, occasionally touching his straining chest. She felt some ancestral pull to him, like never before. He talks bad poetry, and had told her there is a piece of her in every island, in him, in the places she has ignored. "And don't tell me—he makes you feel like a woman, a *whole, real* woman. Oh God, you're having an affair. You went to *write* and horned Pierre instead."

Pierre had driven the distance he usually complained about, to pick up Ata from Blanchisseuse. He couldn't spend another night alone and didn't think she should either. He went for her after work that day and they left soon after he got there, to beat the dying light on the road back down. She offered to drive but he didn't let her.

She didn't say a word, sitting in the cushy seat next to Pierre. He smelt the ocean in her, glanced at her burnt lips and feverish secret. "I guess you got some writing done. Any good?"

"This is the thing, Fraser. I feel terrible. But never so alive . . ."

Fraser's eyes flutter closed.

"I'm sorry. Sorry."

"Don't be, Ata. Not for me." His eyes stay closed. "These things happen in any relationship, and you and Pierre have gone through a lot . . . such differences. You must race and run and write, you must write. I'd like to . . ." He was giving in to sleep.

Ata feels his hand loosening but when she tries to slip hers out, he jerks, fighting it. "Go to sleep. Rest. I'll be here when you wake up."

Vernon's shadow appears on the hot patio floor before he does. He swats at his ear, peers into the cool, dim room, and the soft rumble that comes from his throat sounds like a question.

"Yes, he sleeping," Ata whispers, and steps out into the heat with him.

The nurse frowns, looking at Ata standing next to Vernon's bare chest.

"Yuh get small," he mumbles, and twists away when she looks at him curiously. "You lose some size. Why you get black so?"

Ata walks to the shade of the avocado tree with him, shocked at his many words and uncharacteristic boldness. "I went up on the North Coast."

He smiles sideways and pulls out a crushed pack of cigarettes. "Real t'ings now going on," he says, straightening and smoothing a Du Maurier. "He mudda ain' coming again."

"I know."

"Alot'a dem ain' go able hangle what will go down. E go get bad. Real nasty."

Ata accepts one of the horrible-tasting cigarettes and he lights it for her, sucking in his smoke, hissing.

"I go be right here. I know dem nurses don' like me but I staying right here. Is only if I have to go out for one'r two grocery and t'ing, then I come right back."

These cigarettes have a cheap way of stinking up your mouth more than imported brands. The rank tobacco smell clung to your hands and clothes, rough and rumshoppy as its flavor in the back of your throat. "I don't like these cigarettes," she says as the smoke fingers the stiff, warm leaves around them.

Vernon comfortably rests his arm on a rough branch. "Heh. Fraser never like them neither. He does have all kind'a fancy ones inside there. When they finish and he have none, what yuh t'ink he calling for? Mines . . . He tell me he don' want to stay alone."

Fraser had told all of them that. And the shifts had started again, spread thinner this time as he frightened their nerves away, shrinking rapidly.

Zaboca. Avocado. Ata and Vernon gaze past the hanging fruit at the valley opening its mouth to the city. Their friend's bones, they know, are showing now. He always used to go on about zaboca—calling it that because of the sexy zouk song and the fruit's sensuality. Cursing its fattiness but groaning to eat it—silky creaminess, sliding yellow into green.

"I'll go back in and check on him," she says quietly.

"Make sure you eat too. You can't 'ford to get more maggar."

Terence came to visit later that day. He had lost some weight too but looked better for it. More handsome a little drawn, Fraser pointed out immediately.

Terence's face, with all his goodness-clear eyes, hung from his shoulders, high above the bed. He looked like he was almost ducking from the low ceiling. The gold band was a bit loose on Terence's finger now. He loomed over the bed, blocking most of the light from the window, bringing dusk too early into the room.

"Shall we move you to the living room? You up to it?" Ata asked Fraser.

"What a relief."

They waved the nurse aside and helped Fraser up and onto his feet, holding on to his weak arms, a shoulder under his. Ata busied herself getting Terence a drink and tried to leave them alone, but Fraser asked her to stay.

The pain of the love between the two men squatted in the room, under the stupid candelabrum, a watery fat edema. It had sucked every ounce of pride and joy and gelled there, gray and wobbling like a great ball of snot. Ata focused on it and Fraser gazed at the handsome face of his lover. Terence couldn't look at Fraser for long. Every time he glanced, Fraser's thinning lips and sunken eyes lanced him. A ghoulish remnant of the flesh and blood he knew, but his mind and this emptiness and . . .

"Terence, this is your last visit. I have to ask you not to come anymore. Don't come here anymore. We must say goodbye. I—I don't want you to see me like this, or remember . . ."

Ata ran out of the room crying. Fraser in Terence's arms like a child. Terence didn't object, he just sat and held him, lifted him onto his great lap, and cradled Fraser while their sobs rocked them.

Salt stiffened Terence's perfect features, when he finally walked out of there. Ata crawled into Fraser's bed; he was tucked and peaceful. Beautiful sleep, come.

Ata dreams her lover's arms and he whispers,

> *sky clear and baking a seaside day*
> *but I will seek the comfort of a pommerac tree.*

Red fruit dripping. Saline bag leaking. She wakes to a sticky feeling between her legs. Blood.

"Blood. Blood is what I see sometimes, in front'a me," Sam say to his Queen.

She listening patiently as they drive.

"Blood."

"But yuh daughter need to see you. De po child will start to think you don' like her."

"Mums, when I hold her, de last lil' while, and I look at her good, I see blood. I telling you—" Sammy answer his phone straight up. "Yes. Yes, right now I dropping my Queen in town, then I can come for you. Yes."

Mums don't say nothing more all the way into town. She don't know what else to say so she just hold on to what she knows best—patience, love, and love of God. The work must help him, and time, please God.

Father McBarnette say to Sammy, "When I said I have a trip for you, I mean a long one."

"Tha's okay." Sam nods, looking around the inside the huge, empty cathedral. He had met Father by the side door and was up close, you could almost say, in the pulpit or what they call it. These Catholics have money, boy. Just the sheer size'a the place and the oldy design and windows and thing, like a antique jewelry. "How far you reaching?" he ask the priest. Sam looks at saddy, genkle Mudda Mary, then at Jesus, string up on he cross. Blood again. Dripping down the man face.

"Guapo," Father McBarnette say.

"*Guapo!*" Sam echo loudly. "You know how far Guapo is? That is quite-o, quite-o, that is down in de back'a beyond, behind Gaw—sorry, sorry."

Father smile.

"When you hear *Penal*, Father, you know that is country fuh-so. But *Guapo*, now, you have to go quite past Point Fortin, past La Brea—"

"I know. I want to go there and come back today. I'm going to see something they building down there."

"Oh ho! You going and see the church they say de prime minister building down there? Okay." He don't wait for Father to confirm. "Yes, is Guapo' self we have to reach. I know where. I hear it ain' finish yet."

Father asks Sam to wait a moment and touch him gently on his shoulder before he leaves. The touch feel like Father want him to kneel and confess something. The Father know everything, but Sammy not about to go telling him no tragedy lines. Still, it feel like a kind'a blessing. Sammy grateful even though he not Roman Catholic. Right here, is where people does be kneeling, and taking Communion, whispering secret praise and sucking biscuit and drinking—why they had to call it "the blood of Christ"?

Father come back through the lil' door in the darky pulpit and they set off. He make Sammy promise that this is a private and confidential trip. Never does he want to hear it broadcast round town, that Father McBarnette went to spy on the PM's church in Guapo.

"Never, Father," Sammy agree. "This is not a matter for public affairs. And too-besides, all my private trips is private. They stay right in my car. But you know how Trinis like to maco, Father." He claims he can't be responsible for who might recognize the priest down there.

Father agrees.

Ata bolts upright, squeezing her legs together and pressing her pants into her crotch. Fraser is still sleeping, sound and motionless, and she holds her panicked breath to listen for his. His chest rises and falls again and she dares to move, checks the mattress under her. Relieved that the blood hasn't reached the sheets, she inches to the foot of the bed, and makes it to the bathroom.

In the light, against white, when she releases her hand, it is blood. But her period was only two weeks ago. She squeezes and compresses her stressed insides. No pain but definite bleeding. Not heavy. *Breathe*, she tells herself—*my body is dealing with this, breathe. And if this is happening to me, what about Fraser's insides?* She lets the tears fall onto her legs as she sits on the toilet. Salt red. The nurse stirs in the kitchen. She must have checked Fraser's pulse and temperature by now. It has only just gotten dark.

Night falling fast as Sam and Father McBarnette leave the construction site of the Presbyterian Church in Guapo and head back to Port of Spain.

"Look, what I tell you, Father? Watch behind and you will see the light from Point Icacos lighthouse—tha's how close we is to the bottom'a Trinidad."

"It is a big church, isn't it?" Father had hear too much about the distances and the different routes and roads and want to get Sammy impression of the building, now that he see it himself.

Sam lift himself forward onto the steering wheel. "Is not a nice design, Father. That could never look nice when it done."

Father smile. "'Guapo' means handsome in Spanish."

"Well, dat could never look handsome, is a ugly piece'a work."

The endless driving is the counseling Sam need. The familiarity of roads and potholes, rumors and development, the talk of the land, comfort him.

Sam glance across at Father bearded profile, settling back on he headrest for the long road ahead. "Why ah say so, is 'cause it build like a oversize house. You know them big spanking house, that returnees does build when they just come back? What they send they money from Canada to build? Yuh know the ones? Something like a hotel. It look like one'a that—but megarized. Everything in Trinidad is mega now, yuh know. That same stupid prime minister make it so. They well overdo it—but watch the windows they going and put—house windows . . ."

The dark country sky brush the tops'a coconut trees as they zhupp by.

"Aluminum-frame house windows they buy from Moonan.

Is a contract deal, tha's what it is . . . Father, you talk to the woman pastor? I hear she not easy, she is de one who go behind de PM for the money. You know wha' I mean?"

"It's not good to repeat hearsay," Father murmur, lulling.

"Father, what yuh think about Fraser . . . sickness, and how he getting on now, eh? You t'ink is right?"

Father dozing so Sammy continue, he used to talking to sleeping passengers. "Fraser chasing away good-good friends and now he own Mums ain' talking to him. He doing like he *want* to die. Who want to die? Is not right . . ." He have a feeling nothing in this world would ever be right again.

Is a kind'a black Jesus, Sammy carrying here in his car. Well all right, a black-man of Jesus or "of the cloth," with he lil' wooden cross ressing on his chest, and piece'a white collar shining by he throat. Father wouldn't tell him what he think about Fraser even if wasn't sleeping. He would tell him what God think or what Jesus say. Smart man. No one would never know what a man like he thinking. But Sam still wished he did. He had two hours of driving to Mount Saint Benedict tucked high up in them Saint Joseph hills. Then half an hour back down to home. He will pass and check on his daughter. Even though will be late, he could watch she sleeping face.

THOMAS SMILES at Fraser, who's trying to pucker up and give him sweet-eye, even now. "Look at you—yuh can't do nothing and yuh still trying."

"So you wait till I stuck in bed, to come close? You just want to tempt me. Where de short pants?"

"Nah, I tell meself that go be too much. Look how it turn round now, eh?"

"You too late, man, too late." Fraser mock-steupses and turns his head away, reaching for Thomas's hand on the edge of his bed. "Thanks for coming."

"Well, I had was to come, and see how me good ole pallywal doing." Thomas keeping good cheer to cover his shock. Fraser was disappearing by the day. "You ain' eating enough, man. You can't let dis t'ing fight you down."

"No, it's not that, it's—" Fraser breaks into coughing.

"Like you ketch Alan nasty cold."

The racking seizes him and takes its cruel course. Thomas feels it shaking up through his own thick hand.

"Have a seat," Fraser splutters as it passes. The nurse sticks her head in and he waves her away. Signals Thomas for his glass of water, to wash down the phlegm that wouldn't come up. "Ah boy, ahh." He sinks deeper into his pillow. The feeling of emptiness inside now was beyond hunger, and more comfortable, maybe even clean. Yes, clean. He feels better without food, extremely lucid for moments too.

"Where Alan, by the way?" Thomas asks.

"He's, he's sorting out downstairs, to camp out for a while, now he's decided to stay on a bit longer."

"Good, tha's good."

"Where's Ata?" Fraser asks. "She and Helen and Marriette supposed to be coming today."

"Sammy will bring her just-now. Pierre gone up Blanchisseuse, just for today, so she don' have de car and she had to pick up a few things."

"Oh? Why Pierre gone up there? They quarrel?"

"No," Thomas answers promptly, happy to report. "You know him, maybe he have some document work to do, or something. Maybe he just want to get away too. Yuh know how it does be sometimes." He drums his fat fingers on the mattress and stares at the Casio digital watch he wears when he's out.

"Yes, maybe." Barely a murmur from Fraser. The two pillows are seeping into his head. Muffling him. Pierre should be careful up there. He wonders if Ata has told him. How could she? No. Did he tell her she should—come clean with Pierre straightaway?

"Baking. You could say de sun baking today, ent?"

Sammy seems more normal today, Ata notes. He reverses neatly and slides down the drive, crouching forward into his customary on-the-lookout pose. He checks the rearview, to see the gate closing properly, because he knows no one was left at home. She relaxes a little. She likes his ever-guardedness now. It makes her feel safer, closer to something secure.

"Yuh looking a lil' better but getting too small—don' let Fraser get you dry up like he. He can't help it but you, you have to look after yuhself, yuh-hear? You need some good food. Pierre don' cook?"

She shrugs.

"What happen to yuh friend from de office? I don' see she round much again."

"A good few friends not around much again." Even Pierre, Ata thinks, can't be around Fraser too often. Pierre. "You know, the other day, when you dropped me up the North Coast—"

"Uh huh, yeah."

She tells him how nice it was to have some time for herself, with nature. But Sammy waits for more. She could see he knows that isn't what she wants to talk about. "Well, I had a surprise visitor—"

"What de Jesu Christ—t'ief!" Sammy slams brakes, then accelerates to avoid being hit from behind.

Ata reassures him as they jerk forward, Sammy checking behind, one side, two sides, glancing at her.

"But you ain' learn? You have to be careful—you shouldn't even be up there by yuhself in de first place. You know dis person?"

"Not really—"

"What! You . . ." Sam driving too fast into Saint Ann's but Ata trusts he's in control.

"It's like I know him from somewhere." They reach the vegetable shop and he stops right outside it. "He's familiar but I didn't get a good look at him. He may not even be real."

Sam looks at her in amazement. "Ah waiting—you go and buy yuh lil' vegetable—I right here." This woman mad, he realize, as he watch her get out and enter De Green Corner shop. Her pinky-mauve sleeveless top making her look blacker and she hair always wild anyway. She picks up a pawpaw and hesitates to ask the cashier the price. Sam watch her lift a watermelon, like it real heavy—she weak. She must be weak, with all the stress. And then she man gone up there, by heself. What really going on?

But Sam don't have to wonder long, Ata is already done. Was only two things she needed there.

"Tell me, leh me get this straight." They pull off again and swerve across the tiny bridge. "Dis fella, who you t'ink you know, drop in by surprise, just so—and you didn't jump—you wasn' 'fraid? How he get in—you didn' lock de door, nuh? You need to stop here too?"

Ata nods and he swings up into Hi-Lo's car park. "Actually he appeared as if from nowhere, but no, I wasn't afraid."

Sam parks again, watching her closely, his whole squingey body turned toward Ata.

"I think it's spiritual."

Jumbie.

"He . . . we . . ."

"Ghost. Jumbie. And is a he? What dis t'ing do you?"

She had already gone too far. Ata looks into his little springy face—he'd understand that she couldn't talk to Pierre about this—she told Sam.

Before he could respond, though, "I'll be right back," she says. Jumps out, braces herself, and dashes into the freezing supermarket.

A jumbie take her. Sam slumps into his seat, dumbfounded. This more serious than anything. This is not madness—is obeah kind'a business, and like she ain' even realize! He had hear about some Lagahoo something, where the Lagahoo does be naked and make everybody sleep before he enter the house—he does take, rape, no, he does bite woman leg and suck blood. "In dis modern time?" He must say it aloud. "To she? Now?"

On the North Coast, in the cottage, Pierre thinks he hears a noise coming from the deck. He gets up from hunching over his laptop, and checks. Nothing. He has never felt unsafe here. And he doesn't feel like he could finish the damned report today after all. Maybe a nap would make him feel better. It's just barely midday, though—so why so exhausted? Pierre doesn't want to think of why—only to get through his duties. Do what you can, always do your best.

He pours himself a glass of wine, makes a sandwich, and continues working. Until sleep takes him.

I cannot see the colors of the reef. The ocean's face is flat and opaque, like me. I wait, like the still leaves. For the cleansing lashes, to be.

The words stackle on the edge of a shelf and rush shivering with Ata down another aisle, searching. Almond milk. Dates and cinnamon. What would Pierre be eating up there now? What else could Fraser taste?

Three bands of light. Clouds dragging their heavy selves . . . These laden winds butt against the insides of my chest.

Cassava bread. Yogurt. The open chillers of cheeses and butter face Ata coldly. Judging. Coconut water. Goose bumps and her nipples rise. She glances around again and sweeps herself quickly to the checkout.

"You have a mark on yuh leg? 'Seduce,' you say?" Sam questions as she drops into the car with the two bags. She leans forward, wrapping her bare arms in her long skirt, but the baking-tin heat is already warming her up. Sam pauses and the warmth from the seat, the sunlight, feels good—real. She turns her face upward in the open window, welcoming it.

This is how mad people get on. "Listen to me, Ata." Sam backs the car out slowly, his voice cautious but urgent. "This is not something to play with . . ." This combination of madness and jumbie-business is a dangerous thing. He had hear how some people does have nervous breakdown, but the spirit part . . . "First of all, if is a real man—yuh don' have to lie for me—you know I is a confidence person and I ain' go judge." She shaking her head. "No, what? He not real? No—you don' know?"

"Then how could he appear and disappear like that?"

"He not real."

"I started writing and . . . it's almost as if he's in me."

"Ata, Ata." The car crawls, extending the short drive to Fraser's flat. "Now you getting me frighten." But the woman smiling brightly at him, Sam, as if he-self is the one who off! He can't laugh back with her—is not funny.

She say it is, though. And is okay—most probably her imagination, and exhaustion. She did have a drink.

"Ah was going to akse you dat next, 'cause I know allyou ways. Not to say youall does drink too much, but I know Pierre like he lil' wine."

They almost reach, straining up the steep hill. And Ata quiet, like she thinking the same exact thing he thinking next—'bout Pierre up there, and this thing.

In the floral living room, Helen and Marriette sit with a pillow-propped Fraser. He's well ensconced and rested after a little doze. Thomas is outside somewhere with Vernon, their voices rolling.

"You look a lot better." Ata kisses Fraser and settles herself on the rug next to Marriette. "And this room is particularly lovely at this time'a day."

"Thank you," the turtle replies, nodding slowly. It is. He had made it so and placed that orchid pot just off-center below the window so the patch of sun bounces off the tiles, illuminating the blooms. He had asked them to place the pot there, rather.

Fraser looks at the three beautiful women. "I want you all to be my maids of honor. You don't have to carry the coffin or anything, just walk alongside. One on either side of me and you, Helen, at the back."

"By your head, let that be the head end. Sure, we'll accompany you," Marriette says, almost lightly. They're all determined to make this light. Nothing will make it a dark afternoon. Not even if the rain suddenly pours or Fraser breaks into tears.

"And beautiful fuchsia, summer dresses."

"Morning-glory color," Ata says.

"Yes. No black and boring white. But don't let them pile up awful flowers and wreaths on the, the box—"

"Casket."

"I want that simple and white. No wreaths."

"No wreaths." Helen makes notes.

Marriette spreads the stack of small prints and sketches out on the floor. "Why you don't use a nice photo instead? I sure you have some nice artistic portrait somewhere."

"That's an idea, what about a drawing, or one of Alan's portraits of you?"

But he doesn't want tradition. He had always found the face of the deceased on the funeral program morbid and haunting. He eventually chooses a detail of his church abstract—a cross, cut out of a wall, with bits of white in the blue, like birds. A piece of gray like a hill. Say . . .

Say the right words, please, hills. When the day comes, be gentle.

Nothing must spoil this petal moment. Ata watches the pollen flicker of Fraser's face and lowers her lids.

But we shall welcome him softly, the hills whisper. And a small breeze ruffles the sketches, light as ashes.

"Cremation is out of the question," Fraser says.

Night grows big and bold and still Pierre sleeps. The phone wakes him. He jumps out of bed now, out of sorts and panicked. Fucking Christ, what has come over him? He couldn't have been *that* tired. Ata must be worried. What bloody time is it, anyway? Shit. He turns on the table lamp and his laptop is there, doors wide open as usual. Pierre scans the room quickly. Why is the deck so bright? He switches off the light.

The moon is still bright. Ata should have been here, he thinks, standing against the rail. The wind is quiet, making the waves downright loud. Pierre looks at them. White teeth appearing and disappearing. Hypnotic. The churgly chatter unceasing. What's that patch of gray there—a current? Down the steps, the cicadas must be tucked into the hill itself. What are they doing, screeching at this godforsaken hour? Or is it frogs? A strong breeze picks up, out of nowhere. Pierre can see no rain cloud.

The raped and scarred earth drinks. Coupling a mouth to a breast. Ata broke out of her fitful sleep. Why hadn't he called? Four a.m. He must have meant to but fell asleep. Stretched out on that damp bed. This guilty night, after such a day. Fraser had dismissed his staff but said he was too tired to see them. He glorified Alan as his savior to their faces and brushed off Vernon, like a servant, when he came in. Even Marriette was embarrassed for him.

At that ungodly moment, Alan was standing over Fraser's bed, watching his friend's sleeping limbs spasm. *It's a good thing Alan is here, though,* Ata thinks. *And Vernon too.* As they were leaving, Fraser let Vernon lift him into bed. He hung on to his neck and stared up into Vernon's strong face.

What day of the week is it?

Isn't this also the night the poets were having their spoken-word thing? They had invited God of Design too, with a formal arty card instead of the casual bring-a-fren' guerrilla marketing. But would he show? Would he bless the early days of their yardart initiative?

Slinger was duty-bound on his way, being driven past the unavoidable Savannah. They were preparing the place for Better Village, he noted—Best Village, best chutney dance, stick-fight dance, best choir, best "cultural performance"—so sickening. As if everyone doesn't know that only Black party–stronghold villages won every year. I love this country, but God, what a long, long way to go. Everything so substandard, mediocre, insincere. No gumph in people, only in commercial competition. Maybe there isn't enough poverty for artists, like in Haiti, Jamaica—Guyana, even.

"Did you hear that they really going to hang Dole Chadee?" the manager asked, steering them down Henry Street.

"Yes. I read the newspapers this morning."

Crime is the most compelling art form. The drug lord's contract killers had popped off the witnesses while he paid off the jury. Empty downtown night streets gave Slinger the creeps.

"So you saw the other headlines?"

"Yes, Charles, we don't have to talk about it, thank you."

They entered the little alley leading down the side of an office to the artyard and small performance space. Modern yet Caribbean touches, quite nice. Slinger instantly recognized which artist directed it. He respects the guy and there was a quiet, healthy little distance between them. Slinger likes to keep that so.

"Sling, yuh reach."

All his crew were there and the performances already started. Somebody produced a chair for Slinger and he thanked them overdeeply in theater sign language, sat his holy tail down, and drew on his mask of composure. The whispery ripples round the standing edge of the small crowd dissipated, now that Slinger seemed alive and well.

Is revo–lution
times we trodding
Ah, revo–lution
Luther King so–lution.

245

The young man had the part down pat—the beard, deep solemn tone, Black Muslim look about him. Others nodded, some wearing army-colored T-shirts or fatigues, a lot of rasta tams passing for revolution-cool berets. A stenciled red star over there. Che Guevara must have another renaissance, *again*. Slinger glanced around to see if he could actually spot the iconic print anywhere.

The spoken-word artist, rapper, rapsonian, and poet continued and the selection of beautiful, intelligent young people—a few women wonderfully ethnically adorned—were nodding even more. They like it, this youth who is popularly claimed by the media to be "prophetical." Slinger was sure that this boy came from some protected or privileged middle-class home, like many of them did. Okay, maybe he had really come from a humble, or even rough, background—but what's this juvenile obsession with the word "revolution"? This little gathering of the "conscious" Port of Spainian few? The police wanting their thousand dollars more? . . . *The question should be asked whether the police deserve any salary increase, based on a low level of crime detection and charges, for instance.*

Slinger spotted Che Guevara's face finally, on the top of a checkered canvas sneaker, peeking out from under a hem, near him. Cool. There is something in the new range of style and design . . .

The quiet artist-director watched God of Design's amused observation and smiled to himself. He could barely keep up with the new talent and hunger for something different, so how could this isolated man relate? A few artists were making it to biennale participation and waves of good work were beginning to build. Ebbing and flowing in a world-music modern kind of way. Making way.

Slinger tolerated the performances well. He even had some

good words to say, before his manager whisked him away back to his garden hideaway.

Ata sits out with the sunrise and her notebook. She will call Pierre when it's late enough. Dawny words tease her, naming beauty and ugly. Husbandry is animal rearing. Peach in the sky is sometimes called gold. Names tame almost every living thing—none for the thousands of fragments in me. She asks the hills, *Beyond the colors and the differences, what do you see?*

"IT IS HE." Sam takes the early-morning call and speed-ing on his way, bringing Father McBarnette to see Fraser. He had a few things well lined up to ask the priest, but maybe now is not the time. Father looking calm and cool as normal, though, and too-besides, he must do this regular, 'cause is his job, blessing people in they last days. And is still a good half-hour drive to go. Better not to talk about matters at hand.

"Father—"

"Yes, Sam."

He get him going easy—talking the *real* facts about them street-name heroes. The way he put it can't compare with them ole fellas' rumshop version. It even better than the radio pro-grams, 'cause the man quoting book and history lines just like Bible. Sam wonder if Father have any lines for the famous boast-ing subject—Trini women—even though is a ticklish thing to ask such a man. He try.

A deep chuckle come out from under Father lil' white collar. "'For gait, gesture, shape, and air, the finest women in the world may be seen on a Sunday in Port of Spain.'"

In church, of course! But was a quote, he explain, that a writer had dig up about the beauty of mulatto women. A Englishman report is because the "French and Spanish blood seems to unite more kindly and perfectly with the Negro." He say the English does "eat too much beef and absorb too much porter for a thorough amalgamation with the tropical lymph in the veins of a black."

"So that's why," Father explain kindly, "the British mulatto females looked to them like 'very dirty white women' compared to the 'rich oriental olive' of the 'haughty' French and Spanish half blood."*

Father overexcel in this by-the-book business. Sam hope he don't go and pull too many Bible pages upon Fraser, 'cause he know Fraser don't like that so much. Maybe he do now, though. People does change when they know they time come, and it really looking like Fraser bringing on he time to come. Sam could almost say Fraser lucky, to a point. Lucky 'cause he have choices and he can even ask for blessings and prepare. Sammy don't talk again. The priest stay quiet too.

Ata calls the police station in Blanchisseuse. They say, because she can't reach Pierre by phone it doesn't mean he's missing. But they would pass by later, if they have a vehicle available. She calls the restaurant across from the cottage. The kitchen assistant says they will send somebody to check and give him the message. Ata tries to keep the terrible feeling out of her voice, so it won't be part of the message. If she stays positive enough . . .

*V. S. Naipaul, *The Loss of El Dorado* (1969), p. 174.

Alan explains to Father, quietly in the kitchen, that Fraser is beginning to convulse, and so needs this blessing before he loses all lucidity. Father doesn't ask any questions, he just rests a hand on Alan's shoulder and calmly hangs his holy scarf around his neck. He smooths the familiar fabric as he enters Fraser's bedroom.

Sammy find himself in the yard with Vernon. Vernon don't pay him no mind, he continue hosing down the steep driveway.

"It is he." His phone, again. This time Sam's voice change instantly. He start moving around jerky.

Vernon turns off the hose.

"What, yes, no!" Twisting. "I just bring Father by Fraser." He hop up the drive, hushing his voice so inside can't hear. "No, yes. But I could come." Sam pull the phone away from his ear, pointing to it urgently.

"Who dat?" Vernon asks.

"You sure, Ata? You—" Sam flings the phone into Vernon's outstretched hand.

"Yeah, wha' 'appen? Ah, coming now," Vernon says to Ata, snap the phone shut, shove it back to Sam, and stride away.

Sam try calling her back—voice mail.

Vernon, now with a shirt on, go inside and talk quickly with Alan.

"Not a word to Fraser," he threaten Sam as he leaves.

"Thanks for coming, Father. I know it was short notice." Fraser's weak voice trembles in the dim room.

Father McBarnette stands by his bedside just letting his

strong solid self warm the gloom. He holds Fraser's hand in his, rosary bead pearls between their oyster palms.

Fraser feels their cool smoothness trapped in the silky intimacy. He sighs. "How's the church coming along?"

Father sits on the stool close by. "It's slow. We had some holdups with planning approval—"

"My guys told me, sorry."

"But we're getting there. Everything in a timing."

"Inner timing, hunm." The sedated turtle smiles.

"There was this one old Negro, Jacquet, the *commandeur* of Bel-Air sugar estate, owned by Dominique Dert—yes, Dert Street in town."

Fraser nudges his pillow and waits for the light to unfurl. Stained-glass altar light, red, blue, and green.

Father's words filter down softly. "Poisoning was a special form of revolt that outdid the master's whips and chains. Jacquet was well liked and trusted by Dert, but slowly he killed off one hundred and twenty-five fellow Negroes. Eventually, he went too far with his poisonings, then he went off. Dert never suspected him, but the slaves came to know that their *commandeur* is the poisoner.

"Jacquet gave himself up. He said he wanted to die. It was never quite clear, however, if he was poisoned by someone else or if he took his own poison, himself."

Fraser's eyes are large eggs in glass cups.

"Poisoned blood is in our veins. The Caribs before that. It is not our fault . . . Do not be afraid . . . Let us pray." Father stands and waits a moment for the white rushalings to settle. He kisses his wooden cross.

"I coming wit' you," Thomas announces before Vernon arrives, hurrying out, cutlass ready. Ata's eyes widen. "Don' worry, is jus' a caution."

Vernon grunts approval, taking off as they hop in.

Ata's heart rattles in her mouth as the old jeep tears along the hills. She swallows it when they stop outside the little gate and it drops heavy to the bottom of her stomach.

The empty cottage breathes gappy and loose as they enter. It has no clue and was not responsible, sunning itself and stretching open carelessly. All his things are there, the bed unmade, unlike him. The deck draws them out. Instinct steps lead them down to the sea. Biley reflux wave-sick, she gags. She scans, panicking, where? WHERE?

"LOVE LIFTS US UP WHERE WE BELONG." Fraser wants to hear the Joe Cocker album over and over, and it's making Alan crazy. And then Nina Simone. And the moanfulness, the crusty voices . . . it's too much, too much.

No, they couldn't tell Fraser yet, but with all the confusion he must sense it. Helen and Marriette are around all the time and has set up a stream of people between Pierre and Ata's home and Fraser's. Mrs. Goodman has even reappeared, flitting in and out. All of Ata's family has descended, pulling strings for search parties, the army, lawyers, embassies. Pierre's brother flew in from France and whipped the U.N. might up into a frenzy, with the police. Nothing showed. Three, four days later, not a sign.

"We have to tell Fraser," Alan argues. "He's slipping."

"NOOO!" Fraser screams, "NOOO!" in a voice none of them recognize. "I was supposed to go before him! ME . . . aagh . . . take me, take meeah."

A week passed. And still nothing. Nothing. A nothingness as solid as fat around her. The custardy layer fills Ata's mouth whenever she opens it, seals her eyes, but traps her screamy dreams instead of sleep. She refuses to leave and go back to her family home with her three sisters, though. They let her sit out in the sun some more.

Her long-gone mother soothes her, smooths her hair, and croons to her. She had liked Nina's voice too. Ata can hear her singing *"My baby just cares . . ."*

An iguana scuttles across the crispy lawn in front of Ata. Heat like Vallot's baking jail. Pierre. Pierre a Negro chained to the stake with a headless body: "He was made to put on a shirt. The shirt was filled with sulphur . . . The executioner lit the fire."*

The stench of burning sulphur and flesh sears a hole through Ata's fat. Burns hot torture. A Bergorrat and French planters' ritual. Silk cotton limbs. Cursed deep. New Orleans weep. Trees waving strange fruit, *"blood on the leaves, and blood at the root."*

Ata was still bleeding, every day, it hadn't stopped. She told no one but the hills know. Watching.

The damp valley clouds them up in Fraser's living room. All the kitchen full of overcast friends and family. Almost as full as

*V. S. Naipaul, *The Loss of El Dorado* (1969), p. 192.

the last great party but hushed as a hurricane shelter. They argue over how people do disappear, just so, 'specially on the coast. No they can't—it must have been a crime. Whether she's in any state to go up there again, how much of a loner she is, how odd.

"I find since she start with this writing thing, she behaving more strange. I can't understand what she want to write for, anyway—"

"Exactly. Is not like it have any great war or famine, or any kind'a superfamous story here to write about," Marriette's brother cuts off SC.

Fraser is almost buried under Helen, lawyer-friend, smallee-Indi, and her husband around him on the settee. His eyes, a sharp knee, a fragile hand poke out.

"Youall squeezing him!" Mrs. Goodman tweets and starts tugging at his blanket.

They ease away slightly, then settle again.

"I can't comprehend what Ata must be going through, what happened." Lioness Goddess rubs Fraser's foot on her lap. "I don't understand any of this."

"I undershtand," Fraser slurs.

"Of course, we know why she want to keep going up there—that's where she feel closest to him, to any hope," SC says. "But by herself? I don' think she ready for that."

Gray clouds into green for a moment as Fraser struggles to understand why it is taking this long. How long was it now? In the clear patches there is too much to think about, and say. "Ready," he manages and sees them staring aghast at him.

Alan's smoke seeps in from the veranda and they all turn to look at Fraser's mother. The brother sucks his teeth. Sammy, Vernon, and Thomas getting heated out there.

"Had to be fall, he must'e fall and knock he head or something," Sammy bounces.

"Or he was swimming and a cramp take him," Thomas returns.

Sam springy on his rabbit legs. "Eh heh, them currents strong up there. Dat's why I don' take chances sea bathing meself."

Vernon steups long and low like thunder.

"Is not just currents, it have some evil people . . . and t'ings out there too. Yuh just never know."

"Wha' de hell yuh really saying, small man," Vernon snarls.

"It have t'ings that does go on in the countryside you mightn' know about."

Ata arrives with her older sister and Sammy stops. Vernon watches Sam's agitated little self and thinks this man likes to run his mouth too much.

Ata walks in and numbly receives the hugs from her friends.

"Make some room for the woman to take his pulse," Marriette shouts as Nurse Perfect hovers, waiting for the greeting hubble to end.

Ata's bruised eyes draw away from Fraser's clutch and the brother shifts uncomfortably, asks SC to get him a refill.

In the veranda chair, Mr. Goodman doesn't even try any-more—to keep up any pretenses, to be strong for his wife. Slack and deboned he watches, like the hills, as Sammy hops about.

If small man keep running he mouth, he go say something he sorry for. Vernon half-listens, stiffening. He glances in towards Fraser. What it is he talking about now, so bold-face? How you could look at it like some people lucky?

They have time with they love ones before they go. Sammy prattling, "They have time prepare theyself even if is hard, even though they time come before it should."

"And wha' if they choose they time," Vernon growls.

"What you saying?" Sam squeals louder.

"Hush yuh mouth, boy." Vernon raises his head and side-steps away from him.

"What he saying?" Sam turns to Thomas. "Fraser taking—"

"Ah say shut up!" Vernon spring right up to him in a flash and Thomas grip Sammy arm.

"How come nobody ain' tell me? Since when allyou know he taking he own—" *Bupp*, Vernon throw him down on the tiles hard with one cuff but Sammy ain't taking it so. He scrambling round, kicking and popping fists on Vernon's chest, trying to reach his face.

"Aye, aye, aye!" Everybody rushes out an pins back the fight. Brother, Alan, and two others holding down Vernon, he foaming and hollering "Loose me!" eyes glaring past them at the door. Thomas and Mrs. Goodman holding Sammy, who staring at the killer Vernon.

"Loose me!" Vernon screams and bursts away. Same time Ata and Nurse see Fraser seizing. Lawyer-friend there and grabs his limbs but Vernon pitches her aside as he crashes onto Fraser.

The vicious beast in Fraser thrashes and snaps its teeth but Vernon straps him in his arms and lifts. He flinches as claws scratch his face and a bite breaks his skin, but straightens and strides toward the bedroom. Vernon's tears fall into Fraser's rolling eyes and open mouth.

Ata waits, shaken fresh out of her skin. She sits on the veranda even though they told her go home. Home is worse now. He couldn't be gone, this couldn't be her.

Vernon sits at the end of the veranda on the floor. His bent knees push him back against the wall but his head hangs forward, arms slack.

SC's hand rests on her friend's shoulder bones and the warm weight of it feels like a ton and a magnet at the same time. They

wait, and a few others are inside waiting too, for Fraser's next
waking moment.

Only his fingers move in response.

Alan says Fraser is lucid, in the morning, his word backed by
Nurse Perfect. And the morning is as sore as the tortured night
and her skeleton. Ata says she's okay to drive herself but Sam
and Sis won't let her. "It'll be all right," she reassures them.

She feels them watching her when they get to the cottage.
The yellow distance grief brings between even blood sisters
moves with her and the hills never stop staring now. This must
be what it's like to be off.

They keep an eye on her movements on the deck, especially
when she nears the top of the treacherous steps. Sis and Sam sit
discreetly in the small rock garden, when she picks up her notebook and settles.

No spirit verse or touch. Ata waits but hears no words. He is
gone. Pierre is gone. Only guilt remains.

"She writing," Sam whispers. He doesn't know this sister,
owing to the fact that she only fly in when this thing happen.
They all look alike, though, and this one sprawl off in the sun
like she tanning too, ready to stay for a while. He could imagine how bad Ata must be feeling, considering all what she had
tell him. And this sister have no idea. Guilty—it must be 'cause
she feel like she had meet someone and cheat on Pierre, right
here. Sam watch her writing and a kind'a ease on her face and
how she slouch. It must be madness 'cause is all in she head.
Maybe it wasn't even no jumbie. They say writers does be off.

Too much reading and time in they own head. But with all that happen now, on top of that—he really can't imagine this kind'a loss. Is different to his. Sudden like his but different. And how come she never tell him that Fraser killing heself? Sam watch her writing.

From the time Ata came to visit this place as a shy child she told herself—this is a place for adults. From the time them lovely Maracas waves first chewed her up . . . she promised herself she would come back to this prancy, peacock island. But she never trusted the perfumed strutting . . .

Fraser's tongue and lips are dry, so cracked, hot tar inside. *Cachot brulant*, hot prison cells, used as torture. Sir Walter Raleigh's men, shot by poisoned arrows, were "'marvellously provoked' by thirst; but drink made their condition worse,"* he wants to say, to Alan . . . so unsavory, no man can endure to cure, or attend to, "please."

Ata returns to Alan's dragon smoke filling Fraser's apartment. Alan almost lives on the veranda now, trying to focus on the frog's racket, when the fits come. "It's dangerous now, Ata. He's strong when he's like that, and only Vernon, bloody amazing Vernon, can restrain him. Hasn't left his side in days."

"I'll stay tonight, you need some rest," she tells Alan.

"You're not looking so hot yourself, darling. You don't have to," Helen offered.

"Everybody's exhausted. I want to. You go."

*V. S. Naipaul, *The Loss of El Dorado* (1969), p. 51.

Just then, Fraser starts up again. Ata rushes in, then out, trying not to look.

Late that night, early in the morning, she tries to sleep, on that same settee. Vernon is coiled on the chair by Fraser's bedside, the nurses whispering in the kitchen. Eventually Ata dozes, but wakes in a commotion. Vernon pelts out straight onto the veranda floor, bawling.

Gone.

Sure as her eyes were open and the smoke-weight vanished from the air, even as she runs into the room screaming at the nurses, "What are you doing?" they are tying him up. "Don't do that, stop! Stop!"

"We have to do this before he stiffens." They ignore her and continue wrapping his legs straight, his jaw . . . so that he immediately looks like a dead person. Not Fraser. Not the turtle.

She calms a little. This is how they keep his dignity—practical, cruel . . .

"He went peaceful in he sleep," they tell her.

Roge, this may not be the book you wanted, but I hope it helps to preserve some of the ridiculous and wonderful memories of you.

And now that I understand why people dedicate books posthumously, this is also in memory of my mother, who first taught me that love lives beyond life.

Thank You

To Andy Taitt for edits and honesty. To Jeremy Taylor for generous notes, insight, and encouragement. To Jesse Coleman at FSG. Thanks to Roger England for space to write, and to my friends and sisters who understood my need to write this book. And gratitude to my love, Andy Grant, for fierce strength and an extra heart.